COCO
AT THE
RITZ

COCO
AT THE
RITZ

a novel

GIOIA DILIBERTO

PEGASUS BOOKS

NEW YORK LONDON

COCO AT THE RITZ

Pegasus Books, Ltd.
148 West 37th Street, 13th Floor
New York, NY 10018

Copyright © 2021 by Gioia Diliberto

First Pegasus Books paperback edition December 2023
First Pegasus Books cloth edition December 2021

Interior design by Maria Fernandez

Library of Congress Cataloging-in-Publication Data is available.

ISBN: 978-1-63936-581-4

10 9 8 7 6 5 4 3 2 1

Printed in the United States of America
Distributed by Simon & Schuster
www.pegasusbooks.com

for Dick
and for Joe

PARIS

August 30, 1944

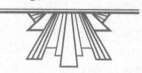

When the doorbell rang at eight thirty on that hot, languid morning, Coco knew they'd come to arrest her. She might have wondered for a moment if someone else was at the door—perhaps the laundress with fresh linen or a porter with a glove she'd dropped in the lobby. But she knew.

Though the carpet muffled their footsteps, she sensed them striding down the hall at the Ritz. Coco and her animal cunning. She knew from the fierce jangle of the bell, from the way the maid's heels clicked so frantically across the floor and the door roared open, she knew.

She crushed her cigarette in an ashtray. Her body trembled, surprising her. Lighting another cigarette, she took a moment to pull herself together. The room was warm, with the white morning sun slanting through the windows, and the air had a stale floral scent, the mixed fragrances of No. 5 perfume, tobacco, and pink roses, which were displayed on the tables in crystal vases.

Until that moment, she hadn't thought she'd be arrested, though one of her acquaintances, the actress Arletty, had been picked up for living with a high-ranking Luftwaffe officer. Arletty, so famous she needed only one name, had flaunted her relationship, attending movie premieres and opera openings with her lover and showing up with him at parties at the German embassy. Coco and *her* lover had kept to themselves, rarely venturing to places where they might be recognized.

Now, she began to worry, as she peeked out the bedroom door and saw the soldiers—the two young men from the French Forces of the Interior—standing in her suite with their grim expressions and guns tucked into their belts. Spatz had already fled Paris with the retreating Germans. And Coco was alone, as she'd so often been in life, with her fame and her money and her secrets, which kept anyone from getting too close.

As she rummaged in her bureau for a fresh pair of stockings, Coco silently cataloged the evidence of her innocence: She had closed her fashion house before the Germans arrived, keeping open only the boutique where her perfume was sold. She never attended a party or a luncheon at the German embassy. Unlike Arletty or her friends Jean Cocteau and Serge Lifar, she avoided the most fashionable nightclubs and theaters frequented by the occupiers. She hadn't gone to the Paris Opera Ballet once in four years, despite urging from Lifar, the company director, who, on a trip to Berlin, actually presented Hitler with a film of himself dancing. True, the *Kommandant* had allowed her stay at the Ritz. What did that prove? Only that she was smarter than most. She knew how to get what she wanted. The great hotel had been her home since she'd given up her apartment on the rue du Faubourg Saint-Honoré in 1933. At the Ritz she found the flawless service she craved and the comfort and security of the family life she'd never known.

Of course, the men have come for her because of Spatz. And that wasn't fair, because her German lover wasn't really a Nazi. He wasn't a cold-blooded killer. His mother was English, after all, and he'd lived in Paris for a third of his life. Why should she feel guilty about Spatz? Anyway, she wasn't going to hide in the closet or jump out the window. She wasn't a coward.

There was a soft knock on the bedroom door. Coco opened it a crack and saw the maid. "Mademoiselle, what should I do?" the maid whispered.

"Ask them to give me a minute to dress," Coco said. "If they take me and I'm not back in two hours, tell the manager at the boutique to call Winston Churchill."

"The prime minister?"

"Yes—his private number is in the book in my desk."

Coco pushed the door shut and flipped through the hangers in her closet, deciding on her No. 2 suit in navy blue jersey, a more casual version of the No. 1 model she'd worn in her working days. From the jewelry box on her dressing table, she took three strands of pearls and a jeweled-enameled cuff. She looped the pearls around her neck and secured the cuff on her wrist. Then she reconsidered the jewelry. No need to call attention to her prosperity, so she stuffed the pearls and bracelet in a drawer.

Coco was sixty-one, though she looked younger thanks to expertly dyed dark brown hair and good bone structure. In middle age, with many love affairs behind her, she had not gained weight; in fact, she had grown thinner. She could still wear the clothes she'd designed after the first Great War: slim skirts, collarless jackets, evening gowns with thin straps and sleeveless chemise dresses.

Arranging her face in a determined expression, Coco smoothed her skirt and opened the bedroom door. Two ordinary youths dressed in brown slacks and plain white shirts stood in the foyer. She eyed the shiny pistols jammed into their belts. Their shirts flashed armbands emblazoned with "FFI" and the Cross of Lorraine, the symbol of the French Forces of the Interior, the loose band of Resistance fighters, soldiers, and private citizens who'd taken up arms in the aftermath of the Germans' departure.

"Gabrielle Chanel, come with us," said the taller youth. He had a spray of adolescent pimples on his cheeks, but his fine brown hair was already thinning.

"By whose order?" she asked, louder than she intended.

"The People of France and the victims of Fascism," said the second youth. He was short and stocky and looked even younger than his partner, with smooth pink cheeks and curly chestnut hair.

The maid was sobbing now, her face buried in her hands. "Do you have any identification?" Coco demanded. They would never see *her* cry.

"You must come with us," said the taller youth.

"Who gave you your orders?"

"If you don't come voluntarily, we'll take you by force."

Coco clasped her hands to stop them from trembling. "On what charge?"

The taller boy spoke in a harsh, unflinching voice. "Treason."

Coco grabbed her purse off the hall table and held her head high as she left the suite, trying to seem as grandly tragic as Joan of Arc but feeling shaken to her core.

The lobby teemed with activity. Men in blue uniforms with gold braid stood stiffly as they spoke to the guests. When Coco appeared between the two FFI youths, all conversations stopped. Guillaume de Lastour, the bald, elderly husband of a woman who'd been one of her most loyal clients, started to doff his hat, but his companion, a portly, middle-aged man, pulled Lastour's arm down, frowning furiously.

Outside, under the hotel's blue canopy, the taller youth nodded toward a battered American jeep parked at the curb. Coco rode in the back seat. The day was bright and clear, the streets jammed with cyclists. The jeep whizzed down rue Cambon, past Coco's boutique at number 31, where already there was an olive drab ribbon of soldiers on the pavement in front. It had been like this every day since she'd put the sign in the window offering free perfume to GIs. "See how popular I am with the Americans?" she said.

The men in the jeep ignored her.

"Where are you taking me?"

The stocky one in the passenger seat looked at her but said nothing.

They passed the Tuileries, where the lawns glistened like green satin and the sandy paths were as bright and gleaming as crushed crystal. The red banners with black swastikas were gone, and tricolors waved once more from the tops of government buildings. Though the coffee in the cafés still tasted like acorns and the Métro only operated a few hours every day, life was gradually returning to normal after four years of occupation. Coco smelled a tang of hope in the air with the white heat of late summer. She was thrilled that the Germans were gone and relieved that they hadn't destroyed Paris. Instead, they had grabbed whatever they could of the city's art and culture, her cuisine and tradition of beauty. They would have stolen the Paris spring had that been in their power.

But now these French boys had taken over. Well, she would survive this. That was the story of her life. She had willed herself from poverty and wedged herself into a world of wealth and power. She beat all the odds. And here she was now at the mercy of these unsmiling adolescents. Didn't they know she had powerful friends who would make them answer for arresting her?

"Do you know how important my name is?" she said to the youths' backs. "No one has done more than me to uphold the tradition of French couture." Silence from the front of the jeep. "You're boys, so I wouldn't expect you to know how vital fashion is for France. Your mothers will tell you." She knew she should stop talking. That was her biggest sin. She didn't know when to keep quiet. But she couldn't bear silence; she had to fill it with the first thing that came into her head.

She knew she'd said too much in the past. Snippets of conversations they might use against her flared in her mind. The intemperate comments she'd made about de Gaulle a few days earlier, while watching the liberation parade from the balcony of José Maria Sert's apartment overlooking the Place de la Concorde. She'd worried out loud that the general would turn out to be another demagogue. That was just talk.

She had not been out much recently. The war wasn't over yet. Just the previous week, German bombs launched from Le Bourget had dropped on the city, killing or wounding hundreds and destroying the Halles aux Vins. Great holes gaped in the pavement where citizens had dug up paving stones to form barricades. Sandbag towers blocked some of the streets, and random gunfire often pierced the air. The Occupation had sparked too much anger and hatred, too much shame and frustration, for the violence to suddenly end. Now, though, it was mostly French fighting French, as it so often was in the nation's bloody history.

Coco lit a cigarette and blew a jet of smoke toward the roof of the jeep. "At least tell me where you're taking me," she said, with as much forcefulness as she could muster.

"No smoking!" bellowed the stocky youth. He lunged over his seat back and grabbed the cigarette from Coco's hand.

They drove for twenty minutes to the Prefecture of Police, an immense stone building on the Île de la Cité. A burnt-out Nazi tank squatted in the street, a great charred insect. Nearby, a large, noisy crowd had gathered. A celebration of some kind seemed to be underway. Women in the skimpy dresses and cork-soled shoes they'd worn throughout the war and men in berets laughed and waved their arms. Schoolboys in short pants scurried about, thrilled by the gathering. A little girl in a starched white dress sat on her father's shoulders, clapping.

As the jeep nudged through the crowd, Coco's eyes traveled to the landing at the building's entrance, and she gasped. A pretty young woman in a gray dress sat on a chair while a man wielding large clippers hacked off her hair. Two brutes with rifles strapped to their shoulders held the girl's thin arms as clumps of gold hair fell to the ground. The girl looked to be no more than fifteen, but she was very brave and didn't cry.

When it was over, the girl was bald. Blood trickled from the back of her white scalp where the scissors had nicked her. The man holding the girl's right arm pulled her to her feet and led her away as the crowd jeered: *Kraut whore! That's what we do to traitors!* A moment later, another young woman, this one a brunette in her twenties, stumbled forward and was pushed into the chair. The brunette looked around at the crowd with a defiant expression, until the man with the clippers yanked her head back and began snipping.

These poor girls! Why were women always vilified and punished for the sins of men? It was men who'd started the war, men who'd committed war's atrocities. Coco felt a sinking in her stomach followed by waves of nausea. She was too famous for the mere humiliation of a shaved head. They'd probably torture her and leave her to rot in the same dank prison where Marie-Antoinette had spent her last wretched years. Well, she'd rather die than see all she'd created destroyed.

Coco's captors led her from the jeep through a side door, up the back wooden stairs, creaky with age, to an interrogation room on the third floor. They nudged her inside, then stepped out, closing the door behind them. She heard the lock turn, then their excited chatter as they clambered down the stairs. Her eyes took in the small, dingy space, furnished starkly with old rickety chairs and a scarred table piled with papers and files.

A big black phone sat at one end of the table. Next to the phone lay a pair of large scissors. They reminded Coco of the scissors she wore every day during her working life to cut away the superfluous froufrous of an outmoded fashion. She'd scissored her way to fame and fortune, and she'd ended up here. She wondered: Were those scissors meant for her?

She heard the lock click, and the door opened several inches, then banged shut. Two men behind the door were talking, and she moved closer to listen.

"If the major shows up, he'll be furious," said one man, his voice edged with panic.

"The roads are impossible. He'll never get here," said the second man.

"The major told us to wait!"

"I'm in charge now."

"He wanted to question her himself. You're not planning . . . But the order from headquarters—he'll be furious you ignored it."

"It'll all be over by then."

The door swung open, and Coco stepped back. Two men entered the room. They were dressed like the soldiers who had arrested Coco, in dark pants and white shirts with the sleeves rolled up. Both wore FFI armbands on their left sleeves. One man looked to be in his early thirties. He had a tall, lean build, close-cropped black hair, a black brush mustache, and nervous dark eyes. The other one looked no older than sixteen, a child really, with a thatch of brown hair and a smooth, hairless face. Yet he was much larger than his colleague, with broad shoulders and thick legs.

The older man, the chief interrogator, shot Coco a savage look, while the boy glanced quickly at her from downcast eyes. The men took seats behind the table, and the Interrogator cleared his throat to get Coco's attention. Her back stiffened, and she stepped forward.

"Your name is Gabrielle Chanel?" he asked.

"You know who I am." Coco's hands shook slightly, but her voice was cool and firm.

The Interrogator consulted a file. "You were born on August 19, 1883, in Saumur."

Coco squirmed at the mention of her birthdate.

"Answer the question, please."

She turned away, ignoring the Interrogator.

He pressed. "Is your birthdate correct?"

"Yes." Coco sighed heavily.

"Before the war you made dresses?"

"Yes . . ." Coco hesitated. "Actually, I revolutionized fashion."

The Interrogator nodded toward the chair in front of Coco. "Take a seat."

"Do you have the authority to detain me? You're not part of the official army," said Coco. As she sat, she removed her hat and gloves and set them on top of her purse on the floor. She started to feel less panicked. She'd sized up the Interrogator. He was an adult—unlike the two who'd arrested her and the second soldier here—but he had a stiff manner. She sensed he was someone who didn't see nuances. She would have to be careful with him.

"I am a captain in the French Forces of the Interior of the Republic of France," said the Interrogator.

"How nice for you." Coco pointed her chin toward the boy, who took notes furiously in a small notebook. "If I had a gun, I'd be a confident bully, too."

The boy stopped writing and raised his head, a look of innocent terror on his face. He was wearing sandals, and Coco noticed that his feet were filthy.

The Interrogator reached into his files, pulled out a photograph, and pushed it across the table toward Coco. It was a snapshot of her lover—handsome, blond, and impeccably dressed in a suit, camel overcoat, and black fedora. "Do you know this man?" he asked.

Coco studied the photograph for a moment with a softened expression, then rearranged her features into a neutral mask. "I've known him for years."

"He's much younger than you, isn't he?"

"A little."

Her lover was thirteen years younger than she. Ordinarily, if anyone brought up the age difference, her cheeks burned with anger. Now she felt a cold tremor.

"Do you know where he is now?" the Interrogator asked.

"No. I haven't seen him in a week."

"He didn't say where he was going? He didn't say good-bye?"

"He *did* come to say good-bye because he's a gentleman."

"He's gone back to Germany, hasn't he?"

"Possibly."

The Interrogator cocked his head to consider Coco. She saw that his mustache needed trimming. He played with the edges of it with his lower lip. "Seeing as you slept in this man's bed for four years, I would have expected you to join him and the other Nazis when they fled Paris," he said.

"Spatz slept in his own bed, and I slept in mine."

"Spatz?"

"That's what his friends call him. It means little sparrow."

"His real name is Hans Günther von Dincklage, correct?"

Coco nodded.

The Interrogator leaned across the table so close to Coco she could smell the fruity staleness of his worn shirt. "Ironic, isn't it, because from the picture, he looks like a big strapping guy. Not a little sparrow."

"It's a childhood nickname—he was a small, sickly boy."

Coco thought with a stab of longing of the first morning she and Spatz had awakened together in bed. Gold light seeping through the curtains had grazed Spatz's long, athletic form, and Coco's heart had swelled with delight. She'd never before slept with such a beautiful man.

The Interrogator glanced at the photograph. "He looks to me like the perfect specimen of Aryan manhood."

"If you say so. His mother is English." Coco took a cigarette case—rose gold with a diamond clasp—out of her pocket. It had belonged to a real Englishman, Arthur Capel, the only man she'd ever truly loved, dead now for twenty-five years. Why did these marvelous men always die or abandon her? Of course, she could take care of herself. But she'd grown so tired of doing it.

Coco removed a cigarette from the case and placed it in the corner of her mouth. She looked at the Interrogator, and he stared back at her, making no move to light it. As she fumbled in her handbag for a lighter, the Interrogator said, "Von Dincklage is German. That didn't bother you?"

Coco lit her cigarette and blew a jet of smoke toward the Interrogator. "Do you expect me to look at a man's passport before I agree to be his lover?"

The Interrogator closed his eyes for a moment to avoid the smoke. "Tell me where von Dincklage is, madam."

"Mademoiselle."

The Interrogator looked Coco up and down, as if he was examining an ancient artifact or an old car, checking for scratches and dents. "Mademoiselle?"

"I am La Grande Mademoiselle. Talk to anyone in fashion, they'll tell you."

"We're not here to talk about fashion. I want you to tell me how I can find your Spatz."

"I have no idea."

"Did you ever see von Dincklage in uniform?"

"Never! He wore bespoke suits from a London tailor and shirts from Charvet."

"He's a Nazi, *and* he's a peacock." The Interrogator uttered a short laugh.

"He wasn't a Nazi; he just wanted them to think he was. He was only trying to get by, to get through the war like everyone else."

"Exactly *how* did he get by?"

"I don't know what he did when he wasn't with me. He was an embassy attaché when I first met him, but don't ask me what an embassy attaché does."

"Promotes Nazi ideology."

"You think we sat around discussing *that*?"

"What did you discuss?"

"What we were going to have for dinner. What most people discuss."

The Interrogator squeezed out a brief, insincere smile. It was the smile, Coco thought, of someone who rarely made use of that expression. She demanded, "Why have I been arrested?"

"For traitorous collaboration with the enemy."

"I love my country," Coco said in a soft voice. "I'm not guilty."

"That's what we're here to discuss." The Interrogator rapped the table with his fingers. "You were either with the Nazis or against them."

Coco gave him a pointed look. "I'm afraid, young man, things weren't so black and white."

ONE

Four Years Earlier

Coco arrived in Paris on a warm Wednesday in July, six weeks after the Germans occupied the city. Though early evening, it was eerily dark. Paris now operated on German time, which meant pushing the clock forward an hour. The streets were empty and silent, the only sound the hobnailed boots of Nazi soldiers strolling the boulevards.

At the Ritz, a giant red flag with a black swastika hung over the massive double doors. Coco's driver dropped her off at the entrance with her suitcase and sped away in his rusted-out Cadillac. She watched him careen onto rue Saint-Honoré, narrowly missing a big black Mercedes. Through the Mercedes' back window, Coco glimpsed a bloodied man between two helmeted soldiers. In the distance, a rifle shot rang out, followed by the strew of a machine gun. Was someone being executed? Coco shuddered.

Since she didn't have an *ausweis*, a German permit, the armed Nazi at the Ritz door refused her entrance. Charlie Ritz, the hotel owner, however, saw her and let her into the lobby. "I've been traveling for two days, and I'm exhausted," she told him, as she started for the stairs.

"You can't go up there. It's reserved for Germans," said Charlie.

"Nonsense. All my things are there!"

"Stop! Don't go any further!"

Coco brushed past Charlie and handed her suitcase to a porter. "Bring that to my suite," she ordered.

"I'm warning you, Mademoiselle. Your suite is unavailable." Charlie's voice boomed. Everyone stared. The lobby teemed with uniformed Germans, and Coco recognized what Charlie was up to: hoping to impress the Nazis with what a big, strong man he was, pushing around little Coco.

The assistant manager appeared and spoke to Charlie. The sink in Himmler's suite was clogged, and the Nazi commander was demanding new quarters. Charlie scurried off to handle the emergency, and Coco climbed the grand, winding staircase. Were the French really barred from the upper floors of the Ritz? She should have called ahead, given the staff a chance to get things ready for her. She'd returned too hastily.

But her nephew André Palasse had been taken prisoner by the Germans while fighting for the French on the Maginot Line, the concrete fortress on the border of France and Germany. Coco had promised André's wife, Catharina, that she'd appeal to the enemy now in control to have the young soldier released. She couldn't do that from André's home in Lembeye, where she'd fled in June, as soon as the first Nazi bombs hit Paris. Coco had bought the large stone house as a vacation home for her nephew and his family, whose main residence was Lyon, where André worked as director of Chanel Silk Establishments. Coco enjoyed taking walks through the woods behind the house with her two school-age great-nieces, but there was little else to do. Mostly, she'd been bored out of her mind. Still, she was determined to stick it out, at least until the bombing stopped. Then one night, while relaxing in the salon with André's family and listening to a Mozart symphony, the tinny voice of World War I hero Maréchal Pétain interrupted the music. "With a heavy heart I tell you today what is necessary to do to stop the fighting," intoned the scratchy voice through the mesh speaker. France had surrendered to Germany. Pétain would become head of a new government at Vichy allied with the Nazis. The nation would henceforth be divided in two: the zone occupied by the Germans, which comprised roughly two-thirds of France, including Paris, and an unoccupied zone that began around Orléans and stretched south to the Spanish border. The German military would command all French forces.

A few days later, Catharina learned that her husband had been taken prisoner. André was like a son to Coco—people gossiped that he *was* her son, by her very first lover, Étienne Balsan, a wealthy aristocrat she'd met while mending trousers in a tailoring shop in Moulins. Immediately, Coco packed for Paris. She and her driver, Marceau, took off in his ancient Cadillac. When they'd fled the city in June, he thought they'd be too conspicuous in Coco's Rolls-Royce, so she'd left the luxurious car behind in the garage.

"Be careful. It's a war zone in Paris!" Catharina had cried, as she kissed Coco good-bye.

"I'm not afraid of the Germans. What can they do to me?" Coco had said, as she hugged her nieces, then settled in the car for the long journey home.

Coco had no idea to whom she'd appeal about having André released. But she'd always been good at steamrolling through every obstacle, no matter how big or insurmountable. She'd think about it after she'd unpacked and taken a bath.

At the door to her suite, she halted abruptly. Radio music drifted from inside. Then a female announcer came on speaking perfect French: *This is Berlin calling. Berlin calling all French wives, mothers, sisters, and sweethearts. Mesdames et mamselles, when Berlin calls, it pays to listen! Il faut que vous faites attention! Most of you listening are alone without your men, your men whom you will never see again, or who at best will come home crippled, useless for the rest of their lives. For whom? For de Gaulle, for Roosevelt, for Churchill and their Jewish cohort."*

Coco pounded on the door. A man's voice shouted over the radio, *"Entrez!"*

At the desk near the window sat a handsome blond man with light blue eyes and a full, girlish mouth that contradicted the virile set of his jaw. He was dressed in a bespoke brown suit, a gray silk tie, and a creamy white shirt. Gold triangles edged in onyx flashed from his spotless cuffs. His thick hair, cut short and parted on the side, was a few shades lighter than his tanned skin.

Coco recognized him immediately: Spatz von Dincklage. She'd met him in the early thirties when he arrived in Paris as an embassy attaché, and she often spotted him while on the town at parties, restaurants, gallery shows, and theater openings. She remembered one evening at the Night in Versailles Ball hosted by Count Étienne de Beaumont, the avant-garde art patron. Spatz and his wife, Catsy, had won the waltz contest, though the competition—heavy with old dowagers and their drunken husbands—wasn't terribly stiff. Coco had noted von Dincklage's extreme good looks. Later, she heard that Spatz had left Paris under some kind of cloud. She hadn't seen him in years.

A heavy odor of stale cigar hung in the air. In the middle of the room sat a card table laden with overflowing ashtrays, dirty glasses, and empty bottles of wine. More empty wine and liquor bottles lay scattered on the floor.

Spatz turned off the radio. "So, the famous Coco Chanel has returned," he said, smiling and flashing two boyish dimples. Coco felt heat rising in her face, the way it broadcast her attraction to him. She wondered what sports he played. Golf? Tennis? Athletic men were usually good in bed. "Are you living here?" she asked, adjusting her wrinkled clothes. She felt dirty and disheveled, embarrassed to be so badly groomed.

Spatz shook his head. "No, no. Just keeping an eye on it for you. Making sure the maids don't steal anything."

Coco eyed the card table Spatz must have brought in and the empty liquor bottles on the floor with a furrowed brow. "Your friends were helping you."

"Sorry about the mess. We had a card game earlier."

"It smells like a cigar factory."

"My friends love their Cuban cigars."

"Where do you get Cuban cigars . . ." Realizing she was talking to a well-connected German who had no problem getting whatever he wanted in occupied Paris, Coco abruptly changed the subject. "This is *my* apartment, and those are my trunks in the hall." She took a cigarette from the case in her purse and, holding it between her index and third fingers, gestured with it toward Spatz. "From my last pack."

He took a lighter from a pocket in his jacket and moved close to Coco to light her cigarette. "I can get you anything you need."

Coco began to sweat, and she wondered if he could smell her. "This will get rid of that awful cigar odor," she said, as she took a bottle of Chanel No. 5 from her purse. She removed the stopper and placed the bottle on the coffee table. "There are crates of perfume across the street in my boutique. You can have as many bottles as you want—for your wife."

"We're divorced, for several years now," said Spatz.

"For your *petite amie*, then."

"At the moment, there's no one special in my life."

Coco found that hard to believe. Spatz was so attractive, his manners so impeccable. She sat on the sofa and crossed her legs, tucking her right foot behind the opposite ankle. She looked at Spatz with a soft expression. "What are you doing in Paris?"

"My work."

"And what exactly is your work?" Coco ran her hands over her hair, tucking it into place. Spatz settled next to her and stretched his arm across the sofa's high back, almost touching her.

"I have an office on rue Raspail." He hesitated a moment. "I oversee textile production."

"For whom?"

"Mostly for the army."

"Which army?"

"Which army do you prefer?"

"I hate the military."

"I much prefer civilian life myself, but here we are." Spatz rose and went to the bar cart, where he poured each of them a glass of red wine. "À la guerre, comme à la guerre," he said, handing a glass to Coco. "I'll see about getting this place cleaned up and your trunks moved in and unpacked. In the meantime, you can have a bath, and afterward, I'll take you to dinner downstairs. The Ritz food is as good as it's always been."

"À la guerre, comme à la guerre," Coco said, raising her glass.

TWO

God, *why did I agree to have dinner with him?* In the bathroom, she undressed and filled the tub. It appeared no one had used it in her absence. The bathmat lay where she'd left it draped over the porcelain edge. The bar of soap was dry in the little china soap dish, and a new jar of blue bath salts sat unopened on the marble sink next to a bottle of Chanel No. 5. She sprayed a mist of perfume into the air and inhaled the scent, annoyed with herself. She had behaved like a silly schoolgirl, blushing and flirting. That was what men like Spatz von Dincklage expected. He was used to women falling all over themselves just to catch his eye. And he played into it, encouraging them with warm smiles and intense looks.

She felt a thrum of desire imagining Spatz in her bed. *If I want him, I can have him,* she thought. *But he's counting on that. I won't be another of his easy conquests.*

After her bath, Coco donned a pair of white silk pajamas with black piping that still hung on a hook behind the door where she'd left them weeks earlier. She lay on the sofa in her salon, lit a cigarette, and flipped through a magazine. An hour passed. At eight, Coco heard footsteps in the hall, then a knock on the door. Spatz had come to escort her to dinner. She waited. Another knock and another. Then the footsteps moved away until there was no sound but the rise and fall of her own breath.

After an hour flipping through magazines, Coco went to the bedroom and turned down the quilt on her bed. She felt sleep coming, deep and heavy. But as soon as she started to drift off, worry over her nephew and her own future pushed her weariness away. She and Catharina had each received a letter from André with the terrible news that he'd contracted tuberculosis. He wasn't being treated, and his condition worsened day by day. She feared he wouldn't survive long in German custody.

Coco wished she had her work to distract her. It had been a mistake to close the House of Chanel the previous year, but there was no question of reopening now under the Germans. Paris wasn't Paris as long as they were in control. The idea of Nazi-run couture was laughable. Suddenly Coco was wide-awake. She pulled her suitcase from under the bed and found the little vial of morphine and the syringe wrapped in a silk scarf. Sitting in the armchair by the window, she pulled her right pajama leg over her knee and injected herself in the thigh. She closed her eyes as the drug washed through her veins. She thought back to her first opening in the middle of the first Great War. It was a grand affair—*tout le Paris* had turned out. Coco had watched it all from behind a screen. From there she could see everything: the buyers, clients, editors, and models. The applause at the end had been deafening. Coco took a bow, but she didn't let herself celebrate the triumph. As soon as you started congratulating yourself, you were dead. Even as the women in the audience were sighing with pleasure, she thought only of the next day's work. Now, there was nothing.

Sitting in the dark as the morphine began to take effect, Coco thought calmly. She had overcome the grimmest of childhoods to become

France's most accomplished and famous couturière. Still, like any ordinary woman, she needed to be loved. She had to have a man at her side. She thought over her long string of lovers: the polo-playing lightweight Étienne Balsan; the foppish invert Dimitri Romanov (*they* never actually slept together); fun-loving Bendor, the Duke of Westminster, the richest man in the world; bookish illustrator Paul Iribe; Igor Stravinsky (she never understood his music, but his intensity had been irresistible); and the love of her life, the dashing Englishman, Boy Capel, her soul mate, taken from her too soon in a car crash. None of these men would commit to her completely, mostly because she couldn't give herself fully to them.

Her heart was empty and that was not a good thing, especially now in the midst of war.

The next morning, Coco awoke groggy from the morphine and furious with herself for not keeping her date with Spatz. She'd been embarrassed by her attraction to him, and she'd let that get in the way of what would have no doubt been a pleasant evening. Maybe he was just being friendly, and now he would think her rude. She was her own worst enemy.

As she washed her face and brushed her teeth, she found herself scheming of ways to see him again. She assumed he was staying at the Ritz, so she didn't think she'd have too much trouble running into him if she planted herself in the lobby or the restaurant.

Instead of calling downstairs to have her coffee and croissant brought up to her suite, she decided to take breakfast in the restaurant dining room. She hoped to run into Spatz.

Coco donned a clean set of underwear and stockings—her last pair. From her suitcase, she removed the elaborate gold dresser set that had been a present from the Duke of Westminster in the middle of their affair and that she'd taken with her in June when she fled Paris. Now she set the gilt-trimmed bottles, jars, brushes, combs, and hand mirror on her dressing table. She sat on the tufted beige stool and leaned toward the triple mirror to scrutinize her face. It seemed every day a fresh line appeared on her forehead, a new brown spot on her cheek. Her dark eyes still sparkled with intelligence and charm, she thought, despite the deepening crow's-feet at the corners. She'd always been attractive, with a small, wiry body, olive skin, and thick dark hair. Her confidence and sense of style had fooled everyone that she was beautiful.

She still knew how to fake it. The trick now was to cover her aging skin with the right foundation. In the twenties her chemists had discovered a formula that looked natural and dewy and wouldn't settle in the crevices of an older woman's face. She applied a light layer of the makeup with a sponge, then, a dusting of powder. Her eyebrows were still gloriously full and dark. She needed only to pluck them a bit on the edges. Next, she coated her eyelashes in several layers of mascara and applied red lipstick.

When her face was done, she dressed in a white silk blouse, a taupe jersey skirt, and a cardigan jacket. She roped three strands of pearls around her neck, secured a white enameled cuff emblazoned with a jeweled cross on her wrist, and clipped rhinestone earrings to her fleshy lobes. After spraying herself with a light mist of Chanel No. 5, she was ready.

A few minutes later, Coco was standing at the entrance to the Ritz dining room. With its towering blue ceiling, creamy walls, and grandly arched windows draped in gold satin, the Ritz restaurant featured the most ornate décor, the most imperious waitstaff, and the most scrumptious cuisine in Paris. It also boasted a demarcation line as clean as the one that separated the nation's occupied and unoccupied zones. The Germans sat on one side of the room, the French on the other. The two sections were separated by a gilt-and-mahogany oval table holding an immense flower arrangement under a crystal chandelier the size of a piano.

As Coco followed the maître d' to a small table on the nearly empty French side of the room, she passed a group of well-dressed Parisians sipping coffee and chatting over plates of eggs and sausage. No one glanced her way or said bonjour. A year earlier, she would have been besieged with effusive greetings. The men would have stood to kiss her hand; the women would have murmured their admiration. Now no one bothered to fuss over her.

Coco spread her white linen napkin across her lap as a waiter poured her a cup of coffee. When he had left with her order—croissant and grapefruit—she scanned the crowd across the room, on the German side. Her eyes fell on a group of balding, jowly officers. Their green-gray jackets (such a nauseating color!) and shiny black belts strained against their heavy stomachs. She noticed that the higher up they were in the Nazi party, the homelier they got, the more gray-faced, pocked, flaccid, and paunchy. A few civilians, men in suits and women in expensive dresses, sat with the officers. But Spatz was nowhere in sight.

Coco ate quickly and made her way to the lobby. Then, as she mounted the grand staircase, a voice behind her: "Mademoiselle Chanel."

Spatz stood at the base of the stairs with one foot resting on an upper step, leaning on his knee and smiling up at her. She felt her heart pound in her chest and was glad she'd taken such care that morning with her makeup. "I'm so sorry about last night. I fell asleep," Coco said.

"I understand," said Spatz. "You had a long journey. You were exhausted."

"If your offer to help me move my trunks is still valid, I'd be very grateful."

Spatz removed his foot from the step and stood to his full six feet. "I have a busy morning, but I can meet you at your suite this afternoon."

"That would be wonderful."

"At two, then?"

"Two."

Coco passed the next hour in her suite reading and smoking. At ten she left the Ritz by the back entrance and walked across the street. Rue Cambon was deserted, the shops silent behind their iron grilles. High in the sky, a cavalcade of immense balloons bobbed, waiting to entrap Allied planes in their trailing ropes. In front of Coco's boutique, a cart of roses had been abandoned, the red and pink blooms starting to wilt under the hot, white sun. Coco wondered what had happened to the flower seller, an old woman with a sharp tongue and two grandsons in the army. Had she insulted a German soldier and been arrested?

Coco pushed open the front door of her boutique. Behind the glass counter, the vendeuse Veronique unpacked a shipment of perfume. "Mademoiselle, you're back!" exclaimed the young woman, clasping her hands over her heart.

"How is everything?" asked Coco.

Veronique lowered her eyes and placed her hands on the edge of the counter. "All right, I guess. Not too many customers."

"We'll get through this. Try not to worry." Coco patted Veronique's hand, then made her way up the mirrored stairway to her second-floor apartment. The two rooms overlooked rue Cambon, a dining room with six chairs around a square walnut table, and a book-lined salon with a roll-top desk and a sofa upholstered in beige suede. This was where Coco dined, entertained, and took care of her business correspondence. There was no bedroom. She slept at the Ritz.

Scattered about was her collection of animal sculptures and figurines. There were two of everything: two porcelain horses flanking the mirror over the sofa, two life-size bronze deer by the fireplace, two gilded dogs in the hearth, two bronze camels and two glass frogs on the side tables, two pearl lovebirds in a jeweled cage. It comforted Coco to see these inanimate creatures paired up. Living things, too, belonged in couples.

No sooner had Coco dropped her purse and lit a cigarette when the phone rang. Veronique was on the other end to say Coco had a visitor—the poet Pierre Reverdy. A moment later the bell rang, and Coco opened the door to find a slender, dark-haired man in his fifties standing on the threshold. For two decades, Reverdy had been her close friend and, though he was married, her sometime lover. Years earlier, he'd moved with his wife to Solesmes in northwest France, and he rarely returned to Paris. Coco hadn't seen him in two years.

"What on earth are you doing here?" Coco said as Reverdy grasped her shoulders and kissed her on each cheek. He was dressed, as usual, to show his contempt for fashion in a stableboy's cap, a tightly knotted green knit tie, and, despite the heat, an old tweed jacket with fraying cuffs and elbows so worn they were almost transparent.

"The Germans are in Solesmes. A few weeks ago, I woke up to find them stealing vegetables from our garden. Later they broke into the house. So, I put Henriette on a train to her sister's in Orléans and moved into the barn. I walled up the windows facing the road so I wouldn't see the Krauts and they wouldn't see me. But eventually they discovered the barn and chased me out. Since then, I've been living in the woods."

He dropped his rucksack, and it hit the floor with a heavy thud.

"Are you hungry? I can order some food from across the street," Coco said.

"No. I can't stay long." As Reverdy sank into the sofa, his eyes fell on the stack of books on a side table. One of his poetry collections, *Cravates de Chanvre*, sat on top. The book was worth a great deal of money, as it featured an original watercolor by Picasso on every page.

"You should put that away. Lock it in your safe," Reverdy said, picking up the book. His face took on an expression of deep pleasure as he turned the pages.

"You think the Germans are going to come in and steal everything?" said Coco.

"It wouldn't surprise me."

Reverdy had given the book to Coco in 1922. They'd become lovers a few years earlier after meeting at an exhibit of Picasso's paintings. There had been much to draw them together. Reverdy's childhood had not been as poor or as grim as Coco's. Still, he had come from the same peasant stock as she. His grandfather had been a carpenter, and his father a wine-grower in Narbonne, a small rural town in the Languedoc region near the Spanish border. In Paris, they'd both created themselves as artists and become part of the elite creative set led by Picasso.

Reverdy kept his seamstress wife hidden away in a flat in Montmartre and lived on and off with Coco in her grand house on rue Saint-Honoré. But he remained contemptuous of her money and had no use for her parties and socialite friends. Coco recalled one day when she was having a lunch in her garden for an important art dealer, and Reverdy walked down the steps with a basket on his arm. Speaking to no one, he elbowed his way through the elegant crowd and began rifling through the bushes, hunting for snails.

Coco found such antics more amusing than embarrassing, and she smiled now at the memory. She believed completely in Reverdy's talent and admired his devotion to his craft. In many ways, she saw him as a better version of herself, an elevated soul and a reminder of what her own life might have been had she taken a different path.

Reverdy closed *Cravates de Chanvre* and tucked it behind the red leather-bound collection of Shakespeare on Coco's bookshelf. "Leave it there, please," he said.

Coco wondered if he knew she'd financed the book's publication. Many times over the years she'd anonymously bought Reverdy's manuscripts through intermediaries and paid editors to publish them and give Reverdy stipends. Perhaps he did know. In any case, he didn't seem to have qualms about accepting her largess. Sometimes he let Coco rent him a room at the Ritz near her suite—all the better to get together for sex.

It had been more than two years since she'd made love to Reverdy and a year since she'd slept with any man. Her last lover, a Spanish sculptor seventeen years her junior, had felt overwhelmed by her extravagant lifestyle and left her after a few months.

As Coco sat next to Reverdy on the sofa, she felt a surge of desire. "I've missed seeing you," she said.

She slid closer to him and put her hand on his thigh. He picked it up and placed it in her lap as he kissed her chastely on the forehead. "I've something to show you," he said. Reaching into his rucksack, Reverdy pulled out a stack of flyers printed in purple mimeograph ink and set it on the coffee table. Coco glanced at the copy on top. Under a crude drawing of the Goddess of Liberty carrying a French flag, the caption read: *To all Frenchmen: Charles de Gaulle has issued a call to arms. We have not lost the war. We must fight back. Out with the invaders."*

Coco's eyes widened. "You've joined the Resistance?"

"What choice do we have but to resist?"

Reverdy explained that he had connected with a Resistance cell while hiding in the woods, and now he was fully committed to their cause. He delivered weapons and secret documents to strange men waiting in darkened houses. He sent coded messages about German troop movements from a transmitter he carried around in his rucksack. He'd also rescued a British soldier from a plane that had been downed by German fire. He'd brought him to Paris and was now hiding him in his room in Montmartre, until he could make arrangements to smuggle him into England.

Coco shook her head. "You've lost your mind."

Reverdy smiled and excused himself to use the toilet. Coco looked out the window to the clear, quiet day. She recalled the chaos of June, when smoke had filled the sky. Bureaucrats from the foreign office on the Quai d'Orsay had burned documents in a huge bonfire by the river, poisoning the air and killing all the birds. At the same time, treasures were hauled from the Louvre, taken to the countryside to be hidden in attics and under floorboards. Who knew if the priceless paintings and sculptures would ever be seen again. Coco hadn't been able to bear the tumult, the mess. Now, at least, some order had returned.

Like most Frenchmen, Reverdy had closed his eyes to what was happening. But Coco understood it was the dawn of a new order. She had felt the shift in the air as soon as she returned the day before, the move toward intolerance and autocracy. She admired Reverdy's courage and wished she could summon some for herself, but she worried about his safety. What was the point of resisting, especially if it got you killed? Who could save André, if not her? For the moment, the Germans weren't going anywhere. It was best to endure them to preserve as much of France's cultural life as possible.

She wouldn't say any of this to Reverdy, though.

"I'll leave you the flyers," he said, reappearing in the salon. "You can slip them under doors at the Ritz and along rue Cambon."

Coco thought for a moment what it would be like to become a heroine of the Resistance. It would be a chance for immortality beyond fashion!

The thought passed quickly, though. "You *have* lost your mind," she said, as she grabbed the flyers and stuffed them deep into Reverdy's rucksack. He shrugged elaborately. He wouldn't hold her failure to help against her. He loved her with an unconditional, familial love. Coco felt he'd forgive her anything.

Reverdy stood, hoisting his rucksack over his shoulder. "I'm leaving Paris this afternoon. You should, too. War is a time to hide, to lay low. You have your country house at Roquebrun. The Germans haven't gotten there yet."

Reverdy brushed each of Coco's cheeks with his lips. "I have to go," he said. At the door, he paused with his hand on the knob. "Get out of Paris, Coco."

"This is my home."

"Resistance is the only response to Occupation."

"Well, I'm resisting leaving the Ritz."

Coco returned to the hotel at two and found Spatz lolling against the wall outside the door to her suite. "I'm afraid I've bad news." He looked at the carpet a moment, then returned his gaze to her face. "The Kommandant needs your suite for visiting dignitaries. I've arranged for you to live on the other side of the hotel." Charlie Ritz had suggested as much the previous day. The more desirable Place Vendôme side of the Ritz was for Nazis. *Privitgast*, private guests of the occupying Germans, were confined to the less desirable rue Cambon side of the hotel.

Coco opened the front door and stomped inside, flinging her purse on the hall table. Spatz followed. "I won't move!" she cried.

"I'm afraid you must." Spatz looked at her severely for a moment, then softened his expression. "I have the key. I can show you your new suite, if you like."

At the opposite side of the hotel, they took the elevator to the top floor and strolled down the long, dim corridor. The rooms on this floor were all occupied by French citizens, the few who hadn't been evicted when the Germans took over. Coco's new neighbors comprised a collection of Nazi sympathizers, including a member of the aperitif wine–owning family Dubonnet, as well as Marie-Louise Ritz, the mother of the hotel's owner.

A few minutes later, they were standing in Coco's new suite—two square rooms and a plain, white-tiled bathroom. "I can't live here!" Coco's eyes darted around the small space.

"I'm sorry, it's the best I could do," said Spatz. He explained that he'd asked the Kommandant to assign her a commodious apartment on the rue Cambon side of the hotel, but nothing was available. Coco could either accept the cramped rooms or leave the hotel. She still had her apartment across the street where she'd just seen Reverdy. But the Ritz was where she *lived*. It was where she always returned after a long workday, after a triumphant fashion opening, after the end of an affair. Before the Occupation, she'd been sure that one day the Ritz was where she would die. Her last exit from the grand hotel would be in a box.

And now? Would the Germans be in Paris forever? Was this her life from now on? She realized she'd felt a knot of fear in her gut since the day the Germans arrived in France. She was losing weight, existing mostly on cigarettes, coffee, and red wine. She must start eating better to keep up her strength. She'd figure out how to get through this, as she'd figured out how to survive so much else.

Midday light filtered through the windows and hung over the floor in a white veil. Once these rooms had been quarters for hotel maids. Coco imagined the poor girls from the provinces who'd come to Paris for adventure and love, only to spend their nights hidden away in this humble spot under the mansard roof, exhausted and lonely. Probably many of them fled home after a few months. Perhaps they married farmers who were drunken brutes. Perhaps the girls couldn't bear their lives and blew their brains out. Coco thought with a shudder, *That's what would have happened to me, if I hadn't had ambition.*

She heard Spatz in the next room, marching around, inspecting every corner. "This can be your bedroom," he called out, loud enough for her to hear through the plaster walls.

Spatz rejoined her in the first room. "This space is larger," he said. "You can move in the sofa and chairs from your other suite and use it as a salon."

"My screens won't fit," said Coco in a dejected tone. Her precious Coromandels, those wooden folding screens painted with birds and flowers that had once graced the boudoir of a Chinese princess and cost more than her Rolls.

"I'll have someone move them across the street."

"I don't trust the workers."

"I'll supervise them myself."

Spatz also arranged for a porter to move Coco's two Louis Vuitton trunks into her new suite. The larger trunk held clothes—suits, dresses, blouses, coats, evening gowns—the last things she had made for herself before shutting her ateliers. Coco later ordered her maid to carry the clothes across the street to the closet in her rue Cambon apartment. It took three trips. The other trunk held shoes, handbags, costume jewelry, hats, and linens. Under the linens were four large scrapbooks bound in green leather in which her secretary had meticulously pasted pictures and stories about Coco that had appeared in the press.

She couldn't resist sitting down and leafing through the scrapbooks—here was a record of her social and professional triumphs, and she enjoyed reliving them. She was no longer the dewy young beauty of the black-and-white photos, with supple arms, a firm jawline, and not a hint of gray in her shiny black hair. It comforted her, though, to think she had once looked like the lively girl in the pictures.

One afternoon when she was going through the scrapbooks, Spatz showed up at her door with two cartons of Gauloises. "I thought you could use these," he said. The Germans had forbidden women from buying cigarettes and allowed men only one pack a week.

"You've saved me the chore of buying on the black market," said Coco, and invited him in. He was dressed in a tan light wool suit, a white shirt, and a blue striped Hermès tie. Coco poured them each a glass of red wine, and they settled on the sofa. "I was just going through my scrapbooks. I hadn't looked at them in years," she said.

Spatz picked up one of the volumes and slowly leafed through it. "I remember you on the town in some of these gorgeous clothes." He looked at Coco and smiled warmly. "At every party, you were always the chicest woman."

The compliment made Coco suspicious. What was he after, flattering her, bringing her cigarettes?

"Here you are with Misia Sert and Jean Cocteau at the Rothschild ball." Spatz pointed to a picture of Coco dressed as Marie-Antoinette in a pearl satin gown with wide panier skirts and a towering white wig. Misia stood to her right in a similar but less extravagant outfit, impersonating an eighteenth-century lady's maid. Next to Misia vamped Cocteau as Louis XVI in a blue brocade coat and breeches. "You three were like the musketeers. All for one and one for all. I never saw one of you without the others," said Spatz. "Are Misia and Cocteau still in Paris?"

"Those two would never leave."

"I hope you'll introduce me to them sometime." Spatz sighed heavily and closed the scrapbook. "I'm so happy to be back in Paris. Except for the past two years, I've lived here for most of my adult life. I was sent here as an embassy attaché in 1927 when I was just thirty years old. I'm almost as much of a Parisian as you."

He opened another scrapbook, this one filled with photographs of Coco with Boy Capel, her British love, who'd set her up in the hat shop on rue Cambon that launched her fashion career. Boy had run a thriving shipbuilding business but still found time to write books on political history and collect art. Coco revered his brilliance and success and adored him for his belief in her. She thought she'd be with him forever, but he was killed in a car crash in 1919. Spatz paused over a picture of the couple lounging on the beach at Deauville.

"Who's this?" asked Spatz.

"My fiancé," she said slowly. "He died soon after that picture was taken."

"I'm sorry—you look very happy with him."

"I was."

Spatz nodded toward a picture of Coco in a long white skirt and a bulky cardigan standing in front of a beach cabana at the Grand Hotel in Deauville with the wind blowing through her hair. "Catsy and I stayed at the Grand Hotel once. I would have had more fun if I'd been there with you," he said, shaking his head.

"Didn't you love her?" Coco asked.

"I thought I did. But we were completely unsuited. Catsy didn't like living in Paris and complained about it constantly. Part of it was, she never spoke good French."

Coco recalled Madame von Dincklage from the few times she'd seen her at parties between the wars. Catsy was a pleasant-looking large-boned blonde. "Is that why you divorced, because of her bad French?" Coco said dryly.

Spatz's expression darkened. "She couldn't have children. At the time, I thought it was important to have an heir, to keep the von Dincklage name going. Now that the world's gone to hell, it doesn't matter."

"What's happened to Catsy?" Coco asked.

Spatz shook his head. "I'm not sure. I haven't been in touch with her recently."

"Did she give you your nickname?"

Spatz explained that it had come from his childhood. "What about you? How did you get the name Coco?"

"My aunts. I lived with them after my mother died. They raised horses in the Auvergne," Coco lied.

Spatz held up a small photograph that had been tucked into the pages of the scrapbook. It showed Coco as a young woman standing in front of a tailoring shop. She wore a dark skirt, a white blouse, and a tailor's smock. Her heavy dark hair was piled on her head in a topknot. "What's this?" asked Spatz.

Coco grabbed the photo from him and shoved it back between the pages. "Nothing."

"I grew up with horses, too," he said. "I'll take you riding in the Bois this fall."

How many other women had he offered to take riding? Coco recalled seeing Spatz at parties dancing with the prettiest women, ignoring his wife. She'd heard gossip about him, that he was an aggressive seducer. One of her clients had had an affair with him and bragged about Spatz's extraordinary prowess in bed.

Spatz looked at his watch and stood. "I'd like to hear more about your girlhood. But I have an appointment. Dinner tonight at eight?"

"That would be lovely," Coco said. *It's only dinner, after all.*

Spatz gave her a warm, knowing look. "This time, I hope you answer the door."

Coco never told anyone the truth about her life, not Pierre Reverdy nor any of her closest friends. She'd lied so much about her origins, she'd started to believe the made-up stories herself. Looking through the scrapbooks with Spatz, however, shook her hard wall of defense. She tried to nap but couldn't fall asleep. She felt herself catapulted down a long tunnel of memory she couldn't escape. Hours later, as she sat at her dressing table redoing her makeup, she was still thinking about her past. She'd had the harshest of childhoods, traveling from village to village in the Auvergne as her asthmatic, constantly pregnant mother trailed after her father. Albert Chanel had been a hard-drinking, barely literate itinerant peddler with no trade or skills except in the art of womanizing, a pursuit enhanced by his exceptional good looks. He had the same thick dark hair and chiseled bone structure as his daughter Gabrielle. Albert scratched out a living selling vegetables, pots, pans, cloth, and underwear to housewives in village squares on market days. He disappeared for weeks at a time and then would reappear, flashing his dazzling smile, to eat a meal and have his laundry washed, sometimes impregnating his sickly wife, only to disappear again.

When Coco was twelve, she saw her mother die in the flophouse where Albert had settled his family in two cramped rooms infested with vermin. Coco, her brothers Alphonse and Lucien, and her sisters Julie and Antoinette gathered around the narrow iron bed where their mother lay, while their father was God knew where. Jeanne Chanel had been suffering from asthma for years, but it had grown worse in the past month, after the death of her newborn son, her sixth child. The previous night, Jeanne had slipped into a coma. Coco held her mother's hand, listening to her agonized gasps for air. There was a demon inside her mother. "Wake up, Mama!" Coco cried. But Jeanne's eyes stayed closed. She wasn't moving except for the horrible gasps. Finally, at five in the afternoon, they stopped. Jeanne's hand grew cold in Coco's own, but still the child clutched it. Her mother had been taken from her, and she felt as though she herself had died. She stood for what seemed like hours by her mother's bed. Then, a harsh voice came from the doorway. "Come along, come along now." Her father.

He loaded Coco and her siblings into his peddler's cart. Stale apples, rags, newspapers, and metal cutlery knocked around the children's feet as an old black horse hauled the clattering cart along the country roads. They left Alphonse and Lucien at a farm as laborers in exchange for room and board. The next stop was Aubazine, an orphanage run by the sisters of the Congregation of the Sacred Heart of Mary. A stark fortress on a high ridge, the orphanage sat in a dark pine forest.

Coco and her sisters slept in an attic dormitory in simple cots pushed up against whitewashed walls hung with wooden crucifixes. They rose at dawn, splashed cold water on their faces, and marched to chapel. If Coco sang "Ave Maria" too loudly, a nun would poke her in the side with a stick. Once she noticed an old hunchback man who'd wandered in from town sitting in a pew opposite her. She felt a surge of pity for him and yearned to sit beside him, to pat his hump and tell him it didn't matter, that he could still be loved. But she dared not move from her place beside a nun. She remained in her seat, feeling utterly alone and unloved herself.

Another time, after a day of lessons in the drafty classroom with the chipped plaster, tasteless meals in the dark-paneled dining room that smelled of boiled cabbage, and brief recreation in the fading light of the walled garden, she lay awake in her cot. After the lights had been turned off, Coco began rubbing her nose violently until she felt blood dripping onto her nightgown. "Help!" she cried. She heard steps on the stone floor and the clicking of rosary beads, which the nuns kept attached to their belts. "There, there, child," said the nun who'd rushed to Coco's side. The nun stopped the bleeding with her handkerchief, then hugged Coco tightly. That was all the little girl had wanted—someone to hold her close.

Coco never saw her father again, though he was out there somewhere in the world. She couldn't bear to be called an "orphan." She couldn't bear to be pitied. So she began to invent stories about three well-to-do maiden aunts who supported themselves by raising Arabian horses that they sold to the military. They lived in a fine house filled with antiques and art and served lavish meals of ham, chicken, eggs, cakes, and chocolate milk whenever she, their favorite niece, visited. She took many of these details from the sentimental novels she borrowed from another girl and read in the bathroom late at night after the nuns had gone to sleep.

The novels helped Coco fight her way out of the black depths by showing her the possibility of reinvention. Later, she beat back the gloom with work. In many ways, the style she created—clean, elegant, pure—was a defense against death, against loss, loneliness, poverty, and sorrow. She had learned from her father to ignore emotional distress, to stomp on it as something unworthy of her attention. Her mother's supplication had brought Jeanne Chanel nothing but misery and death, while her father, the inflictor of this pain, had survived. Coco admired his survival, and it became the driving force in her own life. What mattered was to keep going, to endure.

She applied one more coat of lipstick and inspected her face in the mirror. She liked what she saw. She was no longer a forlorn little girl. She was Coco Chanel, and she was about to dine with the most dashing man at the Ritz.

Spatz called for Coco promptly at eight. Downstairs, when the maître d' beckoned the couple to the left side of the dining room, the German side, Spatz nodded to the right. "Over there, please," he said.

The maître d' led them to a small table in the back right corner. "I thought you'd be more comfortable on this side," said Spatz. Speaking perfect French and dressed in an elegant navy pin-striped suit, Spatz fit nicely with the Faubourg aristocrats who dined frequently on the French side of the restaurant with their bejeweled, over-groomed wives. He ordered a bottle of champagne, which a waiter poured into two baccarat flutes. "I saw in one of those articles about you that after six you only drink champagne and eat steak," said Spatz.

"Don't believe everything you read," said Coco. "But I will have a steak, medium rare."

"Two steaks, medium rare." Spatz handed the menus to the waiter.

"It's all right if you sit on this side of the room?" Coco asked.

"Remember, I'm almost as French as you are." He gave a short laugh. "And my mother is British, from London, an old family with land in Coventry. I grew up speaking English to her. She was supposed to marry the Earl of Derbyshire, but she met my father on a hunting trip in the Black Forest and that was that. I come from a long line of professional soldiers, stretching back to my grandfather Lieutenant-General Georg Karl von Dincklage, who fought in the Franco-Prussian conflict of 1870, when Germany vanquished the armies of Napoleon II."

"You've got war in your blood."

"But I'm not a warrior, though I did fight in World War I, side by side with my father, who was a cavalry major. I had no taste for it. I got out of it as soon as I could and married Catsy. I was just twenty-five."

Spatz paused as the waiter poured each of them another glass of champagne. When the waiter left, Spatz said, "I wanted to clarify something about my wife—my ex-wife. In case you hear rumors, I don't want you to get the wrong idea. Catsy's mother was Jewish. But it was only a coincidence that I divorced her three months before Germany passed the Nuremberg laws prohibiting marriage between Aryans and Jews."

Coco frowned. "A coincidence?"

"Catsy would tell you the same thing. She bears me no ill will."

Still, marriage to a half-Jewish woman no doubt would have ruined Spatz's career. Perhaps opportunism had played as much of a role as love in his divorce. Coco didn't care. No one understood the pressures of expediency more than she.

After Coco and Spatz finished their steaks, they lingered over coffee and caramel flan. Coco took just a bite of hers. Spatz consumed his in four spoonfuls. Afterward, he escorted Coco to her suite. At the door, he bowed and brushed the back of her hand with his lips. She was disappointed he didn't kiss her on the mouth. She felt herself attracted to him in a way she had not been drawn to a man in a long time. He bolstered her confidence. He made her feel young and attractive.

Sitting at her dressing table, she removed her makeup with a washcloth dipped in cold cream. She was ready for a romantic adventure. She winced when she thought of Pierre Reverdy. He would be shocked to find her in the company of a German. And she had to admit it looked bad for a woman who thought of herself as the pride of France to be involved with one of the Occupiers. But Coco didn't think of Spatz as German, with his British mother and English as the language of his childhood. That was where he got his polish. Englishmen were gentlemen.

She washed her face, brushed her teeth, and got into bed. Her heart felt lighter than it had in months. She would not need morphine to fall asleep tonight.

Spatz began visiting Coco every afternoon. He'd call to see if she was in and ask if he could come up. The pretext was to bring her things she might have trouble getting, even on the black market: fine soap, silk stockings, chocolate, flowers, more cigarettes. It was flattering. Spatz seemed so eager to do whatever he could for her that after knowing him for only a week, she broached the subject of her nephew. Could Spatz do anything about freeing André? So far, she'd had no luck enlisting anyone's help in the matter. She tried contacting Pierre Laval, the second-in-command at

Vichy, whom she'd known socially in Paris, but she couldn't get through to him.

As Coco explained to Spatz, "André is suffering from tuberculosis, and he won't survive if he doesn't get medical care." They were sitting on the sofa in her salon sharing a bottle of red wine. Outside the light was changing. The beauty in the fading sky comforted Coco, the pink sunset matching the roses Spatz had brought, which she placed in a porcelain vase on the coffee table. Soon, the days would shorten, signaling the end of summer, and roses would be impossible to get.

"I'll see what I can do," Spatz said.

"It means everything to me that André comes home." Looking out the window to the Ritz garden below, Coco took in the sweet fullness of the flowers, watching their colors fade in the evening light. The following morning the sun would restore the garden to its full glory. This was the point of beauty—to beat back the sadness of the world.

She thought about the first time she'd seen André, when he was just a few hours old, a mewling, wrinkled thing with a head of fine brown hair. He had reminded her of a muskrat. She'd never liked babies, and she resented this one, in particular, as if Julie's love for her infant would dilute her love for Coco. The sisters were just a year apart and exceptionally close. Growing up, Coco had loved Julie more than anyone, more even than their parents. Julie had been her one solace through their grim years together in the convent orphanage after their mother died.

But after the sisters moved to Moulins to take jobs arranged by the nuns, Julie became pregnant by a peddler. He abandoned Julie even before André was born, and over the next several years, as Coco moved to Paris and became a designer, Julie fell in love with a series of men. After the last one, a soldier stationed in town, left her, she grew despondent. One day she deposited six-year-old André on the doorstep of the Catholic church and went home to kill herself by swallowing poison. Coco remembered getting the call from the priest and crumbling at the news. She remembered her despair on the train ride to Moulins from Paris and how her despair began to lift when she saw André sitting on a wood bench in the rectory office, hugging a toy bear. Her heart swelled with a love that surprised her with its intensity. She took immediate charge of the child and vowed to keep him safe. He was a link—the only one she had—to her lost sister.

No matter how intolerable her own life became, she would never consider ending it while André was alive. She couldn't do that to him again. She was glad she and Spatz were becoming close. He was her best hope to bring the young man home. *But if anything happens to André, I will kill myself*, she thought.

Spatz seemed moved by the depth of Coco's distress. He took her hand and squeezed it gently. "I promise I'll do everything I can to free your nephew."

He left the next morning for Lyon and was gone four days. Spatz didn't tell Coco the purpose of his trip. When he returned, he showed up at the Ritz in a new beige linen suit, carrying a large oblong package wrapped in brown paper. "I hope to have good news about your nephew soon," he said. "In the meantime, I brought you something." He handed Coco the package.

She tore off the paper to find a bolt of dark blue silk chiffon, hand-embroidered in a subtle pattern of gold camellias, Coco's signature flower. "Where did you get this?" she asked, running her hands over the luxurious fabric.

"I have my ways." He stood with his hands in his pockets and shrugged his shoulders. "Why don't you make it into a dress?"

Coco unfurled the fabric and wrapped it around her body. She hadn't designed a dress in more than a year, since she shuttered her workrooms and dismissed all three thousand of her employees, except the vendeuse Veronique, who manned the counter where Coco's perfume was sold; the manager of the boutique; an older woman who did the books; and a seamstress whom Coco kept on to make alterations for her former clients.

Coco missed the buzz of the atelier, the mannequins gathered in their little white robes waiting their turn in front of the triple mirrors as Coco sculpted fabulous couture on their slender bodies. She missed the cold bite of straight pins between her teeth, the solid weight of her scissors on a ribbon around her neck. Work was what she had lived for. And now she was idle. It had been a mistake to close her house, though at the time it had seemed the right thing to do. War was coming, and the world of society, of balls and dinners and parties and luxury that had supported her was coming to an end. No one would have money for couture or anyplace to wear it. Or so she had thought.

"The color suits you," said Spatz.

Dark blue was a nice change from black, the color of mourning. Coco had largely been responsible for making black the standard of chic. After the first Great War, she created the little black dress and had women everywhere clamoring to put one in their closets.

As she draped the fabric around her chest and torso, Coco envisioned a gown with soft tiers of fabric in graceful flounces floating from the waistline to the floor. Each ruffle would be finished with picot edging. "I'll have my seamstress make up a dress," she said. She tried to release herself from the fabric but found she was only getting more tangled up in it.

"Here, let me help you," said Spatz, stepping forward. He palmed two fistfuls of chiffon, releasing a space for Coco to move. She spun around and around until the fabric was puddled on the floor, and she was facing Spatz. "I feel like the luckiest man in Paris tonight to be here with you," he said. With his right index finger, he tucked a strand of dark hair behind Coco's ear and leaned in to kiss her. Then, taking her by the hand, he led her to the bedroom and closed the door.

THREE

I hear you're sleeping with the enemy," said Misia Sert over the telephone two weeks later. Misia was Coco's best friend. A faded beauty with failing eyesight, she knew everyone who was anyone in Paris, stretching back to the Belle Epoque.

"He's not the enemy," Coco snapped.

"He's German, isn't he?"

"His mother is English. If you met him, you'd like him."

"We'll see. Bring him to lunch." Misia hung up the phone with a loud click.

Coco had tried to keep her affair with Spatz secret, but one evening at the end of August Jean Cocteau, Coco's *other* best friend, happened to be walking up rue Cambon and saw her exit the back entrance of the Ritz arm-in-arm with Spatz. Cocteau put two and two together and immediately called Misia to tell her about Coco's elegant German.

By then Coco and Spatz had become a couple, sleeping together nearly every night at the Ritz and dining together, mostly in Coco's apartment above her boutique. Her heart melted with love and longing at the sight of him, and the most exciting thing was, he desired *her*. She no longer felt old. She felt young and alluring, as at the start of her career, when men—famous men!—like Igor Stravinsky and Crown Prince Dimitri of Russia fell all over themselves to court her. *"Mein schöner liebling,"* Spatz had whispered in her ear that first afternoon they'd made love. She asked him not to speak German in bed. *"Ma belle, mon amour,"* he'd said, his cheek brushing hers. "No, not French, either," she'd insisted. "English, please."

"Very well, my love," he'd answered.

In English pillow talk with Spatz, Coco smothered the truth of her German lover, as she smothered so many other truths.

Coco's spoken English was rough, but she understood everything that was said in the language. When Spatz spoke English, she could fool herself that he really *was* English, like his English mother and like the great love of her life, Boy Capel. Oh, her life had been sweet in those days. Boy believed in her and encouraged her ambitions. She remembered his first present to her: a white silk gown by Lanvin. He'd given it to her not to wear, but to take apart so she could study its construction.

Spatz, too, understood her need to create. Fashion was her canvas, her blank page. That was why he'd brought her that exquisite bolt of silk chiffon.

At one o'clock Coco and Spatz ducked into a sleek Mercedes waiting with a driver in front of the Ritz. The city felt almost dead, the streets nearly empty. A few cyclists pedaled along. Occasionally, a car whizzed past. The café on the corner where Coco had often taken lunch in her working days had a lone table of customers, three young women sitting with two German officers. Loudspeakers set up in the Tuileries blared treacly Viennese waltzes. A huge "V" hung off the entrance to the Louvre and a banner announced "Deutschland Siegt An Allen Fronten," Germany victorious on all fronts.

It was still Paris, still tall and luminous, with the bridges arched gracefully over the Seine, and the light the exact shade of soft gold as in a painting by Monet. But something strange and horrible hung in the air. It was as if all the molecules of the city had been smashed and put back together, but without the true heart and soul of Paris.

The Mercedes stopped at a red light. A few pedestrians scurried past the windshield. One did not. A gray-haired woman in her sixties peering into the car recognized Coco and planted herself in the middle of the street, her eyes darting madly from the German soldier driving the car to Coco and back to the soldier. "Who is that?" asked Spatz.

"She looks familiar. A seamstress who once worked for me, I think." But Coco had seen scores of seamstresses come and go over the years, and she couldn't be sure.

The light changed. As the Mercedes lurched forward, the woman spat at the car, then picked up a rock and flung it at Coco's window. She heard the jagged chimes of breaking glass, as Spatz pushed her head down with the palm of his hand. "*Scheize*," he said.

Coco watched the woman dart up the street on thick veiny legs. She hadn't gotten very far when the driver screeched the Mercedes to a halt. He pulled a gun from a holster on his belt and started for the door handle. Spatz stopped him with a hand on the driver's shoulder. "Let it go," he said.

The car moved forward, and Coco felt a sharp stinging in her right cheek. "My God, you've been cut!" exclaimed Spatz.

Coco put her fingers to her face, and when she took them away, she saw they were covered with blood. Spatz dabbed his handkerchief on the wound. "It's just a surface cut—nothing serious," he said. For the rest of the trip, he pressed his handkerchief to Coco's face, and by the time they arrived at Misia's, the cut had stopped bleeding.

"Misia's blind, and Cocteau's so self-absorbed he probably won't notice," said Coco, as she inspected her face in her compact mirror and applied a heavy layer of powder to the angry red line on her cheek. She clicked her compact shut and took a deep breath. Turning to Spatz, she whispered, "Please, from now on, let's only have drivers in civilian clothes."

At Misia's gray stone building on rue Constantine an old iron elevator clanked them up to the third floor. In the salon, Misia lay on a burgundy brocade sofa, a beige satin comforter pulled to her chin. She had light green eyes in a flat, round face etched with fine lines. Her once glorious copper hair frizzed around her head in a dyed red nimbus. On a spindly chair next to her sat Jean Cocteau, skinny and sharp-featured with a crop of cowlicks sprouting from a mass of brown hair. Cocteau wore a dandy's jacket pinched at the waist and a green paisley tie that matched the handkerchief triangle in his breast pocket. When Coco and Spatz entered, he jumped to his feet. "*Ich bin sehr erfreut dich kennenzulernen,*" Cocteau said, shaking Spatz's hand.

"So, Jean Cocteau speaks German. It's lovely to meet you, too," said Spatz. He bowed slightly.

"I learned it in childhood from my governess. It's a pleasure to be speaking it again," said Cocteau.

"You don't find hearing so much German unreal, as some of my French friends claim?" asked Spatz.

"Paris is unreal. But I find upheaval invigorating. It's good for creativity."

Misia clucked loudly. "It has the opposite effect on me. I can barely move."

"You were always a lazy cow," said Coco, smiling wickedly.

"Shut up," said Misia.

Cocteau sighed and turned to Spatz with a rueful expression. "I'm sorry, Herr von Dincklage," he said in German, so the women couldn't understand. "I'm used to this. I've been listening to the bitchery of these two for decades."

"No need to apologize," said Spatz, also in German. Then, in French to Misia. "I'm sorry you're not feeling well, Madame Sert."

"I'm worried I'll die before JoJo gets back," said Misia in a dramatic tone.

Spatz smiled warmly. "I would have enjoyed meeting your husband. I admire his paintings."

Coco thought of correcting Spatz but decided not to draw attention to Misia's peculiar situation. In truth, José Maria Sert was Misia's ex-husband. The couple had been divorced since 1927, but Misia remained in Sert's thrall and spent as much time with him as he'd allow. At the moment he was in Madrid with his mistress.

"You're not dying," said Coco in an exasperated tone.

"Perhaps we should come back another time," said Spatz.

"Misia's fine. She just wants attention." Coco elbowed Spatz in the ribs, and he sank into the armchair behind him.

The maid brought in trays of cold ham, potatoes, bread, and haricots verts, and they ate balancing plates on their laps. In the middle of the meal, Cocteau let out a little yelp. "Coco, your face!"

She blotted her cheek with her napkin—some blood had seeped through her powder. Spatz started to explain, but Coco interrupted him. She didn't want to relive the frightening incident or call attention to the fact that Spatz was a German with a Nazi chauffeur. "I cut myself this morning on a ring," she lied. "The stone had fallen out, and the sharp prongs were exposed."

Cocteau narrowed his eyes at her. "You look pale," he said.

"It's just a scratch," Coco said.

Spatz ate quickly and laid his plate on the Louis XIV table next to his chair. "I'm afraid I can't stay for dessert. I have a meeting at the embassy," he said. "Thank you so much, Madame Sert. Lunch was delightful."

Spatz held out his hand to Misia, but she ignored it. Then he turned to Cocteau, who jumped up and enthusiastically clasped Spatz's hand with both his own. "I hope I'll see you again soon," said Cocteau.

"I'm sure you will." Spatz bowed to Misia and, before turning on his heel and disappearing under the arched doorway, kissed Coco on the lips. As soon as the door closed behind him, Coco glared at Misia.

"You were rude."

"He's very handsome, I'll give him that," said Misia.

"You couldn't even lift yourself from the couch and shake his hand," said Coco.

"My grandmother was Jewish!" cried Misia.

"Coco likes to forget unpleasant truths," said Cocteau.

Coco gave him a vicious look. "It's disgusting how you flirted with him."

"*He* flirted with me!"

"I actually saw you bat your eyelashes! You might have been irresistible at twenty, but you're no longer twenty."

"Neither are you, my dear." Cocteau smirked. "Von Dincklage looks to be quite a bit younger than you. Robbing the cradle again?"

"You're the pederast. How old is Marais—twenty-six? And you're over fifty."

Jean Marais, Cocteau's golden-haired, astonishingly handsome lover, was the most famous actor in France. Jeannot, as his intimates called him, had been discovered by Cocteau seven years earlier when he was still in acting school, and they'd been together ever since.

"Did you tell your German how old *you* are?" Cocteau asked in a mocking tone.

Before Coco could respond, the maid entered carrying a silver tray piled with envelopes. "The mail, madame," she said to Misia, and placed the tray on the coffee table.

Misia went through the letters, holding each one close to her eyes to discern the name of the senders. "Look at this," she said, handing a soiled sheet of notebook paper to Coco. It was from their friend Max Jacob, a Jewish poet who'd converted to Catholicism many years earlier and who was living near a monastery in Saint-Benoît in the unoccupied part of France. Coco donned a pair of black-framed glasses from a pocket of her jersey jacket and read out loud:

> *Dear Misia,*
>
> *A short word to tell you that my brother-in-law, the husband of my sister, Mirté-Léa, was arrested by the Germans last week, pulled off the street in one of the Nazis' regular round-ups. We don't know where they've taken him. He is sixty-four, myopic, and in poor health owing to injuries he suffered fighting for France in the*

*first war. That apparently was not enough to protect him. I wonder
if you can send some money to my sister. I would ask Coco, but she
has already sent me a check this month for my own expenses, and
I don't want to impose on her again.*

Coco placed the letter on the coffee table and sighed deeply. "I'll send
him another check."

Max Jacob was the absent musketeer in what Spatz had noted was
their little band of avant-garde adventurers. Together the four friends had
scaled the heights of creative Paris: Max with surrealist poetry; Cocteau
with film, theater, and prose; Misia with arts patronage; and Coco with
fashion. You couldn't tell the story of one without telling the story of them
all. Max never had any money, so the others—mostly Coco—helped him
out when they could. In return, Max acted as their sidekick and court
jester, amusing them by telling horoscopes and performing imitations.
Sometimes, he was a ballet dancer pirouetting with his pants rolled up
to his knees, exposing his hairy gorilla legs. Or he'd pretend to be a lady
opera singer wrapped in veils and singing off-key. The clowning, though,
hid Max's deeply spiritual nature.

"I hope you think of Max when you're in bed with your German,"
Misia scolded.

"Have you forgotten? Max is a Catholic now," said Coco in a sarcastic tone.

"You never took his conversion seriously," said Cocteau.

"Neither did you." Coco picked up her purse and pulled on her gloves
as the maid entered with a tray of pastries. Before passing through the
doorway into the entry hall, she shot Cocteau a fierce look. "You never
take *anything* seriously."

As soon as she returned to the Ritz, Coco opened the center drawer
of her desk and removed a black leather account book. She wrote a check
to Max for two thousand francs. Then, as she fumbled in the drawer for
an envelope, her eyes fell on her passport. Opening it, she saw her birth
year, 1883. Without thinking twice, she took a black pen and turned the

second "8" into "9," shaving ten years from her age. Now she was only three years older than Spatz, no matter what Cocteau or anyone else said.

That evening Spatz took Coco for a walk by the Seine. The river shimmered under a rosy sunset. Children cried as their parents gathered up their toys and games and led them way. Along the quay, booksellers shuttered and locked their display boxes. Couples hurried by, desperate to get home by curfew. Coco and Spatz leaned against the stone balustrade, looking out at the silvery water. "You can't know how glad I am to be back in Paris, away from the hornet's nest of Berlin," said Spatz.

"Aren't you worried they'll forget about you here?" asked Coco.

"I'll be glad if they forget about me. All I want is to stay here with you." He pulled Coco close and kissed her on the mouth. "Paris is home."

"Even with your countrymen stomping all over?" said Coco. "It's bad enough to have German street signs and swastikas hanging off every building, but do they have to parade every day down the Champs-Élysées, in case anyone didn't notice they're in charge?"

"I'd prefer they weren't here, too. Let's pretend they're not." Spatz squeezed Coco's hand. "We'll draw a line around ourselves and not let anyone cross it."

"Fine with me. I have a harem-woman side that loves seclusion."

Secrets. Stolen moments. The erotic charge of forbidden love had always appealed to Coco.

"You're my harem of one," said Spatz. He touched the cut on Coco's face. "It stopped bleeding. I can hardly see it."

"Remember, you promised. No more drivers in uniform."

"I promise." Spatz kissed her again. "Finally, I have what I've always wanted—a woman of true elegance and sophistication."

As the sky turned a deep blue, Coco and Spatz found themselves alone on the quay. The booksellers had all departed, their black boxes lining the pavement like shut coffins. "It must be curfew," said Coco. "We should go back."

"I have an *ausweis*. Let's enjoy this. We have the city to ourselves."

Suddenly, the bluesy notes of a trumpet rang out. "Duke Ellington," said Spatz. "It seems to be coming from an open window in an apartment across the river." He nodded toward the building and crooned in a clear, gentle voice, "*Things you say and do, just thrill me through and through.*"

It was the first time Coco had heard him sing. He had a fine voice. She admired how Spatz knew American songs and the best French wine, how he spoke several languages and dressed impeccably, how easily and comfortably he fit into her stylish world. He draped his arm across Coco's shoulder, and she rested her head on his chest. They stood there for a few minutes in the blue moonlight and the cooling air, listening until the song ended. Then, leaving behind the river and the moon and the dying sounds of the trumpet, they started home to the Ritz.

FOUR

oco stood on a little wooden footstool in front of the triple mirrors in her third-floor atelier, wearing a new dress made from the blue silk chiffon Spatz had brought her. It had a bodice held up with thin fabric straps and a long skirt with tiers of soft ruffles. Manon, the only seamstress Coco had kept on after closing the House of Chanel, had sewn the dress according to Coco's instructions and now knelt on the floor next to her boss, pinning up the hem.

It was the first time in a year Coco had entered her atelier, a large square room flooded with light from the tall windows facing rue Cambon. In her working days, the atelier had buzzed from morning to late at night with mannequins and seamstresses chatting and milling about. Bolts of cloth and boxes overflowing with buttons, sequins, and bits of embroidery had cluttered the floor. Handbags, hats, and shoes had piled up on the tables. Now the atelier was empty, everything cleared away and put into storage, the thin carpet of needles, thread, pins, and fabric pieces long ago vacuumed up.

Coco studied the dress in the mirror from all angles. "Don't make it too short," she told Manon. "Just below the knee."

"Does Mademoiselle have in mind an occasion to wear this dress?" Manon asked.

"I'm going to save it—to celebrate the end of the war."

Manon dropped the hem and made the sign of the cross. "God willing, we will live to see it."

There was a loud pounding on the door, and a moment later, two stern-faced Nazi soldiers burst in with their guns drawn. "Step back," barked the taller of the two.

"We need your files," said the shorter, stockier soldier, who seemed to be in charge.

"My files?"

"Those are our orders—to collect all the files from Paris couture houses."

"Why?"

"We just follow orders, madame."

"This is an outrage!"

The taller soldier stepped forward and poked Coco in the shoulder with the tip of his rifle. "Where are they?"

Coco led the soldiers to a room off the studio where her files were stored in floor-to-ceiling metal cabinets. The tall Nazi pulled on a few drawers. "They're all locked," he said.

"The keys are in my suite across the street," Coco said.

"We've no time to wait," the short Nazi said.

Coco watched, horrified, as the soldiers smashed the locks with the butts of their rifles. "You can't do this!" she cried. She ran to the phone and called Spatz at his office. The receptionist put Coco on hold for several minutes, then told her Herr von Dincklage wasn't in the building.

The Nazis emptied Coco's files, making several trips, carrying armloads of documents downstairs to a German army truck parked on rue Cambon.

When they'd left, Coco said to Manon, who'd hung back through the ordeal, trembling with fear, "At least they didn't take the dress off my back."

The day after the Nazis confiscated Coco's files, Spatz arrived at the Ritz to take his breakfast with her. She hadn't seen or talked to him since the previous morning. "Where were you? I called and called," she said.

"Busy day. I'm sorry." He looked hard at her, and his expression said, "Don't ask me to explain."

Spatz did not have a room at the Ritz, as Coco had originally thought, but kept an apartment on Avenue Foch in the elegant Sixteenth Arrondissement favored by German officers. A month into his affair with Coco, he began spending a couple of nights a week there. He never gave Coco the phone number at the apartment or invited her to visit. He claimed he used it mostly for poker games. No matter where he slept, though, with Coco or at his own place, he usually joined her at eight a.m. in her suite.

When Coco told Spatz what had happened, he pounded the sofa cushion with his fist. "Those fools! I'll have everything sent back and the locks on your cabinets replaced."

"What are they up to?" Coco asked.

Spatz sighed heavily. "The Germans are moving couture to Berlin."

"Couture can't exist outside Paris!" scoffed Coco. She sank into the sofa beside him. A waiter from the restaurant downstairs arrived with the couple's breakfast: a pot of coffee, two sliced apples, and a basket of croissants. After shaking out white linen napkins for Coco and Spatz, the waiter poured each of them a cup of coffee, bowed at the waist, and retreated through the front door. Coco picked up the copy of *Le Figaro* on the breakfast tray and scanned the pages.

"You won't find anything about it in there," said Spatz. He explained that Gestapo agents had broken into the offices of the Chambre Syndicale de la Couture, the organization that had regulated high fashion since 1868. They'd ransacked the files, confiscating all export records and documents related to the creation of collections going back to the nineteenth century. "I didn't know they were raiding individual houses," he said, shaking his head. The Germans planned to keep French ateliers open to supply a workforce to make the clothes, but French couturiers would move their headquarters to Berlin. "Coco, there's a place for you," he said.

"Are you crazy?" Coco set her cup down in its saucer so roughly that liquid spattered the front of her white silk blouse.

"You've been complaining you're bored to death."

"I am."

"This is your chance to reopen your house," said Spatz.

"Not in Berlin!"

Spatz insisted he could finagle a special situation for Coco. She and she alone would remain in Paris. He was sure his bosses would agree. Wasn't she the greatest of all French couturiers? Her atelier on rue Cambon would be a monument to her unique status. He promised he could get her all the materials and trimmings she needed, despite severe rationing.

"I'll think about it," said Coco.

Spatz broke off a piece of croissant and popped it in his mouth. "Very well, darling," he said.

During the next few days, Coco began to consider that perhaps reopening wasn't such a bad idea, if the Germans allowed her to remain in Paris. She'd been so stupid to close the House of Chanel, largely to exact revenge on her workers. Her relationship with them had steadily deteriorated since 1936, when her entire staff walked out in the wake of widespread labor strikes across France following the election of a socialist president. Coco hadn't been able to shake her anger at her seamstresses, who'd scrawled "OCCUPIED" in white paint across the front door at 31 rue Cambon and refused her entry to the fashion house she'd created, which was her life and which she loved above all else. Three years later, it felt good to fire them all. Except Manon, the only one who dared cross the picket line. *A case of cutting off my nose to spite my face*, Coco thought now.

Without work, she felt exiled from her true self. Spatz understood this about her. He validated her ambitions, just as Boy Capel had. At Spatz's urging, Coco agreed to discuss a possible Chanel relaunch with a reporter from *Ce Soir*. Spatz arranged the interview with the venerable evening paper, which now, under Gestapo control, published an avalanche of German propaganda dressed up like legitimate news.

One afternoon, a reporter, Emile Ponson, arrived at Coco's rue Cambon apartment. He was a small man in his fifties with sparse gray hair and deep creases on the sides of his mouth. Like so many Parisians of the time, he had the worn-out look of an old, cracked shoe. Coco puffed on a cigarette as Ponson removed a pen and a notebook from the pocket of his jacket. "All of us who cover couture are very happy to hear you're reopening," he said.

"Nothing is definite," said Coco, talking around her cigarette.

"Will you be hiring back any of your former employees?" Ponson asked.

"I've been in touch with many of them, and they are all ready to go back to work," Coco lied.

"What about fabric? Accessories? Won't supplies be hard to get?"

"It'll be a reduced collection, probably only twenty or thirty models. But I'm looking forward to seeing my seamstresses and getting the ateliers up and running."

Ponson shifted awkwardly in his seat. "You've softened your views since 1936."

Coco gave him a severe sidelong glance. "I'm sure my workers are as bored as I am at home doing nothing."

For forty minutes, Coco patiently answered Ponson's questions. He kept bringing up the strike of 1936, but Coco refused to discuss it. Instead, she nattered on about her plans to update her ateliers with fresh paint and improved lighting. Finally, Ponson closed his notebook, signaling that the interview was over. "Thank you for your time, Mademoiselle," said Ponson. "I hope I'll soon be back to report on your new collection."

Ponson's article appeared on the front page of *Ce Soir* the following day, next to a story about General de Gaulle being sentenced to death in absentia by Germany's puppet government at Vichy. A Ritz porter delivered a copy of the paper to Coco's suite at five p.m. She lit a cigarette and sat on the settee by the window to read:

> *All good things have returned to Paris, we affirm every day, including Chanel. Here she is, the most brilliant and elegant Parisienne, the woman who after the first world war invented the little black dress in jersey. Chanel is here, living at the Ritz, and she is full of projects, full of plans, full of courage. She promises that she will soon reopen her fashion house and resume designing clothes for the chicest of the chic.*

An unflattering pen-and-ink portrait of Coco illustrated the article. *That drawing of me is despicable. I'd never wear a turtleneck!* she thought, and tossed the paper onto the coffee table.

Spatz came in at six. "Have you made up your mind?" he asked after he read the article.

"I don't know," Coco said. "I don't trust the Germans. What if I agree to it and then they confiscate my building and force me to go to Berlin?"

A cloud passed over Spatz's face, and he flinched slightly. Then he quickly recovered. "I won't let that happen."

A week later, as Coco continued mulling whether to reopen her house, Misia insisted on visiting her at the Ritz. Misia said she had a special present to deliver—a little bonsai-style tree that she had made herself (despite her near blindness) from feathers and pearls, Coco's signature gemstone. The real reason, Coco suspected, was she wanted to inspect Coco's new suite.

As soon as Misia arrived, she minced through the two rooms, laid the tree on the bedroom windowsill, and said, "You're so eager to sleep with your German, you're willing to do it in a *maid's* room?"

"How do you know it's a maid's room? You can't see!" cried Coco.

"I can see well enough to know they've stuck you in a cramped little nothing of a suite."

"So it's smaller. I'm saving money!"

Coco didn't tell Misia that she was surprised Spatz couldn't wrangle her something larger. It distressed her to think he had no real influence with the Reich. She'd heard no word about when her nephew might be released, and whenever she asked Spatz about it, he grew impatient. "I'm working on it. These things take time," he insisted.

There was no question of Coco changing addresses, of moving to another part of town. She had to be at the Ritz, where she could keep an eye on her shop across the street, the source of her income. At least she had a lovely view of the hotel garden and surrounding rooftops. She'd moved in a few of her things: a crystal chandelier, which she hung over the bed; her dressing table (though it barely fit in the corner); and pictures of André and his family. Within no time, she felt at home.

As Coco settled into a chair in the small space converted to a sitting room, she watched Misia make an elaborate display of inspecting the meager accommodations. Misia appeared to have recovered entirely from her fright when the Nazis had arrived in June with their bombs and guns. She had been dining with Coco at the Ritz when a fiery explosion outside had rattled the windows. Misia was too afraid to go home, so she and Coco passed the night in silk Hermès sleeping bags in the hotel's basement shelter. The next day Coco had fled to André's house in the south, while Misia barricaded herself with ex-husband Sert in the Right Bank apartment they'd once shared.

Misia didn't miss an opportunity to disparage the Germans. And with the hauteur that came with her pedigree—her father was a famous Polish sculptor and her grandfather a celebrated Russian cellist—Misia now felt she must guide Coco through the Occupation, just as she'd guided the young couturière through the first war and introduced her to the Paris beau monde of money and culture.

As a child growing up in Brussels, Misia had played the piano for Franz Liszt, a family friend. In her youth in Paris, she was painted by the greatest artists of the day, including Vuillard, Lautrec, Bonnard, and Renoir. She was, as Cocteau once described her, the "beribboned tiger" of the Faubourg salons, a regal beauty who married up three times, conquering new social worlds with each husband: Thadée Natanson, publisher of the avant-garde art journal *La Revue Blanche*; Alfred Edwards, the wealthy owner of *Le Matin*, France's foremost newspaper; and José Maria Sert.

Watching her friend, now so frail and diminished, Coco thought of the first night they'd met, at a Paris dinner party in 1916. At the time, Misia ruled the Paris salons. Coco was a mere dressmaker. She didn't say two words to Misia the entire evening, but she knew she'd bewitched the older woman. She could feel Misia's eyes on her throughout the meal. As Coco was leaving, Misia admired the pretty couturière's mink-trimmed red velvet coat. Coco took it off and placed it over Misia's shoulders. "It's yours," she said.

"What a lovely gesture, but I can't possibly accept it," Misia said, returning the coat to her.

Coco handed it back to Misia. "Maybe, then, just wear it tonight. You can give it to me tomorrow." Misia took that as a sign Coco wanted their lives to entwine. So, the next day, she entered the hushed foyer at 31 rue Cambon and climbed the stairs to Coco's third-floor studio. The *pose* was underway. Coco stood in front of the triple mirrors, draping fabric on a mannequin, a tall, thin girl who resembled Coco, with dark bobbed hair and olive skin. Coco unfurled a bolt of black satin over the girl's shoulders and around her hips and kneaded the fabric with her square, large-knuckled hands. Gradually, the outline of an evening dress came into focus. When she was done, she lit a cigarette and stepped back to admire her work. "Yes, that's what I want!" she said, blowing a jet of smoke toward the ceiling, then turning to Misia. "What do you think?"

"It's lovely."

"I'm glad you think so, because I designed it for you."

After that day, Coco and Misia became inseparable. They talked on the phone every morning, never made a move without consulting the other, and sometimes dressed as twins. Still, Coco never lost her envy of Misia's pedigree, and Misia always felt envious of Coco's creative success. The love the two women felt for each other would always be pricked by resentment and competition.

"So where is Spatz?" Misia asked after she'd made her point to Coco about the tiny suite.

"Why do I have to tell you everything?"

"Because you owe me everything."

Coco sighed and shook her head. "I have no idea where he is."

"Off on some Nazi business, no doubt."

"He doesn't tell me where he goes during the day."

In fact, Coco didn't want to know. She preferred to nurture her fantasies of Spatz as a dashing diplomat. At the Ritz, he never mingled with the Nazis. He always took the tiny, rattling lift from a discreet side entrance, the same entrance Coco used on the French side of the hotel.

"Don't you care what the Nazis are doing?" Misia pressed. "This morning I went to buy a new pair of gloves at Maison Charonne and found the windows smeared with anti-Jewish slogans. Poor Monsieur Charonne was so embarrassed, but he's a brave man. He kept the shop open."

Coco stared at Misia. "You can't blame Spatz for *that*."

"Every day the Germans strip the Jews of more of their rights. Who knows where it will end. Look at what happened to Max's brother-in-law. What if they come for Max next?"

"The priests will protect Max," Coco said, as if to convince herself.

Misia slid up on her chair and leaned toward Coco. "Aren't you worried about what will happen if the Allies win? What people will think? You've been living with a Nazi."

"Please. He's not a Nazi. Maybe he's a member of the party, but he's not like the others."

"He *works* for the Nazis. Don't fool yourself that he's a harmless bureaucrat. He's devious. I can tell."

Coco stood up abruptly and started pacing. She wished she was in her old apartment on rue du Faubourg Saint-Honoré, where there were rooms upon rooms and she could close doors on Misia.

The older woman narrowed her eyes. "Does it ever occur to you that Spatz is using you?"

"No one uses me!"

Cocteau had taunted Coco that *she* was using Spatz. For sex, mostly. He was being critical, not out of sympathy for the German but because he thought Coco was fooling herself that she was in love with him. And he was right, in a way. She used Spatz. And loved him. Used, loved—in the end, it was all the same.

"Why is he with you when he could have a young beauty?" Misia said.

"He likes sophisticated women."

"He likes rich old dames who are well-connected."

"You're just jealous."

"I wouldn't take a German into my bed if he was the last man on earth."

Misia grabbed her handbag off the windowsill and, banging her knee on a corner of the sofa, stormed out.

Coco couldn't bear to think that Spatz didn't want her for *herself*. Despite her ferocious independence, she longed to be adored by a man in a lasting union. Enduring love, though, had eluded her, and she felt this as a failure. She had a profound sense that she'd missed what was really important in a woman's life—marriage and children. Even though all she'd seen in her youth was how it brought women misery. But for her, it would have been different. Could be different. Did Spatz see this yearning in her? Did he sense her vulnerability? Was Misia right? Was he using her?

All he had told her about his work was that he oversaw textile production for the war effort. But what exactly did that mean? Most of

France's wool and silk had been appropriated for German uniforms and parachutes. Fabric and clothing for the French had been severely rationed. And now the Germans wanted to move couture to Berlin. Perhaps Spatz seduced her because he needed her help to make this a reality. But she had already said she wouldn't do it. So what did he want?

She brooded over this all afternoon. That evening, as they were sitting in the back seat of a black Mercedes driven by a German chauffeur—in civilian clothes this time—Coco asked Spatz directly. "Don't ruin this by looking for reasons to suspect me," he said, squeezing her hand. "You know I care about you."

"You also care about pleasing your bosses."

Spatz dropped her hand and spoke quietly. "I just found out couture is *not* moving to Berlin after all. At least, for the time being. The Reich has . . . well, let's just say other priorities. So, if you decide to reopen your house, you can absolutely stay on rue Cambon."

"I'm still thinking about it." Coco looked out the window at the wide, tree-lined boulevards of the Sixteenth Arrondissement. They were headed for Bignon's, a quiet bistro on Avenue Foch, not far from Spatz's apartment. Since the Occupation, Bignon's had begun serving German food and become a favorite spot of the Nazi officers who lived nearby, many of them in grand apartments that had been abandoned by their owners at the start of the war.

On rue Suchet, the Mercedes passed the large stone mansion that had been rented before the war by the Duke of Windsor and Wallis Simpson, the American woman he had given up his British crown to marry. *If I reopened, I could count on Wallis for big orders,* Coco thought. She found the thrice-married Wallis dull, but had to admit she wore clothes well, and she owned her share of Chanel couture. But Wallis wouldn't be around for fittings. As unrepentant Nazi sympathizers, the duke and duchess were an embarrassment to Britain, and King George, the duke's brother, had swept the pesky couple out of the way by appointing the duke governor of the Bahamas. Now, their Paris mansion stood empty. A heavy chain bound the tall wrought iron gate; a Nazi guard holding a rifle kept vigil on the front steps.

"Why are the Germans protecting the Windsors' house?" Coco asked Spatz.

Her lover nodded toward the driver and put his right index finger to his lips. "I'll explain later," he said.

With its dark paneling, burgundy flocked wallpaper, and picturesque landscapes in gilt frames, Bignon's resembled the dining room in a French country house. Before the war, the restaurant served simple French food: roast chickens, cassoulets, soups, and fruit tarts. After the Occupation, Bignon's began offering schnitzel, rouladen, sauerbraten, and chocolate cake to cater to German tastes.

Coco and Spatz sat a table near a roaring fire, perusing the menu. "Champagne?" asked the slender, dark-haired waiter in a white jacket and bow tie. Spatz nodded, and the waiter poured two glasses. After returning the bottle to an ice bucket on a nearby stand, he planted himself next to Coco's chair with his feet spread wide and his hands clasped behind his back.

Coco inspected her fork. "This is filthy," she told the waiter in a disgusted tone.

"I'm so sorry, madame." The waiter bowed, then scurried away to fetch a substitute.

"Really? A dirty fork?" said Spatz.

"I did that to get rid of him. He stands too close, as if he wants to get in on our conversations."

Coco took a sip of champagne. "Before he gets back, tell me about the Windsors' house."

Spatz leaned across the table and spoke in a low voice. "The duke and duchess met Hitler when they visited Germany in 1936 soon after their wedding, and they struck up a friendship with him. The Führer promised to restore the duke as King of England with Wallis as his queen after Germany conquered England. In the meantime, at the duke's request, the Reich is protecting the Windsors' Paris mansion. Also their château in Cap d'Antibes. The duchess is insanely fond of her possessions. Once, after the Windsors arrived in the Bahamas, Wallis discovered she'd left her favorite Nile green swimsuit on the Riviera. The duke got a German officer to retrieve it from her bedroom, and the officer had it flown to her overnight. The Abwehr dubbed the mission Operation Cleopatra Whim."

"I don't believe it," said Coco.

Spatz shrugged, as if it didn't matter to him.

It was bad enough that a member of the royal family was keeping property in enemy-occupied territory. But enlisting the Nazis in retrieving a swimsuit was beyond the pale. Coco wondered if Winston knew about it. Coco had gotten to know the prime minister in the late 1920s, during her affair with the Duke of Westminster, when they were both guests at Bendor's hunting lodge in the Aquitaine. At the time, Churchill was chancellor of the exchequer, a plump, out-of-step politician in a pin-striped suit and polka dot bow tie, smoking endless cigars. Churchill's Tory principles appealed to the savage businesswoman in Coco at a time when France and much of Europe were falling in love with socialism. They became friends, and Churchill always visited Coco when he was in Paris. The last time was right before the war. They had dinner together in her apartment. Churchill got drunk and began moaning about Edward abdicating. "He never should have married that woman," Churchill said.

The waiter returned with a clean fork and laid it at Coco's place, then continued hovering.

As Coco sipped her champagne, her eyes roamed the room slowly, stopping on the German ambassador, who sat at a table near the windows with an elegant blonde. "There's Otto Abetz and his wife," she said, smiling tightly and nodding to Abetz when he caught her eye.

"We have a dinner with them next Friday," said Spatz. "He's expecting you to come. He likes to show you off."

"I wish he liked me a little less," Coco said. Abetz kept inviting her to parties at the embassy, and she continued to refuse. She rested her clasped hands on the lace tablecloth. "Can't you tell him that I don't like going out?"

It was one thing to have dinner in an obscure bistro frequented by Germans, and another to go to large parties at the homes of Nazis.

Though Coco had a fatalistic feeling that the Allies were doomed—the Germans had already taken Belgium and Libya—she wasn't on their side and didn't want it to appear so.

"I'll come up with some excuse," said Spatz. He crooked his finger at the waiter, motioning him over. "For me, the veal schnitzel," he told him. "Steak for the lady." Spatz handed the menus to the waiter, who wheeled and disappeared into the kitchen.

Spatz leaned forward and opened his mouth as if to say something. Then he sat back abruptly, just as a tall, elegant man in his sixties walked by on his way to the toilet—Michel Pelissier, a lawyer and old acquaintance of Coco's, whose wife, Amélie, had been one of her best clients. Coco called out to him.

"Michel! What a surprise."

"I was just at your boutique," said Pelissier, stopping and bending to kiss Coco on both cheeks. He wore a gray wool suit and carried a small black-and-white bag emblazoned with double Cs. "I bought a fresh bottle of Chanel No. 5 for Amélie." He held up the bag by balancing the black cord on the tip of his index finger. "I looked for you to say bonjour, but I couldn't find you."

"I don't think I've seen you here before," Coco said.

"It's my first time. My friends suggested it. They live in the neighborhood." Pelissier glanced toward a group of well-dressed middle-aged men sitting at a table near the entrance.

Coco nodded toward Spatz. "This is my friend . . ."

"Nice to see you, von Dincklage," said Pelissier. He took Spatz's hand.

"You've met?" Coco looked back and forth between the two men.

"On the Riviera, several years ago," said Spatz. "I was living on the Côte d'Azur with my wife, my then wife."

"How is Catsy?" asked Pelissier.

"I'm afraid we've lost touch," said Spatz.

"Ah, well, if you do see her, give her my best." Pelissier again bent low to kiss Coco.

After the lawyer had left, Spatz said softly, "That man doesn't like me."

"You're imagining things." Nothing in Pelissier's manner had given her any inkling of awkwardness or hostility. Why would Spatz say that?

Spatz didn't argue, but after their dinners, their desserts of sliced fruit, cheese, and coffee, Spatz took Coco's hand and led her out of the restaurant quickly, not giving her a chance to say *bonsoir* to her old friend.

Though Coco missed fashion with an aching longing, she remained ambivalent about reopening the House of Chanel. She didn't trust the Germans not to change their minds again and move couture to Berlin. What was left of couture, in any case. Materials were scarce—most fabrics, including wool, cotton, linen, and silk, had been requisitioned for German uniforms, parachutes, blankets, and bandages. And the Nazis had instituted a draconian list of restrictions on couture, ranging from skirt lengths to the number of garments that could be shown in a season. Coco had no desire to reopen under such circumstances.

Who knew what the Germans were planning? Every day, it seemed, they passed a new law further restricting the rights of French Jews. First, Jews were barred from the army, then journalism, politics, academia, law, business, and medicine. One day while she was out shopping with Misia, they passed Baruch's lingerie shop on rue des Capucines. A harsh yellow sign in black lettering in German and French hung in the window: JEWISH BUSINESS. The sign was so huge, even Misia could read it. "Poor Monsieur Baruch," Misia said.

The proprietor, Gustave Baruch, was a World War I hero, and he'd propped up his medals, including the Croix de Guerre and the Legion of Honor, under the sign. *As if that will protect him*, thought Coco.

"The next thing you know he and his family will be deported," said Misia.

"You don't know that," said Coco.

"Thousands of Jews already have disappeared," said Misia. "My concierge told me about a family in her building in Montmartre who were arrested by the Nazis and taken away in the middle of the night. Why do you think the Nazis required Jews to register? So it'll be easy to find them and send them away. The Nazis are cagey. They aren't doing it all at once. But you'll see, it's only going to get worse and worse."

At the Ritz later that evening, Coco asked Spatz, "Why do the Germans have to do this? Baruch is a nice man."

Spatz claimed to know nothing about the anti-Jewish statutes or the deportations. "My office has nothing to do with it," he said. "Berlin keeps us in the dark as much as you." He flung his newspaper onto the coffee table. At the bar cart, he poured himself a generous glass of scotch and downed it in two gulps.

With no clothes to design and no business to run, Coco found it impossible to distract herself from the horrors of the war. She tried not to dwell on where the Jews who'd disappeared had been taken and stopped pressing Spatz for answers. His insistence that he was in the dark was unwavering. To avoid the black thoughts overwhelming her, she started taking singing lessons. She'd loved to sing, since her days warbling for tips at La Rotonde, the café-concert in Moulins, where she'd moonlighted from her tailoring shop job. The slight, dark-haired girl with the luminous personality had two songs: "Ko-Ri-Ko" (Cock-a-doodle-do) about a rooster, and "Qui qu'a vu Coco?" (Has anyone seen Coco?) about a lost dog. Though Gabby, as she was known then, had a small, tinny voice, the café's male patrons were charmed by her gamine looks and lively manner, and they began calling her "Coco." The nickname stuck, though she would never admit to Spatz or anyone else how she'd acquired it.

A singing coach, a skinny woman with frizzy red hair who dressed in layers of fringed shawls, came several times a week to Coco's apartment on rue Cambon. Coco had installed an upright piano in the salon, and on music days she spent all afternoon singing scales with her coach.

After her music lesson, she would usually join Spatz for drinks in her rooms at the Ritz. They'd relax with a cocktail or two before Coco dressed for dinner. Some evenings, however, Spatz didn't show up. Usually, he'd send a message that he'd been held up, though he rarely explained why. Invariably, on these evenings, he'd sleep in his own apartment. Coco never asked him who he was with when they were apart. Every man she knew, married or not, had a craving from time to time for the heat and sweetness of a new body. No one had ever been faithful to her, and she did not expect fidelity from Spatz. She assumed he occasionally saw other women. Perhaps from time to time he visited one of the city's more exclusive brothels, where the whores were young, impeccably groomed, and closely monitored by doctors for any sign of disease. But these girls meant nothing to him, she was sure.

She tried not to dwell on his more significant dalliances from the past. One was Hélène Dessoffy, a former client of Coco's, whom Spatz had gotten to know on the Côte d'Azur in the 1930s. Hélène lived mostly in the south. She was not part of Coco's circle, and, except for her occasional visits to rue Cambon, Coco never saw her and knew little about her private life. She'd heard rumors, though, that Spatz had embroiled Hélène in some kind of diplomatic scandal. The rumors were vague, and Coco never asked Spatz about them. She didn't tell him the truth about her life, and she didn't expect him to tell her the truth about his, a willful denial that enabled them to live comfortably as the world went to hell around them.

One afternoon, as her music lesson was winding down, Coco glanced out the window and saw Hélène Dessoffy slip into the Chanel boutique underneath the apartment. Coco noticed with dismay that the silky brunette, who was fifteen years younger than Coco, looked as youthful and beautiful as ever. When Coco went downstairs ten minutes later, Hélène was waiting for her at the perfume counter.

She was dressed in a green jersey suit from one of Coco's distant collections and wore her hair in a simple bun at the nape of her neck. Small diamond studs glittered in her earlobes, and a brown schnauzer lay in her arms. His intelligent eyes fixed on Coco as she kissed Hélène on each cheek. "This is a pleasant surprise," said Coco, trying to sound sincere.

"Is there somewhere we could talk?" asked Hélène.

"I'm afraid I'm late. I'm meeting someone," said Coco.

"Spatz?"

Coco eyed Hélène cautiously. "Yes."

Hélène stroked the schnauzer's furry back. "You know about him?"

"What do you mean?"

"That's what I need to talk to you about." Hélène's voice quavered with distress.

Coco led her to the opposite end of the boutique and motioned for her to take a seat on a large beige ottoman. Coco sat next to her and folded her hands in her lap. Hélène lowered her voice. "Spatz is a spy. He's in the Abwehr, the German intelligence organization that works closely with the Nazi SS."

Coco's heart started to pound, but she kept her voice level. "He works for the embassy, overseeing textile production. But he's not very ambitious and we never talk about it."

"That job is just a cover. He wants to drag you into it, like he dragged me. You could be arrested for treason."

The schnauzer lifted his ears and set a paw on Hélène's sleeve. "That's preposterous," said Coco. She blew the dog a kiss, and he settled back in Hélène's arms. She still missed her own pets, Lune and Soleil, gifts from Boy Capel who were buried at La Milanese, the house she'd shared with Capel long ago.

"No one else should have to go through what I went through," said Hélène. As if in assent, the schnauzer emitted a sharp bark. "Dieter, hush," said Hélène.

"Your dog has a German name?" said Coco.

"He was a present from Spatz." Hélène brushed the top of the dog's head with her lips, leaving a bright red smear on his little skull. "Spatz gave me Dieter when he left France in 1939, so I wouldn't be lonely."

Hélène lowered her eyes as she stroked the dog's ears. "He told me he couldn't bear bloodshed. He'd had enough of it during the first war and would have no more of it. I helped him go to Switzerland and arranged for him to stay with friends of mine. I wrote to him at my friends' address, but French Intelligence intercepted the letters! Every word of love had a hidden meaning to those suspicious men. Because of Spatz, they arrested me and accused me of being a spy myself and kept me in jail for four months."

Coco remembered hearing from acquaintances on the Riviera that Hélène had a serious drug problem. She was known to use opium daily and often seemed to people who encountered her to be in a drug-addled fog. She looked sober enough now. Perhaps, though, she'd been in jail for drugs, not espionage.

"I risked my life for Spatz," said Hélène. She started to cry softly.

She still loved him! That was why she had come, thought Coco. She was jealous. Spatz had spurned her, broken her heart, and now she wanted Coco to be as miserable as she was. Warning Coco about Spatz's so-called spy activities was just a pretext. She was being overly dramatic, trying to scare Coco. Standing abruptly, Coco told the younger woman, "I appreciate your visit. But I must go. I'm already very late."

In her suite a few minutes later, Coco found Spatz reclined on the settee with his newspaper. She lit a cigarette and puffed on it nervously. "Hélène Dessoffy just showed up at the boutique," she said. Her hands were trembling.

"Oh?" Spatz folded his newspaper and gazed over the top of it with a furrowed brow.

"She says you're a spy."

Spatz slapped the paper on the coffee table. "Every German is a spy to the French."

"Why did she go to prison?"

"She's a drug addict."

"You didn't enlist her in espionage missions?"

Spatz sat up and clenched his hands together with his elbows on his knees. "Look, this was all before the war. My job was to improve relations between our nations. That meant forging friendships with the French and placing articles favorable to Germany in French journals. If you want to call that *spying*, fine. Most people call it propaganda." He straightened his back and folded his arms across his chest. "I'm not happy about what happened to Hélène. For a while I thought I loved her. But the drugs." He shook his head. "There's no future with someone who's addicted to drugs." He grabbed his newspaper and, shaking it out, resumed reading.

Spatz didn't know that Coco used morphine from time to time. When they were together and she had trouble sleeping, she took Seconals.

Coco stamped out her cigarette in a crystal ashtray on the side table and picked up a copy of *Les Parisiennes* lying next to it. Amid the articles about gardening, new ways to wear turbans, and the best diets were several full-page propaganda ads issued by Vichy. In one, an illustration of a Frenchman working in a German factory was juxtaposed with a picture of a young mother at the dinner table in Paris with her little son. The caption read, *Father works in Germany to protect our liberty at home.*

Who believes this rubbish? Coco lit a fresh cigarette and, puffing furiously, flipped through the pages with a sharp snap of her wrist. Another feature, titled "A Day in the Life of an Elegant Woman," showed a series of black-and-white illustrations in which a slender, dark-haired Parisienne and a tall, dashing blond man strolled down the Champs-Élysées, took in an art exhibit, dined at a restaurant, and relaxed at home. The man wore the same dark suit, white shirt, and striped tie in every frame, but the woman's outfit changed from a short dress to a jacket-and-skirt ensemble to an evening gown and a *robe d'intérieur*. The couple looked happy. They weren't hurting anyone. They could have been Coco and Spatz. Love wasn't political. Love was a country without borders.

Spatz rarely said a word against any of his countrymen. He never discussed Nazi ideology, though he was loyal in his defense of what the Nazis had accomplished at home. Germany had won her self-respect back. People had jobs, food, medicine. There were new factories, new roads, and new schools. But success had come at a terrible cost. Spatz wouldn't discuss the violence, the killings, the rounding up of citizens. Once, when Coco deplored the Gestapo's execution by firing squad of an innocent seventeen-year-old French boy in retaliation for an attack on Germans by the Resistance, Spatz shrugged. "Nothing is perfect," he'd said.

As Coco tossed the magazine onto the table, a piece of paper fell to the floor. Picking it up, she saw that it was Reverdy's flyer. He must have slipped it between the magazine's pages the day he visited. She glanced at the crude illustration of the Marianne, the French Goddess of Liberty. Coco thought of herself as deeply patriotic, a kind of living Marianne. Her work had been part of the nation's cultural glory, her perfume business a significant contribution to France's economy. How had she so easily fallen into bed with a German?

Throughout her life she'd pushed for more status, more money, more fame, more proof that she was no longer a poor, loveless orphan. It was never enough. She'd never felt secure in her position at the top of French life. The hierarchies were too ambiguous. With the Occupation, though, the lines between insiders and outsiders had been starkly drawn. Deep in her heart, she knew she'd made the wrong choice. But everything in her biology, her background, and her environment pushed her to align herself with those in power. She was doomed from the start.

Coco crumpled Reverdy's flyer and stuffed it under the sofa cushion. She wouldn't think about the poet. She would think only of the man sitting opposite her and the strong, solid feel of him in her arms. "Let's not go out tonight," she said to Spatz. Coco squeezed next to him in the armchair and began to unclasp his belt. "Let's have dinner ordered in, and . . ." She couldn't finish the sentence. He was kissing her too hard.

FIVE

The worst part of the day for Coco was when Spatz left in the morning after breakfast. "Time to go," he'd say, palming his fedora and setting it on his head before walking out the door. At these moments, they were an ordinary bourgeois couple, with the man going off to his office and the woman left behind with nothing important to do. Only they weren't an ordinary couple. Spatz was an enemy of France who worked out of an office in the former Hotel Lutetia, where God knew what he actually did. He never confided in Coco. Sometimes, though, he told her about his lunch dates, golf outings, and poker games, mostly with low-ranking German officers and Frenchmen he'd known before the war. Coco got the sense he spent most of his time socializing.

Meanwhile, Coco was bored and antsy. Each day after Spatz left and she finished dressing, she'd head across the street to her boutique to chat with the vendeuse Veronique and take care of whatever correspondence there was related to perfume sales.

One morning during the first fall of the Occupation, Coco found Veronique slumped over the glass display case, sobbing. "My God, what is it?" said Coco, draping her arm over the young woman's heaving shoulders.

"My husband, Henri, has been dismissed from his job!" She spoke in gulps between sobs.

"Isn't he a teacher at the L'École Sebastian?"

"Was!" Veronique stood straight, wiping her tears with the backs of her hands. "It's the law now. He's a Jew!"

"I didn't know. . . . You're Jewish, too?"

"No. But my children are." Veronique had two daughters, ages ten and eight. "Henri thinks we should leave. Go to the unoccupied zone, where my sister lives."

"But *you* have a job."

"I can't work here anymore. Henri won't let me."

"Why?"

Veronique looked at the floor a moment, then directly at Coco. "Monsieur von Dincklage." Spatz always said bonjour to Veronique on his way upstairs to see Coco in her apartment. And if he was waiting for Coco to meet him downstairs, he'd pass the time chatting with Veronique.

"He had nothing to do with Henri losing his job."

Veronique had stopped crying now, and she spoke in a cold, severe tone. "He's German."

"So what?"

"Henri doesn't want me to work for someone who lives with a German."

"And you do everything Henri tells you?" Coco shook her head, then reached in her handbag and pulled out a wad of franc notes in a money clip. She removed the clip and handed the cash to Veronique. "This will help you for a while. It's what I'd owe you at the end of the month, anyway."

Veronique bowed her head. "Thank you, Mademoiselle. Is it all right if I leave now?"

Coco clicked shut her purse. "Suit yourself."

After Veronique left, Coco locked the front door. She deplored the laws that denied Jews their jobs. Everyone had a right to work—and to fight and compete in business. Glancing at the shelves holding bottles of Chanel No. 5, she wondered what sales would be this month. At the start of the Occupation, her Jewish partners, Paul and Pierre Wertheimer, had fled to New York and no longer had access to her perfume's unique floral essences from Grasse. Pétain and his Vichy functionaries were cowards, allowing the Nazis to interfere in French commerce. But there was nothing she or anyone else could do about it. Reverdy and the rest of the maquisards were fools to think they could halt the German war machine.

On the phone in her apartment upstairs, Coco started calling her former vendeuses. None of them were available—they'd either left Paris or found other jobs. Then she remembered Angeline, a curvaceous blonde with a flirtatious manner whom Coco had fired for sleeping with the husband of a client. Angeline was ecstatic to have her job back and agreed to return to work the next day. "I'm warning you, behave yourself this time, or you're never getting another chance," Coco told her. "There's a guard on duty. He has keys and will let you in."

When Coco arrived late the following afternoon, Angeline was at her post behind the perfume counter talking to a dark, wiry man in worker's clothes. The pretty vendeuse stood ruler straight, her elbows digging into her sides and her hands clenched in front of her, as the man leered at her across the glass countertop. Angeline had taken the boss's warning to heart. Coco was used to seeing strange men in the boutique. They often stopped in to buy perfume for their wives as special-occasion presents. But there was something familiar about this man's leer, also his round head topped by tight, graying curls, and his rough, square hands. When he looked up, Coco saw with a jolt that it was her younger brother Alphonse Chanel.

"Gabby! Still my glamorous big sister," he cried, opening his arms wide. He grabbed Coco by the shoulders and kissed her on each cheek. "How can you women stand it here?" Alphonse said. "Those German bastards are everywhere. I almost tripped over a few just walking down your street."

Coco shushed him. "Don't talk like that. You're in Paris now."

Still the same Alphonse, thought Coco. Years earlier, she had pushed her brother out of her life, and now here he was, no doubt wanting something. "Let's go upstairs," she told him.

In Coco's salon, Alphonse went straight to the long suede sofa and stretched out. "Had a hell of a time getting here. Had to take three trains, and they were all late," he said, as he arranged himself on the cushions, careful to keep his scuffed boots, with their worn soles, off the sofa. Once he was settled, his eyes flitted around the room, taking in the Coromandel screens and animal sculptures, the leather-bound books and gilt mirrors.

"Still, it's a good thing you didn't bring your Bugatti. It would have been confiscated," said Coco.

"No more car, Gabby. It's at the bottom of a ravine. In smithereens." Alphonse smiled, showing the white, even teeth he and Coco had inherited from their handsome father.

Coco scowled. "That's the third car I've bought you that you wrecked."

"The Bugatti was the best." Alphonse grinned.

"You're not getting another one, if that's why you're here."

Alphonse fished around in his pockets and pulled out a folded newspaper clipping—the *Ce Soir* story about Coco's reopening. "Is this true?" he asked.

Coco glanced at the clipping. "No."

"Because if it is—"

Coco cut him off. "I'm sorry you came all this way to find out that my situation hasn't changed, despite what the newspaper wrote. I'm not resuming your allowance."

For years, Coco sent monthly checks for three thousand francs to Alphonse and their younger brother, Lucien. She stopped the money flow in 1939 when she closed her house, explaining to her brothers that she could no longer afford the stipends. That had been a lie, and she winced now to think how gullibly Alphonse had accepted the news. Since she'd cut off his allowance, Alphonse had run a café-tabac in Saumur. But Coco suspected he spent most of what he earned gambling and playing poker.

Lucien was hardly better. He made a living peddling cheap shoes at local markets. Coco was embarrassed by her brothers. The funds she'd given them were mostly bribes. The Chanel brothers understood that in exchange for Coco's financial support, they were to keep away from rue Cambon and never talk about their sister to the press. Lucien, a sweet-natured man who was devoted to his wife and children, rarely left Clermont-Ferrand, where Coco had bought him a house. But Alphonse showed up occasionally in Paris, often to nudge Coco into giving him money to cover his gambling debts or to pay off a girl he'd gotten pregnant and promised to marry, though he already had a wife and a mistress and children by both.

"Alphonse, there's no more money," said Coco.

"It looks like there's plenty," he said, running his hands along the sofa's luxurious fabric.

"I still don't have an income, except from the perfume and a few things sold downstairs. We're in the middle of a war. Who knows what's going to happen? The Germans could take everything I have."

"The damn Germans. I hear Julie's boy's a prisoner. What's his name?"

"André."

"Never met him. But I hear he's a nice fella."

What a family they were. Uncles and nephews who were strangers. A sister who shunned her brothers.

Alphonse plumped up the fringed satin pillow at his back. "If I were younger, I'd join the Resistance," he said. "I'd like to kill a few Krauts myself."

Coco shook her head sharply. "You can't talk like that," she repeated. She wondered if Alphonse knew about Spatz. Had he heard rumors? Fortunately, Spatz had told her he wouldn't visit that night—he was playing cards with friends and staying at his apartment.

"That's how I feel," Alphonse continued. "The French need to stand up for themselves."

"Hush. Talk like that will get you killed."

Alphonse affected a nonchalant pose. "I don't care. It's true."

Coco knew she had to get him out of there. Her brother—just eighteen months her junior—had always amused her with his tough, scrappy ways, but in Occupied Paris, he was a ticking time bomb of insolence. "You better get going now," she said. "Travel is dangerous these days."

Alphonse made no effort to move and, in fact, looked entirely settled on the sofa. "Why don't we have dinner?" he asked. "I'm starved."

The thought of appearing in public with her shabby brother while he spouted noisy insults to the Germans terrified Coco.

"I'll call the Ritz and have dinner sent over. We can eat here. But then you have to go—you can't stay; there's a curfew. You don't want to be arrested."

That seemed agreeable to Alphonse, so Coco called the Ritz dining room and ordered two steaks, cooked medium rare, with sides of potatoes and vegetables, to be delivered to her apartment on rue Cambon.

An hour later, a butler arrived with the food. He was an elderly man in the blue-and-white livery of the Ritz, complete with spanking white gloves. Once Coco and Alphonse were seated at her square walnut table, the butler poured their wine and filled their water glasses. Then he stood behind Alphonse's chair, with his nose in the air and his hands folded at his back.

Alphonse picked up his knife and fork, looked at Coco with a mischievous glint, and said, "Tell that geezer behind me to fuck off. It bugs me having him back there!"

The butler's eyes widened with shock, and his mouth began twitching nervously. He slipped into the pantry off the dining room and shut the door. Coco burst out laughing.

"Ah, Gabby, just like old times, huh?" Alphonse winked at Coco and popped a big chunk of steak in his mouth.

He still ate in the frank manner he had as a boy, mouthful after mouthful with no pause for polite chatter. Coco swallowed only a few bites of her steak, pushed her plate aside, and lit a cigarette. She studied Alphonse as she puffed. He'd been a wild, uncontrollable child, stealing money from the patrons of the flophouses where the Chanel family lived and frequently fighting with other boys. He was a great source of worry and vexation to their mother. But Coco admired Alphonse's strength and energy. He was so different from timid Lucien, six years her junior, who rarely spoke and cowered in the corner if anyone scolded him.

The Ritz butler emerged from the pantry carrying a coffee service on a large silver tray. Just as he set the tray on the sideboard, the front door opened, and a moment later Spatz stepped into the dining room. His eyes grew wide when he saw the scruffy man at Coco's table.

"I wasn't expecting you," said Coco. Her throat had tightened, and she could barely squeeze out the words.

"I left my clubs in your closet. It's golf day tomorrow," said Spatz, leaning in to kiss Coco on the lips. Then he turned to Alphonse and extended his hand, as if this country peasant were a visiting dignitary. "I'm sorry, we haven't met. I'm Hans von Dincklage."

"Alphonse Chanel." Coco's brother stood and took Spatz's hand.

"My brother was just leaving," said Coco.

"I think I'll have my coffee first," said Alphonse. He scowled at the butler and pointed to his cup.

Spatz looked at Coco. "Your brother?" He smiled. "I'm learning more and more about the mysterious Coco Chanel."

The butler asked Spatz, "Would you like something to eat, Herr von Dincklage?"

Coco saw her brother's eyes spark.

"No, thank you," said Spatz. The butler bowed and scurried back to the pantry as Spatz helped himself to a glass of red wine from the bar cart. He remained standing and spoke to Alphonse in a cordial tone. "What brings you to Paris?"

Alphonse opened his mouth, but Coco didn't give him a chance to talk. "You better leave now. You'll miss the last train."

"There's one at eleven thirty."

"Not anymore. The curfew's at eleven."

"I don't care about the Krauts' damn curfew. They can kiss my ass."

Spatz cleared his throat. "Monsieur Chanel, do you play golf? I'd like to get Coco on the course in the Bois, but she won't go until I take her riding first. She tells me she had horses growing up at your aunts' house. You must be an expert rider, too."

"I see Gabby's been at it with her stories again," Alphonse said.

Coco rapped her knuckles on the arm of her chair as her foot shook frantically under the table. "Alphonse, really, you can't be out past curfew."

"Let your brother relax," said Spatz. "It's *I* who must be going—I've an early tee-time. I'm afraid I won't be joining you for coffee." He nodded to Alphonse. "A pleasure to meet you. Have a safe trip home."

Alphonse took Spatz's hand for a moment, then dropped it as if it were a hot coal.

Spatz squeezed Coco's shoulder. "I'll see you tomorrow evening, darling."

"*Herr* von Dincklage," Alphonse said in a snide tone when Spatz had left.

"What do you mean?" said Coco.

"I heard the geezer call him *Herr*. His French is better than mine, but he's got a little accent. He's a Nazi, isn't he?"

"He's not a Nazi."

"My God, my sister is shacking up with a Nazi! Wait 'til I tell Lucien our Gabby is a traitor!"

"He's working on having André released."

"You believe that?"

Coco threw her white linen napkin on the table and hurried to her desk in the next room. A minute later she returned with a check and handed it to Alphonse. "Here's five thousand francs," she said in a flat tone.

Alphonse glanced at the check and slipped it into his pocket. He pushed back from the table and strode toward the door.

"Good-bye, Alphonse," Coco said. "Please don't come here again."

Coco returned to the Ritz and spent a tortured two hours worrying about how Spatz would react. Would he abandon her? Have her thrown out of the hotel? Worse, denounce her to the Nazis for harboring someone with anti-German views? Or would he denounce Alphonse and have *him* arrested? Alphonse was still her brother. She didn't want anything bad to happen to him.

Coco injected herself with morphine and fell into a deep sleep.

In the morning she went to her boutique, mostly to distract herself. Business was moribund, just a few Nazi officers, talking to one another in German, laughing, sniffing bottles of perfume, looking entirely care-free and pleased with themselves. Coco scuttled up to her apartment to await her horrible fate.

Spatz came in just after three, still wearing his baggy golf knickers and sporty tweed jacket. "Bonjour, darling," he said pleasantly.

Coco hung back, waiting for the guillotine blade to fall.

"Is everything all right?" he asked. "Did your brother bring bad news?"

"No. Nothing like that."

Spatz came over and put his hands on her shoulders, looking down into her face. "Your brother is an interesting character," he said.

Was it possible Spatz didn't care? "Yes, interesting. Not at all like me," said Coco.

Spatz kissed her forehead and laughed. "Every family has a few interesting characters. They embarrass us, but we still love them."

Coco sank into the sofa and felt her fear deflate with the cushion. "I'm sorry he made that remark about the Germans."

"Sometimes I feel the same way, darling." Spatz smiled. "Now, let me go across the street to get cleaned up, and we'll have a drink before dinner."

"I'll join you in a minute," said Coco. "I've some correspondence to tend to."

She sat at her desk and opened the middle drawer, where she kept her documents. The evening before, when she'd written Alphonse his check, everything was in its place. Now, however, she saw that her address book, which she always kept on the right side of the drawer divider, was on the left side underneath some insurance papers. Someone had tampered with it. Spatz? What was he looking for? The addresses of people who were possible enemies of the Reich? Or sympathizers he could enlist in his cause? Coco shook off these thoughts. She was imagining things, letting Misia's suspicions infect her.

Later, as she sat on her settee at the Ritz sipping wine with Spatz, she said, "I was so rattled by my brother showing up last night that I stuck my address book in the wrong place in my desk. It took me a minute to find it."

"But you *did* find it," said Spatz. An almost imperceptible cloud crossed his face.

He *had* snooped in her address book. Certainly, he had.

SIX

Spatz knew Coco didn't like to be seen with him in public, so after a while he stopped coming home with tickets to the opera and the ballet. One evening, however, as he walked through the door of her suite, tossing his hat on the entry table, Coco announced, "We're going out tonight."

"Really? I was looking forward to a quiet night with just *you*." Spatz put his arms around her and drew her close, nuzzling her neck.

Coco pulled away. "It's the opening of Cocteau's play, *La Machine à écrire*. It's a light comedy about a typewriter. Harmless stuff. We're due at the theater in an hour. I promised him."

Spatz regarded her with a lascivious glint. "There's no time for . . ."

Coco cut him off with a playful swat at his shoulder and retreated to the bedroom. "I'll just be a minute," she called to him as she changed into her new blue silk chiffon dress. She'd decided not to wait for the war's end—an impossibly distant, even improbable event—to wear it.

"Beautiful," said Spatz, when she was twirling in front of him.

At the Théâtre Hébertot, the Germans had bought out the best seats. When Coco and Spatz arrived, almost the entire orchestra section was filled with Nazis in uniform and their female companions in gaudy evening dresses and furs. As Coco and Spatz took their seats in the first row of the balcony, Coco spanned the crowd, her eyes fixing on Otto Abetz, the German ambassador, in the middle of the fourth row. Next to him sat his wife, Suzanne, the black satin straps of what Coco recognized as a Chanel gown hugging her white shoulders.

As soon as the lights dimmed, Spatz fell asleep, his chin tucked against his collar. Coco herself fought to stay awake through the first scene of frothy dialogue. Suddenly, a commotion erupted at the back of the theater, the double doors burst open, and a group of French thugs rushed down the center aisle, flinging stink bombs onto the stage. Screams rang out as the stench of rotting food and animal excrement filled the theater. One thug sprayed black ink into the face of the actress playing the lead, then pushed an actor standing next to her into the orchestra pit. Gagging, Coco and Spatz fled to the street.

The air was frigid. Coco pulled her fur around her body as Spatz lit a cigarette. He placed it between Coco's lips, and she drew in a lungful of smoke. Spatz took the cigarette, now ringed with red lipstick, and puffed on it as his eyes wandered up and down the street. "Where's the goddamn driver? I told him to wait."

"I'm not surprised about this," said Coco. "The French fascists hate Cocteau. That right-wing critic from *Je Suis Partout* has been attacking him in print as a degenerate homosexual."

Spatz snorted. "But Cocteau's friendly with Germans. I've seen him at lunch at the embassy. And he's a member of the Group Collaboration, the consortium of French and German artists."

"None of that counts in the face of his relationship with Jean Marais."

Suzanne and Otto Abetz emerged from the theater and ducked into a shiny navy blue limousine. Coco and Spatz watched the sleek car speed away. "Abetz will shut down this play for sure," said Spatz.

"Isn't there something you can do?" asked Coco. Their car pulled up, and Spatz threw his cigarette on the pavement, crushing it with the toe of his shoe. He nudged Coco into the back seat and settled in next to her. As the Mercedes lurched from the curb, Spatz shot Coco a severe look. "Don't expect me to solve all the problems your family and friends are having with the Reich."

He wasn't solving *any* of them. Though Spatz had repeatedly assured Coco that he was "investigating the situation" with André, Coco had heard nothing about when her nephew might be freed from the stalag where he'd languished for almost a year. Her sense that Spatz didn't have much influence with the Occupiers continued to grow along with her disappointment. Spatz was ineffectual. He didn't seem to care about getting ahead. Coco couldn't understand a man who lacked ambition. She'd never before had a lover who wasn't driven in some way—by power, or money, or artistic achievement. Sometimes she was completely at a loss for why she lived with Spatz. For André, she would tell herself. And for all else she valued. She must get through this war with no losses, with her perfume business, her wealth, her reputation, her friends intact. Above all, she must get André home.

As Spatz predicted, the next morning the Nazis closed *La Machine à écrire*. "There will be no more performances," said Jean Marais, who called Coco in a panic later in the day. "I'm in Toulouse filming. I heard it from my director—news travels fast among actors. As soon as he told me I tried Jean. But he's not answering the phone. Will you check on him?"

Coco threw on her fur coat, took the clanking lift to the ground floor, and walked out into the cold day. Snow fell silently, dusting the city in ghostly white. A few cyclists pedaled along, unmindful of the icy pavement. Occasionally, a black Mercedes whizzed past. On rue de la Sourdière, a handwritten sign announcing "Milk Here" had been tacked to the front door of a funeral parlor that was doubling as a distribution center for rationed goods. Below the sign, a poster depicting a French family—father, mother, and two children—asked, "Are your papers in order?" A line of forlorn citizens stretched around the block: men in threadbare coats; women in cork-soled shoes, their dirty hair hidden under turbans; and scrawny children clutching the hands of the adults. There was no soap, no shampoo, no butter, no meat. Glancing into the alley, she saw a group of adolescents pawing through dirty bins overflowing with garbage, scrabbling for something salvageable.

At Cocteau's apartment in the Palais-Royal, Coco banged on the door. When there was no answer, she asked the concierge to unlock it. Entering the foyer, she walked into a thick blue cloud and took in the rich, sweet smell of opium. "Cocteau!" she called. No answer.

She found him in the bedroom, lying on his side under a brown satin quilt in the big brass bed. Opium paraphernalia littered the bedside table: a box of sticky black liquid, a silver stick for stirring, a small lamp, matches, an amber pipe. Cocteau appeared to be in a deep sleep. Coco shook his shoulder but couldn't rouse him. Placing an ear in front of his mouth, she felt his soft breath. "Thank God, you're alive!" she said, and reached for the telephone.

The ambulance arrived fifteen minutes later and rushed Cocteau to the hospital. When she told Spatz about it later, he arranged to have Cocteau transferred to a private clinic outside Vichy in the unoccupied zone. "I pulled a few strings to get him in," Spatz said, "but you'll have to pay for it."

It wasn't the first time Coco had bankrolled Cocteau's rehabilitation. Twice before she'd sent him to clinics to kick his habit. The cures worked for a while, but Cocteau always relapsed. Coco feared he'd die, and she couldn't let that happen. She needed him in her life. They'd been friends since Misia introduced them more than two decades earlier, and he was one of the few artists in Paris who treated her as an equal. She saw her best, creative self reflected in his eyes.

Misia's dinner party in honor of Cocteau and his new play had been planned for that evening, and she had no intention of calling it off, even though the play had been cancelled and the guest of honor hospitalized for a drug overdose. "What am I going to do with all the food? And the wine? It cost me a fortune on the black market," she told Coco over the phone.

Coco agreed to attend with Spatz, but she couldn't shake her anxiety over Cocteau. She was in a foul mood throughout the dinner. Spatz didn't help things by flirting with one of the guests, Antoinette d'Harcourt, a lovely, dark-haired aristocrat in a sable-trimmed velvet dress, a leftover gem from Coco's 1928 fall collection. During the soup course, Coco overheard Spatz at the other end of the table complimenting Antoinette, his voice going all soft and silky. "That neckline suits you; it shows off your beautiful clavicle."

It made Coco feel old, as if she was losing her allure. And it resurrected unpleasant memories of Emile Weisberg, the furrier who'd provided Coco with the trim for Antoinette's dress—he was Jewish. Bile rose within her. "Weisberg is a money-grubbing invert, like all of his kind, a worshipper of gold above all else," Coco blurted. Coco had drunk several glasses of wine, and she slurred her words.

The table fell silent. Spatz glared at her, and Misia shook her head with indignation. Antoinette and the others—her husband, Duke François d'Harcourt; the journalist Boulos Ristelhueber; and Serge Lifar—stared at their plates.

Coco didn't stop. "Weisberg overcharged me," she fumed. "I knew what he was up to. He gave me inferior skins, saving the best ones for that phony Jean Patou. He had a big crush on Patou." The unfairness of it all. Coco's anger was still fresh, and so the ugly words had tumbled out of her mouth.

Misia cleared her throat loudly. "Catherine d'Erlanger had to sell her jewelry," she said in a desperate attempt to change the subject. "You know that 'stop and go' necklace of ruby and emeralds, the one Catherine's husband gave her for their tenth anniversary that cost him millions of francs? Well, now the d'Erlangers are broke. So, Catherine took the necklace to Cartier for an appraisal, and it turns out the rubies and emeralds are nothing but bits of red and green glass!"

"Baron d'Erlanger was always an idiot," said Coco. She was only momentarily distracted, however. A beat later, she was back on Weisberg. "That damn furrier cheated me for years. He and his—"

Spatz stood abruptly, interrupting her. "We need to go, darling. I've an early meeting."

Sitting beside Coco in the back of the Mercedes on the way home, Spatz lashed out. "Your tirade against the Jewish furrier was ugly and embarrassing," he said.

Coco ignored him and stared out the window at the quiet Seine.

They were driving fast toward the Ritz. The boulevards were empty and dark. To conserve energy, the streetlamps had been turned off by German command, and the buildings flashed purple in the car's bright headlights.

"I don't understand how you could be so vulgar," said Spatz.

Coco bit her lip and picked at the cuticle on her thumb. She should have kept her mouth shut. She hadn't meant to rage on so about Weisberg. Truth be told, she had nothing against him for being Jewish or a homosexual. What rankled was his shady business dealings. Once the snake of nastiness had bit Coco, though, the venom released had to run its course. Watching Spatz flirt with another woman had sparked the darkness in Coco that so easily flamed up.

As the Mercedes crossed the Pont de la Concorde, Spatz asked, "Were you aware that Antoinette d'Harcourt's maiden name was Rothschild?"

"I know who she is," said Coco.

"Then you know her tribe."

"The Rothschilds are a tribe of their own."

"I wish you'd try to control yourself."

"I'm the one with Jewish friends."

"That doesn't excuse your behavior."

"I've heard *you* say Jews were shirkers and profiteers in the first war, that they got rich instead of fighting on the front with you and the other golden Aryans."

Spatz stared out the window at the black street. "Sometimes you embarrass me," he said.

"And sometimes you embarrass me!" Coco snapped back.

Spatz turned slowly and looked at her. "Why, because I'm German?"

"Because it's been almost a year, and André is still in prison. I keep telling my friends that you're working on it, and they keep asking."

Whenever Spatz dared criticize her, Coco threw the matter of André back at him. She worried about her nephew and was desperate to get him home, but she also used André as a weapon against Spatz, a way of proving her continuing independence.

"I've told you before," Spatz said slowly, "these things are complicated. I'm doing all I can."

They rode in silence the rest of the way. When the Mercedes stopped at rue Cambon, Spatz told Coco he'd be spending the night in his own apartment. "*Bonne nuit*," he said coldly, when the driver had opened the door for her.

She stepped out and stormed upstairs, injected herself with morphine, and promptly fell asleep.

The next morning, she awoke with a headache, but her anger had passed. At eight, Spatz showed up at the Ritz with the newspapers. "Bonjour, darling," he said. "I'm sorry I was harsh with you."

"It was my fault. I got carried away," said Coco.

They shared a pot of coffee and, having resolved the tension between them, chatted casually about their plans for the day. Spatz said he had a meeting at the German embassy and lunch with a small gathering of French and German businessmen who were working together. He left Coco with a kiss.

His manner was so affable and suave that it reinforced the impression that had been building with Coco for weeks—that despite appearances, Spatz really didn't hold much sway with the Nazis, that he didn't have the influence or strength of character to help André. She had only a vague understanding of how power flowed among the Germans in Paris. The ambassador, Otto Abetz, was an imperious man weakened by his overwhelming vanity. She'd met Spatz's friend, Captain Theodor

Momm, who was not as handsome as Spatz but, it seemed, considerably more hardworking. The other ranking Germans she met seemed much alike—cold, officious, impersonal. She wondered if this ambitious crew didn't really take Spatz seriously.

Maybe he was simply too polite, which might explain his outburst the previous night over her comments about Weisberg. Though Spatz never said anything against the Jews, Coco never heard him deplore their deportation, the seizure of their property, or the race laws that so circumscribed their lives. When she told him that Veronique had quit because her Jewish husband had lost his job and he didn't want his wife working for someone who lived with a German, Spatz just shook his head. He simply accepted the Nazi way and didn't object when other Germans made anti-Semitic remarks. She was never sure if Spatz held the same anti-Semitic views as the other Nazis she met in Paris. Perhaps he was just too elegant to openly express his ugliest opinions.

"Spatz has corrupted you completely!" shouted Misia over the phone later that afternoon. "I never heard you say such terrible things about Jews before you took up with him. I wouldn't like him, even if he wasn't a Nazi. He's a stupid lug. Boy Capel must be rolling in his grave."

"Did you just call to berate me?" Coco asked.

"And think how Max would feel. . . ."

Coco shut her off by slamming down the receiver on the phone. Dinner was more than three hours away, but Coco went to the bar cart and poured herself a glass of red wine, then retreated to the sofa. By mentioning Boy, Misia had dropped her in a soak of memory. And next to Boy, Spatz and every lover faded.

Who could compete with him? Boy was a rich, brilliant Englishman, owner of a thriving oil-tank business, educated at Oxford, a lover of poetry and art. He'd met Coco in 1909, when she was making and selling hats out of the Paris apartment of her first lover, Étienne Balsan. Unlike Balsan, Capel had recognized Coco's talent and took her dreams seriously, giving her the money to set up a boutique on the Parisian street that would forever be associated with her name.

They were lovers for more than a decade. And with André, whom the couple had taken charge of after Julie's death, Boy was the closest Coco ever got to having a family of her own. She had yearned to bear his child. Until she'd spent time with André, Coco had never thought much about becoming a mother. But the skinny, doe-eyed child had fascinated her. Coco and Boy had sent André to boarding school at Beaumont, Boy's alma mater in the English countryside. But on his vacations, André went to work with Auntie Coco. She recalled his serious little face as he played on the floor of her atelier with his toy train and his impatience at the long hours he had to wait for Coco to finish so they could go out for ice cream. "How long does it take to make a stupid dress?" André had often protested. Coco laughed now at the memory.

She was overjoyed when she became pregnant by Boy in 1918, and eagerly awaited his baby, imagining what the child would be like. Coco was sure it was a girl, a little sister for André. She imagined her as beautiful, slim, and dark-haired, with Boy's black eyes and long lashes. She would go to university, Oxford or Cambridge, in England and study all the subjects her mother had missed in her shoddy convent education: philosophy, English, Greek. She would play the piano and sing and make a superb marriage to a man as accomplished and aristocratic as Boy, a man who adored her and would always be faithful. She would not have a career. She would never have to become a horrible bitch to assert her authority over a staff of seamstresses. She would be happy.

Boy was in London, and Coco was alone in their apartment one night three months later, when she started to bleed. By morning, she'd lost the baby.

Coco had been only thirty-five. There was still reason to hope. A baby perhaps would convince Boy to marry her, though Coco knew that was unlikely. A scrappy French dressmaker was hardly a suitable wife for a rising British captain of industry with social and political ambitions. By the end of the year, Boy had married someone else—Diana Wyndham, the daughter of an English lord. The only way Coco could cope with Boy's marriage was to pretend it hadn't happened, and her friends knew never to utter Madame Capel's name. "If you do, Coco will cut you out of her life," Misia warned Cocteau and Max. In fact, little had changed for Coco—Capel still loved her and lived part-time with her in France at La Milanese, a stuccoed villa fifteen miles outside Paris that was quiet and remote from prying eyes.

On Christmas Eve 1919, returning to his wife after a visit with Coco, Capel crashed his Rolls-Royce in Cannes and died instantly. Coco drove all night to the scene of the accident—desperate to feel close to Boy by standing at the spot where he took his last breath. Boy's body had been removed from the crash site, but his charred Rolls lay in the ditch. Coco walked around the wreck slowly, running her hand along every inch of the blackened metal carcass. Then she sat on a large stone by the side of the road and sobbed for three hours.

When she returned to Paris, she called Max Jacob. In many ways, he was the opposite of Boy—destitute, playful, homosexual. He'd come from a middle-class family in Quimper and fled to Paris as a young man to become a poet. Coco met him when Picasso, who'd befriended Max when they were both struggling newcomers, brought him to a dinner party at Misia's. Max told her once how he converted to Catholicism: he'd come home one day from the Bibliothèque Nationale, where he'd been conducting research on mysticism, and saw a vision of Christ on the wall of his humble room. Of course, to Coco, Max was ever a Jew, as she was ever a Catholic peasant girl with mistrust of the Jewish faith bred in her bones, a prejudice as fierce and primal as the mistral wind that raged through the Auvergne in winter.

That didn't stop them from becoming close. Coco came to rely on Max for amusement, comfort, and consolation. When she was unhappy, he would spend hours sitting with her, trying to understand her. He was available to her in a way that Misia, with her jealous nature, and Cocteau, with his ambition and nonstop working, were not.

When she called Max after Boy Capel's death, he came immediately.

He found Coco lying on the sofa in her salon, an ashtray overflowing with cigarette butts on the table in front of her. Her face was drawn, her skin the color of ash. Max sat at her feet and promised to show her something that would pull her from her despair. He took a notebook from his jacket and drew a quick sketch of Jesus Christ—sturdy beard, flowing robe, halo behind His head. And Max gave Him a new hairdo—short on the sides showing the tips of His beautiful ears, a side part, and one long section in front extending to His chin. "The Jesus Christ bob," he said, handing the notebook to Coco.

She sat up and smiled weakly.

"I got the inspiration at church last Sunday morning," Max told her. "I was falling asleep; I'd been out late the night before. Then I saw Him standing behind the altar. That's when I noticed His new hairdo. Christ had been to the *salon de beauté*! No more flowing, shoulder-length tresses for our Lord, Jesus Christ." He ripped the sketch from his notebook and handed it to Coco.

"I'll show it to my hairdresser," she said, stroking Max's shoulder.

"Tell him it was divinely inspired."

"Do you think he'll believe me?"

"Yes! That's what I told Paul Poiret when he asked for advice about the colors for his next collection. I told him I had a vision. He must use only black, blue, and purple. He looked at me with that fat dumb look he gets and said, 'Really? The colors of a bruise?' Yes, I told him, the colors the flesh becomes when it's been beaten senseless. He believed me! And paid me handsomely—five hundred francs."

"That's good, Max." Coco squeezed the poet's hand. "You always manage to cheer me up."

"I'm so sorry about Boy."

"I don't want to live without him."

"He was married."

"Still." Coco looked out the window toward the Champs-Élysées, as if solace lay in the darkening sky above the trees.

"What would become of dreams if people were happy in their real lives?" Max asked.

GIOIA DILIBERTO

"I know that line," she said, on the edge of tears again. "It's from one of Reverdy's notebooks. You're lucky, Max. You have someone who will never leave you."

Max looked puzzled.

"God!"

"Thank the Lord." Max closed his eyes and made the sign of the cross elaborately.

"Do you do that when you're with your family?" she asked.

"Only when they're not looking."

Now it was Coco's turn to bolster Max. Just a few days after her anti-Semitic outburst at Misia's apartment, another letter came to the Ritz from him:

> *My dear Coco,*
>
> *If only I could have hidden my family in a painting at the Louvre.*
>
> *If only I could erase Hitler like I erase a drawing from one of my sketchbooks.*
>
> *First my brother-in-law and now my sister Mirté-Léa. She was taken from her home yesterday in one of the Nazis' round-ups. I suppose it is only a matter of time before the Gestapo comes for my sister Julie and my brother Gaston. I'm not worried about myself. The priests will protect me. They know I'm devoted to Jesus Christ.*
>
> *I had not meant to bother you with more of my troubles, but I wanted to thank you for your most recent check, and I can't avoid mentioning my heavy sadness.*
>
> *Je t'embrasse,*
> *Max*

Coco read the sentences slowly, then folded the letter back into its envelope and put it in the bureau drawer where she kept all the letters she wanted to save—from Max, Boy Capel, Serge Diaghilev, Igor

Stravinsky, the Duke of Westminster, Winston Churchill. They marked a record of her rise in the world, her important friendships, her triumphs. She liked to think she was someone who didn't dwell in the past, but sometimes when she was alone, she enjoyed sifting through the letters, pulling one out to again scan the news, the compliments, the declarations of love. She'd done that more frequently in the past two years, since closing her house and having more time on her hands. Usually she came away cheered. But later that afternoon, Coco took Max's letter out and read it again. Was he overstating the bleakness of the situation? With his eccentric sensibility, he easily lost grasp of reality and sometimes fell into dark moods. But the Nazis had already taken one of his sisters and a brother-in-law. That was real. Coco wondered for a moment if she should speak to Spatz—could he do anything for Max? No, Spatz couldn't deliver André, let alone come to the aid of a homosexual, Jewish, avant-garde poet. She thought of Boy Capel again and remembered how Max, alone of her friends, even more than Misia, had recognized the depth of her grief—honored it, in a way—and then guided her through the harrowing days afterward.

Perhaps Max's relatives would be released soon, Coco thought. Then she did the only thing she could think to do for poor Max. She took out her bankbook and wrote another check to him for two thousand francs.

SEVEN

C oco insisted that Cocteau write to her every week from the clinic to detail his progress. His treatment plan called for enemas, massages, and electric baths, which did little to ease the torture of his withdrawal from opium. He suffered horrible shaking, vomiting, crushing headaches, and hallucinations. Still, he stuck with it.

Two months passed, and one morning Coco got a call from Cocteau's doctor. "I thought you should know, Monsieur Cocteau's treatment was a success. His withdrawal ended more than a month ago."

"Why are you holding him?" asked Coco.

"We're not. He's free to go, but he wants to stay. He says the clinic's a great place to work. I thought you should know. You're paying the bill."

Coco left that afternoon for Vichy in a Mercedes and driver provided by Spatz. The clinic hid behind a copse of trees, a stone mansion on an emerald lawn surrounded by gardens. It was a cool Wednesday in June, the visitors' parking lot empty. A fleet of workers were scattered across the grounds, mowing, watering, and clipping.

Coco checked in at the front desk, and a squat, middle-aged nurse escorted her to Cocteau's room on the second floor. Cocteau half reclined on the iron bed, propped up on one elbow, a notebook open on the starched sheet. He wore a pair of navy flannel pants and a white shirt with the cuffs rolled back, displaying his frail wrists, as narrow as a girl's. "Coco!" he cried. "What are you doing here?"

"I should have let you die, Cocteau!" she screamed. "Do you know how much this place costs me? You've been here two months, but the doctor says you were cured weeks ago."

"After the cure, the deluge, the most dangerous time," said Cocteau. His right hand held a pencil posed in midair for dramatic effect—he was ridiculously proud of his slender hands with their long, graceful fingers.

A cloud of confusion crossed Coco's face. She kicked a pile of scrunched papers on the floor and looked up, astonished to see Max Jacob standing in the doorway holding a ceramic pitcher. "The flood of health. When you feel too good to paint and write," said Max.

"What the hell are *you* doing here?" asked Coco.

Cocteau explained that he'd sent for Max. Marais was back in Paris filming another movie, and Cocteau had been lonely. Max had needed comforting, too. His brother-in-law, the antique dealer, had died while imprisoned by the Nazis at Drancy, probably from a beating, though Max never found out for sure. After her arrest, his sister Mirté-Léa had also disappeared into the hands of the Nazis.

The night nurse moved in a cot for Max, and he and Cocteau wrote ten hours a day.

"Here's more water," said Max, setting the pitcher on Cocteau's bedside table.

Max was short, portly, and bald, with large brown eyes that gazed intensely beneath thick black brows. He wore a brown cassock and a crude wooden cross on a chain around his neck—the uniform he'd adopted for his life in the monastery at Saint-Benoît. No one at the clinic suspected that Max wasn't really a Catholic monk.

"You look like a rabbi at a costume party," Coco told him sharply.

"I feel comfortable this way, closer to God," said Max.

Coco took in the room—the iron bed, Max's cot, the tall, disheveled stack of papers on the small wood desk. More papers, pens, paintbrushes, ink bottles, and books littered the floor. Several of Max's gouaches were scattered around the chair where he now took a seat.

"I don't mind paying for doctors and treatments, but not if you don't need them," Coco said to Cocteau.

He sat up, swinging his legs over the side of the bed. "Who says I don't need them?"

"You've been using this place like a hotel!"

"Jean finished a book," Max announced.

Coco picked up a few papers off the floor and glanced through them. "This looks like your handwriting, Max."

"I got a lot done, too."

Coco opened her hands, and the papers drifted back to the floor. "You've been here the whole time?"

"On and off."

"They allow it?"

"The staff doesn't care. I'm invisible when I want to be."

Coco walked around the room. She picked up bottles and read their labels, leafed through books, searched inside the wardrobe, and glanced under the rug. She didn't trust Cocteau and suspected he was hiding drugs. Finally, she sat on the bed next to him.

"We miss you in Paris," she said. Turning to Max, she added, "We miss you, too." Then, to Cocteau, "Why don't you come back with me? My car's outside."

Max shook his head and fingered the cross around his neck. "It's too easy for Jean to get opium in Paris."

Coco stood, her fists digging into her bony hips. "I'll get you a room at the Ritz, on my floor, so I can keep an eye on you."

Cocteau held up a long index finger. "One more week?"

"No!" Coco hauled Cocteau's suitcase out of the wardrobe and flung it onto the bed.

"I'm writing seven pages a day."

"I don't care if you're writing a hundred pages an hour. This place costs twice as much as the Ritz." Coco pointed her chin in Max's direction. "I'm paying for his meals, too?"

"He does party tricks for his supper. Tells fortunes for the staff," said Cocteau.

Max grabbed Coco's hand to read her palm, and she pulled it away. "You never let me," he said.

She looked hard at Max, then softened her expression and held out her hand.

Max's fingers felt rough and fleshy as they cupped hers. "The lines from the base of the fate line are strong," he began. "I've seen them this strong only in Picasso. A fierce temperament. Strength, everywhere strength—good and bad strength. The life line is glorious. You will live to a very old age. Wealth will grow. Fame, too. Fame will play too large a role in your life. Only the line of the heart becomes weak. This troubles me—it grows fainter and fainter as time goes on. Love slips from your grasp."

Coco snatched her hand away. Cocteau grinned. "That settles it."

"It settles nothing," Coco snapped.

"You always pick the wrong man," Cocteau taunted.

"Yes, I heard about your German," said Max. His brows knitted together severely.

"He's not what you think," said Coco defensively. Then, turning to Cocteau, "At least Spatz is a *man*."

"My boys keep me young," said Cocteau.

Coco turned to Max. "What about you? I hear you've been prowling the bars around Saint-Benoît."

"Once in a while, I need a boy," Max confessed.

"You're a bad influence, Cocteau."

He'd started tossing shirts in his suitcase in a haphazard manner. Coco removed them, folded them neatly, and returned them to the suitcase. "My boys are the guardian angels of my work," Cocteau said.

"I thought I was!" Max cried, as he gathered his pens and inkwells and placed them in a bag with his notebooks.

"No, I am!" Coco laughed. She put her arms around Cocteau and drew him to her. "Poor, poor Jean. I'm glad you're coming back." She reached for Max's hand. "And what about you, Max? Why don't you come with us, too?"

Cocteau's face darkened. "He can't come. His papers mark him as a Jew. If he tried to cross into Occupied France, the Nazis would arrest him."

"The Nazis." Coco snorted. "They're too busy getting fat on French pastries to care. Besides, I'd watch out for you."

Cocteau raised his eyebrows, giving Coco a knowing stare. "No one is safe with the Nazis."

"You seem to be getting along pretty well," Coco said in a mocking tone.

Max threw his bag over his shoulder, preparing to leave. "Please. I'm happier in Saint-Benoît, where I'm just a lowly monk."

"You take care, Max. I'm sorry you can't come with us," said Coco. She looked at Cocteau, and for a moment their eyes locked. It was as if a blast of dread had blown into the room.

The German driver dropped off Cocteau at his apartment and then Coco at her boutique. "I found this slipped under the door," said the vendeuse Angeline, handing Coco a small, square envelope. Inside was a short message from Pierre Reverdy: *Meet me at 143 rue de la Santé as soon as possible. Take the Métro, and make sure no one follows you.*

Coco hadn't been on the Métro in years, but she followed Reverdy's instructions. She bought a ticket at the Madeleine station and caught a train just as it rumbled in. There were no young people in sight. They avoided the Métro for fear of being nabbed by the Nazis who patrolled it and sent to compulsory work service in Germany. Coco crammed into a middle car with a couple dozen old men and women, many of them bedraggled looking and coughing loudly. She got off at Glacière and walked the four blocks to rue de la Santé. Number 143 was a modest brick apartment building with a scarred black door and cracked concrete steps. She found Reverdy in the small apartment on the top floor sitting at a table with a typewriter and a mimeograph machine. "Ah, Coco, sit down. I'll just be a minute," he said, nodding toward an armchair in the corner.

Reverdy removed the black ribbon from the typewriter and inserted two sheets of paper—one white and one blue—under the roller and began to type. *Vive La Résistance! Help Us Throttle the Krauts!*

As the keys struck, they cut through the blue paper, creating a stencil. Carefully, Reverdy removed the stencil, then wrapped it over the drum of the mimeograph machine. As he cranked the lever, the ink seeped through the stencil onto the white paper being fed through it. "It takes an hour to run off a hundred pages. We can talk while I work," he said.

The smelly purple ink burned Coco's eyes. She felt tears welling up and blinked them back. There had been moments in the past few weeks when she couldn't stop crying, when she worried that she'd made a terrible mistake in taking Spatz into her bed. First Misia, then Hélène Dessoffy had planted in her head the idea that Spatz was using her. He said he loved her, but she couldn't be sure. What exactly did he want from her?

Still, she was too fearful to help Reverdy. In the Métro, she'd seen the posters with the names of Resisters who'd been caught and shot. "My feeling about your flyers hasn't changed. You'll have to find someone else to distribute them," Coco said.

"That's not why I needed to see you." Reverdy released the mimeograph lever and rubbed his biceps. "You're on an official blacklist of collaborators."

"What?" Coco felt her breath catch.

"The Resistance is keeping track."

"I'm not a collaborator!"

Reverdy sighed heavily. "You're living with a German. I saw your name on the list that was just released by de Gaulle's resistance group, the FFI. It came over the teletype in a safe house in Toulouse. I wish you'd take my advice and get out of Paris. And leave *him* behind."

Reverdy returned to cranking his machine. "I've got to get this done. I have to get out of here myself."

In the following days, Coco thought about moving to La Pausa, her country house outside Roquebrun. But she could never stand the country for more than a weekend. By Sunday evening, she'd always be desperate to return to Paris, to the gossip, the glamour, the grittiness. She decided that Reverdy had exaggerated the danger. That was what happened when you lived like a hunted animal. You expected to be killed at any moment. He was projecting his own fears. So what if she was on a Resistance blacklist? Would a *Resistant* really murder in cold blood one of the most famous women in Paris?

She was no more of a collaborator than any of the other celebrities who remained in Paris, tolerated by the Nazis. Sartre still published books written in his Left Bank apartment. Édith Piaf still sang at the Moulin Rouge. Picasso still sold paintings from his studio on rue des Grands Augustins. Like Cocteau, who never stopped working, the Germans left them all alone. Were they on the blacklists, too? At least *she* didn't do business with the enemy.

Nevertheless, Coco decided to lay low, confining herself to one of the shortest commutes in Paris: fourteen steps from her Ritz suite to the elevator; six floors down to the back lobby; twenty-nine steps to the back lobby door; forty-four steps across rue Cambon to the Chanel boutique; three flights up to her apartment.

She continued to decline all invitations. Then, one evening Spatz announced that he'd arranged a private box for the reopening of Longchamp. The racetrack had shut down at the start of the Occupation, but the Nazis were eager to partake of all Paris had to offer, so they'd had it reopened. Spatz knew how much Coco loved horses, and he thought she'd be thrilled. But Coco recoiled. "I won't go," she said.

"Why not?" Spatz wanted to know.

The races always drew a gaggle of press and photographers, and Coco didn't want to be recognized and photographed with Spatz. She did not confide this concern to him, however. Instead, she told him she wasn't in the mood to have people make a fuss over her, which always happened when she appeared at the track.

"I promise no one will see you," said Spatz. "We can drive right up to the entrance and slip in and out."

And so in the end, Coco agreed to go.

When the couple arrived at the track, a light midmorning rain had begun to fall, and umbrellas dotted the lawns and half-empty viewing stands. The sparse crowd was mostly German. Many of the celebrities, journalists, couturiers, and salon hostesses who'd flocked to Longchamp in peacetime were unwilling to mingle in public with the Nazis and stayed away.

In the back seat of the Mercedes on the drive to the track, Spatz had studied the yellow racing form, and he told Coco that Bold Prince had an excellent chance to win in the first race. Coco gave him fifty francs, and he sent his driver to place a bet.

As soon as she was settled in her seat overlooking the finish line, Coco trained her binoculars on the track below where stableboys led the horses onto the course. She scanned the surrounding lawn, and her eyes fell on a group of middle-aged German officers with their heavy stomachs squished against the rail. *God, they're ugly,* Coco thought. *I have the most handsome German in Paris.*

She passed her binoculars to Spatz, who held them to his eyes. "My mother raised horses," he said as he scanned the crowd. "She kept them at our summer estate near the seaside town of Kiel. She taught me how to ride, starting with a little pony when I was two." Spatz handed the binoculars back to Coco.

"I worry about my mother. There's been a lot of bombing around Kiel," Spatz said. He'd once shown Coco a picture of Lorry von Dincklage—a slim, delicate-featured blonde still beautiful in her seventies. "I'll take you to Kiel someday. We'll ride together on the beach."

Coco wondered what Madame von Dincklage, now a widow, would think of her son's romance with a dark little French dressmaker more than a decade older than her child—probably not much. "My aunts, the ones who raised me, bred Arabian horses that they sold to the military," said Coco. "I used to worry on the day every year the cavalry officers came to make their selections that they would pick my favorites."

Spatz looked sideways at her, and Coco realized he knew she was lying. She'd forgotten for a moment that Spatz had met her brother Alphonse. But her love of horses was true. As a young woman, Coco's life had opened up as she rode near Royallieu along the path behind her lover Étienne Balsan's château, then into the forest. The gleaming horses and earthy scent rising from the track sharpened her memory. She half expected to see visions of her youthful self galloping bareback while clutching her horse's mane, stopping by a stream and dismounting by sliding over the horse's tail, picnicking with Étienne in a clearing near a copse of dense pines, racing her horse across an open field—first with Étienne by her side on his own spirited stallion and later with Boy Capel.

She loved the elegance and beauty of the horses, the way they threw their legs in front as they ran and leapt over fallen logs with balletic grace. It occurred to her that the only time she'd ever been truly happy was on horseback. It was on those horses, for the first time, that she had felt hopeful about the future. She did not feel hopeful now. What if someone recognized her? She didn't want to be seen in this sea of Nazis.

The starter's bell rang, and the horses shot from the gate. The race was over in a flash. "Look!" Spatz said. He pulled Coco to her feet and pointed to the board posted above the track. Coco saw that Bold Prince had won, and she was four hundred francs richer. It seemed like a good omen. Then, her gaze traveled to the seats below her. Two men, one gripping a large camera, the other holding a reporter's notebook, had turned and were staring hard at her. Coco slumped in her seat and pulled her hat low over her forehead.

The rain had stopped, and sunshine bathed the track in a golden glow. Near the winner's circle, Génevière Fath, the beautiful blond wife of the couturier Jacques Fath, had appeared like a vision from another world in a sumptuous blue silk dress with a flouncy tiered skirt. An ermine stole draped across her lunar shoulders; on her head perched a towering confection of faux flowers and lace. Soon, she was joined by mannequins from other couture houses, all similarly swathed in opulent fabrics, furs, and jewels. Paris couture continued to operate at a vastly diminished level. The extravagant materials on display here were probably all that the Nazis had allotted the few houses still open.

Before the war, it was de rigueur for couturiers to parade their mannequins in the latest fashions at the racetrack. But these couturiers might as well have had "COLLABORATOR" stamped on their foreheads. Coco was glad she'd closed her house and kept a low profile.

Spatz noticed the intent look on her face and misinterpreted it as longing. "You could be out there with your own mannequins. It's not too late to reopen," he said.

Coco noted with satisfaction that most of Paris's esteemed designers, such as herself and Cristóbal Balenciaga, had either shut their ateliers or, like Mainbocher, who was living in New York, had fled Paris. Mainly, the mediocrities remained. Their mannequins vamped for photographers from *Le Figaro*, *Ce Soir*, *Le Matin*, and the German magazine *Signal*, as flashbulbs popped. Jacques Fath and a handful of other couturiers smiled from the sidelines, occasionally scurrying up to adjust a neckline or hem.

It was as if the war weren't happening, as if ordinary dressmakers didn't have to close shop because they couldn't get fabric and thread. As if there were no propaganda billboards on buildings emblazoned with pictures of bloody French soldiers over captions that read, *C'est Angleterre Que a fait cela*; and concierges on the streets at dawn scrubbing away the phrase *Vive de Gaulle!* that had been scrawled in desperation in black chalk on house fronts during the night. No banners with giant swastikas hanging from the monuments, and no invaders patrolling the streets during blackouts, greeting every yellow cube in the windows with pistol shot. It was as if there were no masterpieces being looted from the museums, no posters in the Métro warning Resistance fighters that their families would be executed, no Jews disappearing.

"Couture is dead," Coco said sourly. "The Germans have killed it."

Spatz frowned at her. "You mustn't talk like that."

"The Americans will probably take over now. They're go-getters. They'll fill the vacuum."

"If the Allies win," muttered Spatz.

The couple left before the last race, hurrying from the viewing box to the waiting Mercedes. The photographer and reporter Coco had caught staring at her skulked by the car. The camera was in her face, then it drew back. Click, click, click, click. It didn't stop until the car had lurched from the curb.

The next day, Coco's picture with Spatz at Longchamp surrounded by Nazis splashed across the society page of *Ce Soir* next to a photo of Géneviève Fath in the latest gown from her husband's atelier.

Coco felt as embarrassed as if the photographer had snapped her nude getting out of the tub. She folded the paper and stuffed it in her desk, returning to it several times during the day to stare at the Longchamp picture, as if the more she looked at it, the less offensive it would be. She blamed Spatz—she never should have let him talk her into going to the track.

To show her loyalty to France, she decided to go to Misia's Bastille Day party at José Maria Sert's apartment. Spatz had not wanted her to go—the Germans had outlawed the holiday. Coco waited until he'd left the Ritz to meet a friend for dinner, then she slipped out.

Sert was in Madrid visiting his mistress, and while he was away, Misia had moved into his apartment overlooking the Place de la Concorde. As neutral Spain's ambassador to the Vatican, Sert enjoyed a wealth of privileges, including abundant supplies of fine food and wine that he was happy to share with his ex-wife. Through a doctor friend in Madrid, Sert also had access to morphine, which he supplied to Coco and Misia every month. The little vials of clear liquid cost four times as much as they had before the war, but Coco and Misia didn't think twice about paying the exorbitant black-market price.

Misia had been careful not to call her party a Bastille Day celebration, but of course everyone knew the significance of the day, July 14, the anniversary of the Revolution. Coco arrived at the Place de la Concorde to find a crowd of men and women marching around the square holding lit candles and waving French flags. She looked frantically about for German soldiers. None were visible at the moment, but she knew it wouldn't be long before Nazis arrived to put a stop (most likely violently) to this flaunting of French patriotism. Entering Sert's building, she made her way to the artist's apartment, where Cocteau and Serge Lifar were lounging on the cushy red sofa, smoking cigarettes. "Why are you monopolizing Lifar?" Coco said to Cocteau. He slid to the far end of the sofa to make room for Coco's bony, silk-clad rear.

"Did you see those people with French flags in the street?" she asked, frowning.

"Vive Bastille Day!"

Coco looked up to see a tiny elderly woman with a nest of dyed black hair and a tricolor flag in sapphires, diamonds, and rubies pinned to her cream linen dress. She was Countess Virginie de Fontenay, and before the war she'd written a popular column, "Carnet d'un Mondain," that ran every Friday on the front page of *Le Figaro*. She'd been born into a grand aristocratic family that had lost all its money (while hanging on to some of its jewels), and she'd never married. She'd often interviewed Coco.

Virginie took out a notebook and pen and began scrawling notes. "A story about Bastille Day is the last thing you'll get past the censors," Coco warned.

"I wouldn't in a million years write for the papers now!" cried Virginie. "I'm working on a memoir about the Occupation. I'm calling it *The Darkest Days I've Known*."

"I hope you aren't planning to go outside to interview those people in the street," sounded a male voice at Coco's side. It belonged to her old acquaintance, the lawyer Michel Pelissier, dressed impeccably as usual in a navy blue suit and light blue shirt with a red-and-blue-striped Hermès tie. Cocteau and Lifar exchanged glances. "Come on, let's see if there's caviar at the buffet," Cocteau said to the ballet master. The two men rushed away with Virginie de Fontenay following as she scribbled in her notebook.

"Those two don't want anything to do with me," said Pelissier with a laugh. "I make them feel guilty."

Months before, Pelissier had chastised Lifar for dancing at a ceremony at the German embassy to celebrate the Nazi triumph over France. Later, at a dinner party, Pelissier had cornered Cocteau and berated him for attending receptions at the German embassy.

Pelissier had the courtly manners and elegant looks Coco admired in men, but she found him pompous and judgmental. Still, this was the first time she'd seen him since running into him at Bignon's, and gauging by his friendly manner, he didn't seem to hold her relationship with Spatz against her. She assumed he made a distinction between Lifar's and Cocteau's activities with the Nazis and her more innocent *horizontal* collaboration. Pelissier also made an exception for Sert, who had helped save Colette's Jewish husband, Maurice Goudeket. Misia had prevailed on Sert, who prevailed on his mistress, the wife of the German ambassador to Spain, to prevail on *her* husband to arrange for Goudeket's release from a German deportation camp.

"I'm worried about those people down there in the street," Coco said, accepting a glass of champagne from Pelissier. "They're going to get shot."

"I'm worried, too. I'll go down in a minute and see if I can talk some sense into them," said the lawyer.

"I wouldn't," said Coco. "They'll shoot you, too."

He shrugged. "Did you hear de Gaulle's speech on BBC Radio this morning?" Coco shook her head. "It was very moving. He talked about France's need to persevere, about our hope, our pride, our honor."

Pelissier looked hard at Coco, and she wondered if he was delivering a rebuke to her, a more indirect version of the censure he'd directed at

Lifar and Cocteau. "All your friends are here tonight—your French friends," said Pelissier.

"Not everyone," said Coco.

"No. Not Max Jacob. Have you heard from him?"

"He's getting by."

Voices singing "La Marseillaise" rose up from the street, at first softly but growing louder as they reached the most stirring verse and the one most likely to provoke the enemy: *"Aux armes, citoyens! Formez vos battaillons! Marchons, marchons . . ."*

"They're going to end up dead," said Coco, nodding toward the windows.

"I'll talk to them," said Pelissier. He had just drained his champagne glass when gunfire rang out, followed by the sound of shattered glass. Coco dropped to the floor and sprawled on the carpet under the coffee table, inches away from Pelissier's pomaded gray head.

Stray bullets shattered the windows in the salon and dining room. Sert's jade lamps and gold plates filled with sausages, hams, and fruit from Spain had careened to the floor and smashed to pieces. Bottles of wine lay on their sides, leaking black circles into the carpet.

Misia slumped on the sofa with a dazed expression. "Are you hurt?" asked Coco.

Misia shook her head, and Coco patted her arm.

The following night Coco refused to go with Spatz to a party at the home of the German ambassador, Otto Abetz. She feigned a headache and climbed into bed with a glass of wine and her cigarettes. She was starting to drift off when the door creaked open.

"You can't hide forever." Spatz stood in the doorway dressed in black tie and tails, his camel cashmere overcoat draped over his shoulders.

"I'm sick."

"Abetz will be disappointed."

"If I don't show, it makes *you* look bad," Coco said harshly. She was wide-awake now.

"Don't start a fight."

"Abetz wants to show he's got the French in his pocket. Isn't that your job?" Her tone was bitter.

"I have to go." Spatz turned on his heel, closing the door behind him with a loud click.

The next day, Spatz failed to appear for breakfast. Coco assumed he spent the night at his own apartment, probably to avoid waking her by coming in late. She ate her croissant and drank her coffee alone, dressed quickly, and headed across the street. She found Angeline restocking the shelves with a fresh supply of Chanel No. 5. It was nine o'clock. The boutique wouldn't open for another hour. "I'll be in my apartment, if you need me," Coco said. She started for the staircase when the front door opened. Otto Abetz walked in with a tall, bulky man Coco immediately recognized as Hermann Goering, the commander of the Luftwaffe.

Goering had a red, beefy face and a barrel chest glittering with medals. His black-brimmed hat sat high on his head like a crown, and his shiny black boots clicked across the floor in the manner of a man who knew people would do what he wanted. He smiled coldly at Coco as Abetz introduced them.

"So nice to meet you, Maréchal Goering, and to see you again, Ambassador," said Coco. She could feel beads of moisture blooming on her forehead under her bangs. Her armpits were soaked.

"I was hoping to meet you last night," said Goering.

Coco lowered her eyes. "I'm afraid I wasn't feeling well."

Abetz's icy blue eyes held her in his sight. "I brought Maréchal Goering here so he could see an example of what's created by French genius," he said.

"I closed my couture house. I sell only perfume now and a few scarves," said Coco.

Goering shifted his feet, clattering his medals. "I'd like to bring something back to my wife in Germany," he said. The French words in heavily accented German filled the air like a bubble of Nazi evil.

Coco turned to Angeline. "Can you check the storage room?"

"My pleasure" said the vendeuse. She curtsied slightly and scurried off.

A few minutes later—a seeming eternity during which Coco made small talk about the weather with Goering and Abetz—Angeline returned carrying an armload of clothes, which she dropped on the counter.

Goering pawed through the sweaters and silk blouses and pulled out a smart little mink jacket. "Emmy will love this," he said.

It was the most expensive item in the pile. "Are you sure?" asked Coco. "It's from several years ago and isn't the most up-to-date model." Coco thought the jacket wouldn't fit Madame Goering, who looked like a large, raw-boned woman from the pictures Coco had seen of her—including one in which she and Eva Braun were scowling at each other at a Nazi rally.

"It's perfect," said Goering. He made a great show of patting his jacket and pants pockets, as he stared at the ceiling. "I'm afraid I have no money on me."

Coco caught Abetz's eye, but the ambassador abruptly looked at the floor. "That's all right," Coco said to Goering. "Angeline will wrap it, and you can pay later."

"Would Madame Goering also like some perfume?" asked Angeline, holding up a bottle with a shaking hand.

"How about two bottles?" said Goering.

When they'd left, Angeline started to cry. "What do I do if they come back?" she asked, as Coco put an arm around her and squeezed her shoulder.

"Let's hope they don't," Coco said.

That evening, Coco met Spatz at Bignon's. The couple sat at their usual spot in front of the fireplace and were served by their usual slim, dark-haired waiter. "The La Tâche," said Spatz, handing the waiter the wine list.

When he'd left, Coco lit a cigarette. "Goering came to my boutique today to buy a present for his wife," she said, blowing smoke out of the side of her mouth.

"He went to the right place," said Spatz, taking Coco's hand and kissing it.

"Isn't that an amazing coincidence? I don't show up at the party, then I get a visit from a high-ranking Nazi, who acts like he has the right to loot what's left of my fashion house?" Coco's voice was hard with sarcasm. "Goering took the most expensive thing I had left—a mink jacket. But he had no money on him. He also got away with two free bottles of perfume."

The waiter returned with the wine, poured Spatz and Coco each a glass, and stood by their table, hovering. Coco looked sharply at Spatz and opened her eyes wide, signaling him to say something to dismiss the waiter.

Spatz cleared his throat loudly, and the waiter stepped even closer to the couple's table.

"The lamb chops," said Spatz.

The waiter hurried away. Leaning across the table, Coco spoke in a low voice. "You tell Goering he owes me fifteen thousand francs."

"Let it go, darling."

"Let it go? Goering has enough money to buy all of France!"

"Do you really expect me to ask him to pay you?"

"No." *But another man would*, Coco thought. Another man would stand up for her and not let her be taken advantage of by a brutal thug.

EIGHT

The incident with Goering convinced Coco she had to get out of Paris. Reverdy was right. It was impossible to lay low enough to avoid all unwanted notice. It disconcerted her that the Nazis seemed to be aware of her every move. She couldn't stand to feel she'd lost her privacy. She'd feel safer and calmer at her country house near the Spanish border in the unoccupied zone.

"I won't stay long, and you can visit me," Coco told Spatz.

"You've packed for six months!" he said, eyeing the four large suitcases lined up in the entry of her rue Cambon apartment. The truth was, Coco didn't know how long she'd be away. That morning, she had gone through the clothes she stored in a small room off the salon and decided to take enough things to last a couple of seasons. They filled two suitcases. A third suitcase held books, and the fourth contained a stash of cigarettes, champagne, perfume, makeup, soap, shampoo, and face cream.

"It's really not that much," Coco said.

"I thought you didn't like the country for more than a weekend."

"I have to get away."

"Do you really think decamping to La Pausa will fool people that we're not together?"

I hope so, Coco thought.

She called Marceau Larcher, the chauffeur who'd driven her to Lembeye in June, and a few hours later he picked her up at the Ritz in her car. It was the first time since the start of the Occupation that the black Rolls-Royce, tricked out with mirrors, a collapsible bar, lights, and a spare tire in a snug black leather case, had left the garage. Cars were verboten for French citizens. Coco decided to risk being stopped by German soldiers, confident that a call to Spatz would prevent her Rolls from being confiscated.

The trip turned out to be uneventful. They drove for nine hours and reached Roquebrun after dark.

La Pausa sat a few miles outside town, high on a ridge overlooking the curvy shoreline of Monaco. The house was dark except for a large lamp over the front door that cast the entry in a pool of welcoming light. The maid Céline greeted Coco. "Soup's on the stove, if you're hungry, Mademoiselle," she said. Céline was a slight, seventy-year-old woman with a tight salt-and-pepper bun. Her real name was Marthe. Coco called her Céline because she believed it a more suitable name for the servant of a grand lady in a grand house.

"Thank you for waiting up. But I'm too tired to eat. I'm going straight to bed," said Coco.

Céline handed her a lantern, and Coco made her way to her bedroom in a far corner of the house.

La Pausa drew its name from Gallic legend. When Mary Magdalene fled Jerusalem after Christ's crucifixion, she is said to have traveled through Roquebrun. The lovely flower gardens and olive trees lured her to rest for a few moments of contemplation at a spot next to what would someday become Coco's property. Coco thought it the perfect place to pause her own eventful life.

The white stucco villa had three wings framing a brick courtyard and sat on nine acres of flower and olive gardens. Coco had built the house in 1928 during the dying days of the Jazz Age and her waning affair with the large, blustery Duke of Westminster. She had entertained Winston Churchill here, when he was staying with British friends at a nearby villa. This was where she had tried to conceive a child with Bendor, as the duke was known by his intimates, though she could never become pregnant after her miscarriage with Boy in 1918. Her next lover, the bookish illustrator Paul Iribe, had died suddenly of a heart attack one summer afternoon while playing tennis with Coco on the villa's tree-shaded court. They were in the middle of a game when Iribe lowered his sunglasses to look at Coco across the net and fell dead. A maid inside the house heard Coco scream and called an ambulance. Coco laid her head on Iribe's chest and felt life leave him. How quickly he was no longer there. By the time the medics removed his body, he was as gray and cold as stone.

So much loss, so much death.

In her bedroom, Coco padded across the plush brown carpet and drew the beige satin drapes. She undressed, slipped on her pajamas, removed her makeup, and brushed her teeth. Before getting into bed, she took a thick book bound in green leather from her suitcase. Misia had given it to her a few days earlier, after Coco told her about Hélène Dessoffy's visit to rue Cambon and Spatz's insistence that he wasn't a spy. "Don't fool yourself," Misia said.

She handed the book to Coco with a few pages marked by torn pieces of paper. The title stamped on the cover in gold leaf read, *When Hitler Spies on France.*

The book had been the talk of the salons when it first came out in 1936. Coco remembered seeing it on a table in Misia's salon and chatting with her about some of their acquaintances named in its pages. But she'd never read the book. Now Coco turned to the first page Misia had marked and read that the author, a respected intelligence agent named Paul Allard, had uncovered reams of classified documents, including dispatches from German agents. Among the papers were Spatz's correspondence with his superiors in Berlin. The book included excerpts, mostly advice on how the Germans could best win the hearts of the French. In one, Spatz reported:

> *My many society friends in France have allowed me to form an ever-growing group of French sympathizers, which will allow me, I believe, to do my best in the tasks entrusted to me. . . . Our influence will only spread slowly, and we will not see . . . immediate results. I ask you for articles in the major French newspapers about the "bourgeois life" of the SS. It would be good to include photographs showing, for example, Nazi officers doing their marketing, to prove with this that the S.A. officer is not a savage but a citizen.*

Coco flung the book to the floor and lit a cigarette. *That proves nothing!* After the first Great War, there was an epidemic of spy-itis. The French thought every foreigner was suspect. Spatz's job as an embassy attaché required him to come up with ideas to improve relations between the French and the Germans. It was propaganda, exactly as he'd told Coco. He wasn't doing anything sinister.

Coco tried to comfort herself with this thought before falling asleep.

A day after Coco arrived at La Pausa, she got a call from Cocteau, asking if he could come down for the weekend. Marais was home—he was between movies—and Cocteau found it impossible to work in their small Paris apartment. He was trying to finish a new play, and he needed a quiet place to write with no distractions. Coco's driver fetched Cocteau from the Roquebrun train station on a Friday afternoon, and twenty minutes later, Cocteau stood in the white-walled salon at La Pausa, his eyes sparking with glee. "I had nothing to do with this!" he said, as he handed Coco a copy of the latest issue of *Aux Écoutes*, the venerable journal of French culture. Coco had been reclining on the fawn leather sofa reading a book. She sat up and laid the book aside. "Read the top of page four," said Cocteau as he crossed the salon to the bar cart, where he poured himself a generous glass of red wine.

Coco opened the journal and read out loud:

Jean Cocteau, the prolific writer and director, and Coco Chanel, the famous fashion designer, were married last weekend at l'Eglise St. Roch. The couple, who have been close for many years, apparently decided the time was right to tie the knot. Monsieur Cocteau would confirm no details, but when asked about the marriage, he did not deny it. Mademoiselle Chanel, who has made glorious wedding gowns for some of the most gorgeous women of Paris, was married, our sources tell us, in a simple beige jersey suit. The Cocteaus will make their home at the Ritz, where Mademoiselle Chanel has lived for many years.

Coco doubled over in laughter and tossed the journal onto the coffee table next to a crystal ashtray. It was full of lipstick-ringed butts and ashes that overflowed onto the leather top. Late afternoon had come, and outside the light was fading, turning the sky as deep red as the wine in the half-empty bottle on the cart.

"The news of our marriage was also picked up by *Le Petit Parisien* and *Le Figaro*. No one besides *Aux Écoutes*, though, claimed to have spoken to me."

"Did they?"

"No! They never even tried."

Cocteau said his mother had alerted him to the item in *Aux Écoutes* in a phone call the evening before, and he'd rushed out to buy the journal and the afternoon papers at a kiosk near his apartment. "Maman said, 'Why don't you admit it to me, Jean, since it's in the papers.' I didn't protest too much. She's old and ailing and it gives her peace of mind to think I'm not like my father." Cocteau *père*, a doctor and secret homosexual, had shot himself when Jean was just eight. "Did *you* plant the item?" he asked Coco.

"Me? Why would I?" said Coco through a puff of laughter.

Cocteau shrugged. "I don't know. To deflect attention from you and Spatz, perhaps."

Though she had nothing to do with the item, it struck Coco that the false story might actually help her—people who read it were likely to believe it and discount the rumors they might have heard about her living with a Nazi.

"It must have been one of *your* friends—to stifle talk about you and Marais," said Coco.

The hard right-wing that abhorred homosexuality had continued its relentless attacks on Cocteau for his "unnatural" relationship with the dazzling actor. The vitriol against him had not let up in the Fascist press.

"It doesn't matter. It won't stop my enemies," said Cocteau.

"At least you made your mother happy."

"For a few minutes."

"These days even a few minutes of happiness should be prized." Coco poured herself more wine. "To better days," she said, raising her glass high.

"To better days," said Cocteau.

Coco was enjoying the peace and beauty of the countryside and her time away from swastika banners, gray-green uniforms, and the German language. She missed Spatz terribly, but it wouldn't be long before he came for a visit. In the meantime, she had Cocteau and then Misia, who arrived on Monday night, a few hours after Cocteau departed.

No sooner had Misia stepped through the door with her suitcase than she told Coco that Max Jacob's sister Delphine had died. "She'd been in a stupor of grief since her husband's death in a German prison last year. I just got a letter from Max about the funeral in Quimper," she said. "He's in a bad way. We should check on him."

"In Saint-Benoît? That's a six-hour drive, and you just got here," said Coco.

"Max is despondent. Thanks to the Nazis' latest anti-Jewish laws, he's lost the copyright to his books, and he can no longer receive royalties. It was only a tiny sum, but he depended on that money. I'm worried about him. And you should be worried, too." She shot a look at Coco.

They left the next morning in Coco's Rolls. Though they passed no checkpoints along the way, and the Rolls wasn't stopped, the trip was hardly pleasant. Coco and Misia bickered through the six-hour drive, sitting in the back seat and picking at each other, while the driver ignored them, his eyes relentlessly fixed on the road. They loved each other and couldn't live without each other, yet they couldn't spend two hours together without fighting. Misia never stop nagging Coco about the shamefulness of her affair with Spatz. Coco didn't see how her romance was any more deplorable than Sert's relationship with a German woman, which Misia tolerated without complaint.

Max wasn't home—he rented a second-floor room in a modest brick house on Place du Martroi—so Coco and Misia set out looking for him. The two women drew stares in their identical beige jersey Chanel suits. When Coco had an outfit made up for herself, she often had a duplicate sewn for Misia. In town, huge flags emblazoned with swastikas flew from the government buildings. The street signs had been newly painted black with yellow lettering in German. Nazi soldiers in impeccable uniforms and shiny black boots paraded down *la grand rue*, the principal commercial street in town.

The women found Max on the riverbank sitting under a chestnut tree shaded by fragrant pink blossoms. "Max! We've been looking everywhere for you," said Coco. She eyed his monk's cassock and the cross on a long chain around his neck. "I see you're still dressing the part." She kissed him on each cheek. "We'd have been here sooner, but I couldn't get Tante Brutus here out of bed."

"It's pointless to get out of bed these days," said Misia in an imperious tone. "Except to see you, dear Max."

"I'm sorry about Delphine. I hope you're feeling better."

"A bit," said Max.

"Was it a nice service?" asked Misia.

"Gorgeous. It was the first time I'd been in Quimper in many years, and after we buried Delphine, I spent a couple of hours marking the scenes of my past. I stopped at the café where I used to hold court, reciting poems for the local literary men. They were young, intelligent,

and beautiful—and they admired my work!" Max shook his head rue-
fully. "Those days are over. It's very different now in Quimper. At the
café, there were only old men sitting at the marble-topped tables. I
drank a coffee and felt a poem coming on. So, outside, on the street,
I performed my old ritual. I forced myself to conjure a new image each
time I reached a lamppost. If no image came, I stood until inspiration
struck. This method had always worked for me. And it worked for me
that day, too." Max closed his eyes and recited the first lines of the
poem he'd written for Delphine:

> *No flowers you said no wreaths*
> *But April doesn't feel that way*
> *They're a gift from the Lord*
> *Look! You're already in Paradise*

"Did Picasso show up for the funeral?" asked Coco.

"No, and neither did Cocteau, but he was in the middle of directing
a film," said Max.

"Those selfish monsters," said Coco.

"It takes one to know one," said Misia.

Coco glared at her friend. "Go to hell."

The women treated Max to dinner at the hotel next to his rooming
house. Afterward, as they settled in the car, Coco rolled down the
window and called out, "Please, Max, put on some normal clothes. At
least get rid of that big, swinging cross."

"I still don't understand what got into Max," said Misia when they
were on the road. "Converting to Catholicism is one thing. But posing
as a monk?"

"Max thought it was the only way to repent his sins," said Coco. "I
remember the night he hit bottom, when he landed in jail in Montmartre
for drinking and soliciting a male prostitute. The next morning, he called
me to meet him for Mass at Sacré Coeur."

"You went, guilty Catholic that you are."

"No more guilty than anyone else," Coco snapped. "Anyway, I found Max in his regular spot in the third pew from the back of the church. I slipped in next to him just as he was having a hallucination. He thought I was the Virgin Mary, scolding him for being a sinner. 'Mother Mary, Mother Mary, I'm sorry!' he kept saying.

"After that, Max knew he had to get away from Paris, from the compulsive behavior that was eating his soul and causing his delusions. So, he moved to Saint-Benoît, where the monks took him in. He prayed with them, meditated, and went to Mass twice a day, and because of his devotions, he entered a period of great productivity. In a few months, he completed a new edition of poems, the libretto of a comic opera, and two illustrated novellas."

"Poor Max, exiled from Paris," said Misia heavily.

"Max loves Saint-Benoît, where he feels closer to God."

Coco recalled the many times he'd tried to kindle her faith by urging her to pray and go to church. She wished now she'd taken his advice. Turning to Misia, who was drifting to sleep with her chin on her chest, Coco said, "We should pray more."

"What are you talking about?" Misia said groggily. "I've never seen you pray in your life—not since Venice, anyway."

Only once had Coco experienced a moment of religious fervor—decades earlier, in 1920, in Venice, where Misia had taken her after Boy Capel died to distract Coco from her grief. While kneeling at the altar of an old medieval church, Coco was blessed by a priest who gave her a card inscribed with the prayer of Saint Thérèse. Later, in Paris, Coco collected more religious cards, which she kept in a small leather case with a handwritten note: "I am a Roman Catholic; in case of serious accident or transportation to hospital, I request a Catholic priest come to me. If I die, I request the blessing of the Catholic Church." She always carried the case in her purse, but she hadn't looked at the cards or said the prayers in years. The spiritual was too elusive for Coco—too soft and uncertain. Coco was hard, with sharp edges, and she sliced through life, ignoring every obstacle. She couldn't help the resentment and bitterness that bubbled up in her and often overflowed, leading her to lash out. She said terrible things about everyone, even her best friends. *Especially* her best friends. They understood her, and they were the ones most likely to forgive her in the end.

Friends like Misia, who, slumped in her seat, had fallen back asleep and was snoring loudly.

"Why don't we have a dinner party at La Pausa?" Spatz suggested that night on the telephone. "I'd like to meet some of your Monaco friends."

"Who?" Coco heard a drawer opening and closing, then paper rattling.

"I have in mind Stanislao Lepri, Leonor Fini, Jean-Louis de Faucigny-Lucinge and his wife."

Lepri was the Italian consul for Monaco; his lover, Fini, was an Argentine painter. Prince Jean-Louis de Faucigny-Lucinge was a wealthy art collector, and his wife, Liliane, a former fashion model. Coco wondered if Spatz had gotten the names from her address book. "Why these four?" she asked.

"They sound interesting. I'd like to meet them."

Though she'd brushed off all concern after seeing Hélène Dessoffy, Coco realized she'd been unsettled by the woman's accusations and also the mentions of Spatz in Misia's book about German spies. It occurred to her that Spatz's suggested dinner party guests were all German sympathizers, though she wasn't sure about Liliane. Perhaps Spatz wanted to ingratiate himself with Monaco's elite. He couldn't single-handedly move the tiny principality, which so far remained neutral, to the German side. Still, it wouldn't hurt for him to have friends among Monaco's most influential citizens.

The dinner party would be the following week. Coco's vendeuse in Paris took care of the invitations. Spatz said he'd bring wine, champagne, and flowers. Coco was in the salon discussing the menu with Céline a few evenings later, when she looked out the window and saw Pierre Reverdy pedaling a bicycle up her driveway. He parked the bike at the side of the house next to an empty garden shed. Coco met him at the door.

Reverdy looked shocked to see her. "You're here. . . . I thought you'd be in Paris," he stammered.

"What are *you* doing here?" Coco asked.

"Business." He smiled slyly.

"What business?"

"I'm expecting a drop tonight."

"On *my* property?"

"If all goes well."

"Usually there's a German guard in the gatehouse. It's your luck he's not here tonight."

For a moment, Reverdy's eyes flared; then he smiled. "I guess I did pick the right night."

Inside, Coco showed Reverdy to a guest room where he could wash up and change. Twenty minutes later the two friends were sitting on the terrace eating a ham frittata prepared by Céline.

"I'm happy to feed you and give you a bed, but I don't want you using my place for Resistance work," Coco said.

Reverdy paused between bites. "Are you afraid your spy will find out?"

"Spatz is not a spy!"

"Don't be naïve. His textile production job is just a shield. It's classic espionage. He picks up secrets from you and your friends and reports them to his superiors."

"What secrets?"

"Let's say I tell you that I'm using your garden as a staging post for Jewish refugees escaping from France to the Spanish border. You tell Spatz. He tells his boss. That's it. That's spying."

"I'd never betray you."

"Good."

"You're *not* using my garden, are you?"

Reverdy regarded Coco with an intense, meaningful look but said nothing.

"God, is Céline helping you?"

"Better you don't know what goes on when you're not here."

"How does she get you past the guard?"

"As I said, better you don't know."

"It has to stop. And you can't stay. Spatz *will* be here in a couple of days."

"I'll be gone tomorrow morning."

Reverdy explained that he was on the run. A week before, he'd fled the Left Bank apartment he shared with two radio operators. One evening when he was alone cooking potatoes on the stove, he glanced out the window and saw two Gestapo agents in black leather trench coats exit a beat-up Citroën and head for the apartment entrance. "I slipped out the bedroom window down the fire escape," he told Coco. As he clattered down the narrow iron steps, white rectangles of windows flashed by, and muffled chatter from behind the windows trailed his descent.

Then he was on the ground. His eyes darted around like a trapped animal's, looking for an exit. He saw a gravel pathway leading to a tall wrought iron gate. He expected soldiers to appear, sirens to wail. He listened for boots running behind him, for shots ringing out. But the streets were clear. He walked toward a sliver of brightness leeching from the sidewalk—the entrance to the Métro. With the last of the change in his pocket, he bought a ticket. He switched lines several times and dashed out at Les Gobelins. He begged a few coins off a passerby and from a phone booth called a friend who had long been part of the Resistance. The man met him at a café on rue Berbier du Mets, where he handed Reverdy a rucksack with clean clothes, money, a flashlight, a small shovel, a flask of whiskey, and new identity papers.

Reverdy changed in the alley and set out for Gare Austerlitz, where he bought a ticket to Saint-Benoît. "I was to receive my instructions from my contact—one of the priests. I thought I might see Max, but he never showed up for Mass. There was a Nazi guard at the door. I'm worried. Maybe Max has been arrested."

"I just saw him."

"He's a Jew, and the Nazis in Saint-Benoît know it, no matter how he dresses."

Coco felt a stab of guilt. She should go back to Saint-Benoît and check again on Max. Tell him to hide himself.

A plane buzzed overhead, and Reverdy jumped up. He pulled a flashlight out of his rucksack and beamed it at the black sky. "There it is," he said.

In the flashlight's white trail, Coco saw a parachute slowly falling from the sky. A moment later it landed in her garden with a heavy clonk. Reverdy dashed to the bushes, and Coco watched as he disentangled a large suitcase from the parachute. Inside were two wireless radios wrapped in rubber. Miraculously, they'd survived the fall. "What in God's name are you going to do with those?" Coco asked.

"I'm not going to tell you." Reverdy dug a hole behind an olive tree with his shovel and buried the parachute. He carried the radio transmitters into the house and laid them on the kitchen table. "Go to bed, Coco. You don't need to worry about this."

But she did worry. Obviously, she did.

Coco awoke before sunrise and found Reverdy gone. So were his transmitters. *He's buried them in the cellar somewhere, and he's planning to use them to send messages to his pals in the Resistance when I'm not here.* She hadn't ventured into the vast cellars of La Pausa for years, not since the house was first built and the architect wanted her to see every inch of his masterpiece. Now she took the narrow stairs behind the pantry and made her way through the dank, low-ceilinged rooms, past the wine cellar, the laundry, the furnace closet. She found the transmitters in a remote corner, buried under a stack of old newspapers. They were heavy, but she managed to carry them upstairs and put them in the trunk of her Rolls.

When Coco returned to the house, Céline was in the kitchen preparing to bake bread. "You're a fool to help Reverdy," Coco snapped.

"I'm sorry, Mademoiselle," said the maid. She twisted her apron between her fists and began to cry softly.

"Never again let him in when I'm not here. You could get yourself killed."

Céline hung her head. "Yes, Mademoiselle."

Coco roused her driver from the gatekeeper's cottage where he bunked, and they took off for Saint-Benoît. A dense fog lingered in the morning air. There were no cars on the road, only a couple of mangy dogs. The Rolls passed a one-legged young man hobbling along on crutches. Coco wondered if he'd lost his limb in the war. She felt a wave of pity for the boy and wondered if he wished that the bullet had killed him and released him from all worldly pain. *Death wouldn't be so bad—it would be the end of suffering and misery.* The thought passed, though, as soon as the young man faded from her sight. No doubt he wanted to live. Coco wanted to live, too. She couldn't bear for the world to go on without her.

Outside Saint-Benoît, Coco saw a gravel path that led to the river and directed her driver to take it. He was forty, with thinning brown hair, gentle hazel eyes, and a timid manner. "Stop here, and open the trunk," she told him when they reached the riverbank. They each carried a transmitter to the river. Coco heaved hers into the water, but the driver hung back. He wore a faded black suit that sagged on his lanky frame. "These are worth a lot of money," he said.

"Get rid of it!" Coco commanded.

"What if someone sees us?" His eyes darted around.

Coco recalled when she and the driver had left Paris at the start of the war. As his old Cadillac rounded a corner, they confronted a shiny pair of eyes—a big yellow cheetah stood in a pool of light from a streetlamp. A bomb must have hit the zoo, and the big cat had escaped. He stood perfectly still in the middle of the road, his head erect and his body tense. He stared at Coco with his glowing eyes, and she stared back, willing him to run away. But he wouldn't move. So Coco got out of the car. The driver screamed for her to get back in. Men were such cowards! But she wasn't going to let that animal hold her up. "Go on, get out of here!" she yelled at the big cat, and the beast ran off. "You see?" she said, when she was back in the Cadillac. "I know how to give orders."

Sometimes, though, you had to do things yourself. She grabbed the transmitter from the driver's arms and hurled it into the water.

By midmorning, the fog had lifted, and the sky was a bright, hard blue.

At the abbey, a priest told Coco that Max had, indeed, been arrested, but he was released after a few days. She found her old friend in the courtyard reading the Bible. "Let's go somewhere to talk," Max said.

They drove to a secluded park, where a sign warned DOGS AND JEWS PROHIBITED. Max hesitated in front of it. "Come on, you're with me," Coco said. She'd brought a wicker hamper with food she'd found in the pantry at La Pausa: bread, cheese, apples, pastries, and wine. As Coco arranged the white china and silverware on a cotton blanket, Max told her about the frightening incident that had led to his arrest.

He had been standing in the nave with a group of high school boys, ready to lead them on a tour of the Benedictine abbey. The sun slanted through the plain glass windows, splashing pale gold light over the mosaic floor and up the vaulted columns. A few monks scurried about, their brown robes whipping around their ankles. The students squirmed and giggled, then fell into a sullen silence as Max began his introductory history. "Saint Benoît was born in 480 A.D. to a wealthy family. He studied—" A commotion stopped him in mid-sentence.

German soldiers with guns drawn stormed up the long aisle, the harsh clicking of their boots echoing off every surface of the vast basilica. Soldiers grabbed each of Max's arms and led him outside. As he looked into their smooth, youthful faces, their light eyes, gold hair, and rosy cheeks, they resembled the angels romping around Christ in the painting above the altar. "The war wasn't their fault. They were just performing their duty," Max said. "A parent in town had probably complained that a Jew was giving tours of the abbey to Christian children. In the courtyard, a soldier aimed his rifle at my back and marched me off to jail. The priests convinced them to release me. I was forbidden to give any more tours. The Germans posted a policeman at the gate to keep me out, but the officer tired of this vigil after just a day, and I resumed my tours with no further incident."

In the village, Max told Coco, the soldiers saluted and clicked their heels. They were virile and strong, and the local girls took note. Some of the German boy-warriors were billeted in private homes, in bedrooms next to the girls' bedrooms. They passed each other in the corridors at night on the way to the toilet, the girls in diaphanous nightgowns, and the boys admired the lovely bodies underneath the clingy fabric. They could hear each other breathing through the thin walls. In the morning, the girls passed the Germans' bedrooms, and if the doors were ajar, they saw them shirtless, shaving in front of their mirrors. The girls served the soldiers breakfast—eggs and freshly baked bread—and the Germans were grateful. They brought presents to the girls, flowers and chocolates, and sat with them in the gardens behind the hedges where no one could see. Max watched love unfold with the roses and hydrangeas, and he loved, too.

"I loved my incredible, astonishing Lord, and alone in my room I prayed," said Max. He took Coco's hand. "I want you to pray with me now." Coco closed her eyes and bowed her head as Max implored, "Since You are God, and since You know all, tell us when this war will end."

As they finished their lunch, sitting on a blanket spread on the ground, the sky blackened, and wind churned the air. Soon a hard rain began to fall. "I know a place we can go," Max said. He helped Coco to her feet.

They drove in Coco's car to a deserted mansion, which sat atop a wooded hill five kilometers out of Saint-Benoît, in the village of Bonne. The stone Italianate house, painted gray with burgundy trim, had seen better days. The paint was peeling, the windows were dirty. It looked dismal even as the rain stopped and bright sunshine burst through the clouds. What had once been a lovely garden behind a tall wrought iron fence was now a brown jumble of weeds and dry earth. "I heard the priests talking about this place. It's one of several deserted homes in the area—the Jewish owners forced out by the Nazis," said Max.

Coco's driver dropped them at the front door, then left to find a farmer with an air pump—the pressure was low in the tires.

As he drove off, Coco and Max pushed open the front door and entered a high-ceilinged marble hall. Soft sunlight angled in through the open windows. A few pieces of antique furniture were scattered about, and an intricately woven Turkish carpet covered the floor. On the walls hung large paintings in gilt frames—mostly impressionistic landscapes and sentimental, idealized nudes.

Max led them up three flights of stairs—past the rooms displaying more mediocre art and antiques—to an attic studio. The large space, sun-drenched from an immense skylight, held a dressmaker's form and an old sewing machine. For a moment Coco was back in her atelier and not in the attic of an abandoned house. She sank into an old armchair, and the cushion released a cloud of dust. "What's wrong?" asked Max.

"It reminds me of my workrooms," said Coco. "I miss them."

"Maybe you can reopen after the war."

"I can't think about that now."

They heard the crunch of gravel outside and went to the small oval window that looked out on the garden and the driveway. A group of men in dark suits, a couple of them wearing swastika armbands, stepped out of a white van parked near the entrance. An attractive woman with upswept reddish hair followed the men. "Oh God, that's Fraulein Lichten," said Coco.

"You know her?" asked Max.

"She works for the Einsatzstab Reichsleiter, the organization that oversees looting. She's an acquaintance of Spatz's. I met her once. She came into the boutique to buy perfume."

Max gave her a stricken look.

Coco started to say something, and Max held out his hand palm forward to stop her. "We won't discuss him. I've never passed judgment on your lovers, and now's not the time to start."

They could hear the Germans knocking around on the floors below, working out what they were going to take and what would be left behind. Laughter. The creak of heavy frames banging the walls.

"What would that German woman do if she saw you with me?"

"Probably tell Spatz."

"Would that be bad?"

"I don't like people knowing my business. Especially awful women like Fraulein Lichten," said Coco. "You never know with those types. You hear her down there barking orders."

"Reminds me of someone I know." Max smiled at Coco, and she rolled her eyes.

"I wonder what they'll do with the loot," Max said.

"Goering likes nudes. And tasteless luxury. Maybe it'll all end up in one of his mansions."

Coco wiped the dust from an old trunk with her palm and sat on the edge. "I hope we're not stuck up here forever."

"Do you want to tell me why you're really here?" Max asked.

Coco smiled. Max could always tell when she had an agenda. "Now's as good a time as any," she said. She removed from her purse a gray felt jeweler's case and handed it to him. "Open your present."

The box held an exquisite bracelet, a fringe of diamonds on a slender diamond link, from a collection Coco had designed in the thirties. "It's beautiful, but too small for me," Max said, holding out a hairy, thick wrist.

Coco laughed. "It's yours, should you ever need it."

It made Coco feel good to help Max. And the others—Serge Diaghilev of the Ballet Russes, the composer Igor Stravinsky, Cocteau. She was generous, too, with her lovers; her nephew, André; and, for years, her brothers. But usually there was a quid pro quo—she was buying access or love or, in the case of her brothers, bribing them into silence. She didn't feel that way with Max.

For the next twenty minutes Coco and Max sat on the floor of the studio. The Germans were still wandering through the first floor when the sound of tires crunching gravel rose up from the driveway. Coco went to the window. "Oh God, my driver with the car," she said.

When Coco and Max appeared downstairs, the Germans stopped talking and stared. "Mademoiselle Chanel! What are you doing here?" said Fraulein Lichten.

"I was visiting my friend," said Coco, nodding to Max. "He's a monk at the monastery in Saint-Benoît. We thought we'd take a drive and came upon the house. We were just looking around."

Lichten looked Max up and down, taking in his monk's cassock and the cross around his neck. Then, turning to Coco, she asked severely, "Is that your car that just pulled up?"

"Yes. We're leaving."

"Do you have a permit?"

"No."

"If I were you, I wouldn't take it out again."

Coco and Max spent the rest of the afternoon touring the countryside and dined that evening on the terrace of a roadside bistro attached to a farm. Moonlight brightened the drive back to Saint-Benoît. "It was a lovely day," Max said when the car stopped in front of his boardinghouse. "A day almost outside the war."

"Until we ran into Fraulein Lichten."

"I hope you don't get in trouble at home."

Coco smiled and squeezed Max's hand. "I can handle Spatz."

A few days later, Spatz drove himself to La Pausa in a Reich-owned Mercedes. He arrived at noon with a trunk stuffed with champagne bottles, tubs of Russian caviar, and filet mignon steaks packed in ice. As Spatz's arms overflowed with bouquets of white roses, Céline rushed out of the house, wiping her hands on her apron, to take the flowers.

"Are you ready for tonight?" Spatz asked Coco, as they kissed.

"It's a lot of work for Céline and Ugo." Coco nodded toward the caretaker, a stocky man in workers clothes who was arranging lanterns along the stone walkway.

While Spatz played golf at a nearby course, Coco spent the afternoon sunning herself on the terrace above the quiet blue sea. The olive trees were in full bloom, their fresh white flowers singing out against the dark pines on the hillside. But the glorious weather didn't ease Coco's black mood. She was not looking forward to the evening. Spatz *was* using her, at least in this case—using her house, her staff, her hospitality, to meet and court a group of people who might be sympathetic to the Germans. Coco had no idea to what end, but she resented it, and she brooded on it for hours. Hoping to numb her feelings, she drank a glass of champagne, then a few glasses more, though the alcohol only deepened her distress.

That evening, Leonor Fini and Consul Lepri were the first to arrive. Leonor was a small, delicate woman of forty with auburn hair and a lively manner. Though born and raised in Argentina, she had lived in France for two decades. Her lover, Lepri, was in his sixties, portly and bald and dressed in a bespoke Italian suit. "How are things in Berlin?" Lepri asked Spatz, as he took a glass of champagne from Ugo, who, dressed in a black suit and white shirt, acted as butler on dinner party evenings.

"The trains aren't running on time, and the air raids are annoying. But people are getting by," said Spatz.

"Just like we're getting by," Coco interjected.

Spatz shot her a sharp glance.

An arpeggio of laughter rose from the entry hall and, a moment later, Jean-Louis and Liliane de Faucigny-Lucinge stepped into the room. "What a view! I could see the spires of the cathedral from your driveway!" cried Liliane. She was a cheerful gumdrop of a woman in a pink silk sheath and a froth of blond curls.

"A plane just now flew overhead, narrowly missing the top," said Jean-Louis. He was a few years older than his wife, a slender, elegant man with gray-streaked hair slicked back on his head and lively dark eyes.

Coco led the couple into the salon, where she introduced them to Leonor and Lepri. Ugo offered them champagne from a silver tray, and they each took a glass.

"I don't think the Germans will bomb Monte Carlo," said Coco.

"Did you see the Cinema des Beaux-Arts is showing *Vol de Nuit*?" said Liliane.

"I saw it when it first came out. Nothing's more exciting than a night flight over mountains in dangerous weather," said Leonor.

"Just ask Hitler's deputy, Rudolf Hess," said Coco.

"It's a French film," said Spatz impatiently.

"I wonder what happened to Hess? Wasn't it a few months ago that he crashed a plane in Scotland on the grounds of the Duke of Hamilton's estate?" said Jean-Louis.

"Hess survived, but he was taken prisoner by the British," said Lepri.

Coco raised an eyebrow at Spatz, and he quickly looked down at the carpet.

"What was Hess doing flying over Scotland?" asked Liliane.

"I'm speculating, but I think he was hoping to enlist Hamilton's aid in convincing Britain to broker a peace favorable to Germany," said Lepri. "Hamilton hates Churchill almost as much as Hess does."

"What do you think, Spatz?" asked Leonor.

"I think we should all have more champagne." Spatz strode to the bar cart and lifted a bottle by the neck from a silver bucket.

Spatz refilled Coco's glass, which she quickly emptied. "The Germans don't know how to talk to the British. I do! You know Churchill and I are great friends." She held her glass out to Spatz, but he shook his head and returned the bottle to the bucket.

Céline announced dinner, and the party moved to the dining room. Before taking her spot at the head of the long mahogany table, Coco opened the doors to the terrace. The white taffeta curtains billowed out, and she felt the warm evening air against her skin, drawing her back to her first days at La Pausa, to her romance with Bendor, the Duke of Westminster, and her friendship with Churchill. Bendor and Coco loved visiting the Riviera, and she had built the estate so the couple wouldn't have to stay in hotels. At the time, Coco had wanted to marry the duke. He was twice-divorced, tall and athletic, with a beefy face that was almost handsome and a galumphing exuberance that reminded Coco of a Newfoundland puppy. Early in their affair he introduced her to his old friend Winston Churchill, the pudgy, reddish-haired chancellor of the exchequer. Coco had sat next to the future prime minister at a dinner at La Pausa, then joined him as his partner the next weekend at Bendor's hunting lodge in Mimizan. Together, they tromped through the woods hunting boar. The out-of-shape Churchill watched in fascination as Coco scrambled up a steep hill, then elbowed her way through a dense thicket of ferns to corner a huge boar. Coco fired once, hitting the beast square between the eyes and sending him crashing to the ground. Afterward, Churchill told her, "You are a great and strong being, fit to rule a man or an empire."

The Germans should let *her* talk to Churchill, she thought. Hess was crazy. Look at how he'd bungled things with his idiot mission. She'd make sure whatever peace was brokered was as favorable to France as it was to Germany.

Céline had laid a platter of steaks, bowls of haricots verts, scalloped potatoes, and a basket of bread on the table. "We should do something after dinner," said Jean-Louis, as he took a generous helping of potatoes.

"Plan a mission?" asked Coco snidely.

"Play cards," said Jean-Louis. He glanced around the table. "Bridge, anyone?"

"An excellent idea!" said Spatz.

"I love bridge!" cried Leonor.

"It's settled, then. A round of bridge after dinner," said Jean-Louis.

Céline returned and whispered something in Spatz's ear. He pushed out his chair and stood. "I've a phone call," he said, and disappeared into the salon.

Leonor leaned toward Coco and spoke softly enough that Lepri across the table couldn't hear. "God, he's handsome. If they all looked like that I wouldn't mind the Germans sticking around."

"Most of them look like toads," said Coco. "And they've got bad breath."

"I hear Hitler has bad breath, too."

There was the scrape of a chair, and Spatz was back at the table.

"Has another cabinet minister crashed in Scotland?" asked Coco.

"My golfing partner left his jacket in my car."

"What a relief. Goering and Goebbels are still loyal Germans."

Spatz scowled. He'd come to expect these bursts of sarcasm from Coco. Holding forth around the table, she raged against the idiocy of Hess, then moved on to the unattractiveness of the Nazi high command and the frumpiness of their women. She was glad she'd closed her ateliers. The Germans had ruined fashion, as they'd ruined all of French culture.

Spatz talked over her, raising his voice as he turned to Leonor. "Tell us about your upcoming exhibit at the Galerie Georges Petit."

Coco's eyes held a sinister glint. "I've seen your work. It's cubism, exactly what the Nazis consider degenerate. What did you have to do to get the Germans' approval—promise your firstborn to the Third Reich?"

Leonor went pale. "My new canvases are more traditional—" she began feebly, but Coco interrupted.

"I'd like to know. It can't be because the Germans love your art. If they did, they'd just swipe it. Have you met Fraulein Lichten, who loots for the Nazis? I have, and she's a witch."

"Someone from cultural affairs . . . from the . . . the embassy came to my studio. . . ." Leonor stammered. "There wasn't any problem."

Coco continued to natter on about Nazi looting and the Germans' poor taste in art, ignoring the glum, downcast looks on her guests' faces. At the end of dessert—a delicious chocolate mousse—Jean-Louis thanked Coco for the dinner and said he and his wife had to be going.

"What about bridge?"

"I'm afraid we can't."

Coco turned to Leonor. "You'll stay for at least one round?"

"We should retire, too," said Lepri. "Leonor and I need to get an early start tomorrow for Paris."

Coco and Spatz stood in the doorway as the cars that had brought their guests wound down the curving drive and slipped into the velvet night. Spatz shut the door violently and shouted at Coco. "For once, I wish you'd just fucking shut up!"

He turned on his heel and strode toward the guest wing to spend the night alone.

Coco watched him stomp away, a tall, blond German in an elegant suit, and she saw him then as Misia saw him, an enemy of France and of herself.

NINE

The following day, Céline told Coco that Spatz had left early while she was still asleep. "He asked me to tell you he was on his way to Berlin," the maid said.

Coco returned to Paris that evening. Her head ached, and a heaviness had settled in her bones. For the next week, she sat in her suite, indulging her misery, imagining that she and Spatz were finished. *He doesn't deserve me*, she told herself. *He'll regret screaming at me and taking off without so much as one word of apology.* She hoped Spatz was as miserable as she was. She wanted to punish him. If he phoned, she vowed not to take the call. When he returned, she'd refuse to see him.

But he never called. Ten days passed, and finally one evening at ten Spatz showed up at the Ritz carrying an enormous bouquet of red roses. When Coco saw him standing in the little salon looking even more handsome than she remembered, her heart melted. "Let's not fight, darling," he said, hugging her tightly.

They made love twice that night and fell asleep in each other's arms, their quarrel forgotten.

"How would you like to go to Spain for a few weeks?" Spatz asked Coco the next morning.

They were sitting side by side on the sofa in their bathrobes, drinking coffee.

"With you?" Coco asked.

"No. I need to stay here." Spatz cleared his throat. "You've been complaining about how difficult it is to run a perfume business during war and how depressing Paris has become. I thought you'd welcome the change of scene."

"Are you trying to get rid of me?" Coco said in a joking tone.

"Hardly." Spatz kissed her neck as he cupped her right breast. Straightening his back, he spoke in a matter-of-fact tone. "An associate of mine, a Frenchman I just saw in Berlin, is coming over today to talk to you about traveling to Madrid. Will you hear him out?"

Coco shrugged. "I suppose."

"We should dress. He's due here in an hour."

At nine, a chubby man in his late thirties arrived at the door. Spatz introduced him as Baron Louis de Vaufreland, a French aristocrat with close ties to the Germans. "Herr von Dincklage tells me you had a nice sojourn in Roquebrun," Vaufreland said to Coco as he settled in an armchair near the fireplace. He had wispy brown hair combed over his balding head, and he was dressed in an expensive suit that was a size too small for his lumpy body.

Vaufreland pulled an envelope from a pocket inside his jacket and handed it to Coco. "Here's a train ticket to Madrid and a visa—all the documents you need to get across the border into Spain."

"I have no plans at the moment to go to Spain." Coco shot Spatz a sharp look.

"Herr von Dincklage says you have a perfume distributor in Madrid. Don't you need to talk to him about sales in Spain?"

COCO AT THE RITZ

"Why are you so interested in my business?"

"You're a friend of the Reich. As am I."

The room altered around her. Shakily, she took a cigarette from the pack on the coffee table, and Spatz stepped forward to light it. "Listen to what he has to say, darling."

Coco exhaled a jet of foul smoke toward Vaufreland, and he turned his head to avoid it.

"We'd like you to talk to your British friends in Madrid. We'd like to know what people are saying about the . . . um . . . political situation," Vaufreland said.

"And if I don't feel like leaving town?" Coco took a last drag on her cigarette and stamped it out in an ashtray.

Vaufreland's face darkened, and his tone turned harsh. "Mademoiselle Chanel, would you like to see your nephew released from prison?"

"Spatz has been promising—"

Vaufreland cut her off. "Do you know how many French soldiers are in German hands? A million. And do you know how many die each day? Thousands upon thousands. Do you want your nephew to be another statistic?"

If she refused, would the Germans execute André out of spite? Would they put him in front of a firing squad? Or chop his head off with an axe—a method Misia claimed Hitler used on his most despised enemies? An image of henchmen in black hoods dragging André into a prison courtyard filled her mind. She felt as if someone had slugged her in the chest.

"All right," Coco said, her voice raw. "I'll do as you wish."

When Vaufreland left, Coco snapped at Spatz. "I suppose he's not a spy, either."

"He's working with us."

"But you want *me* to become a spy."

Spatz took Coco's face in his hands and kissed her gently on the mouth. "Think how happy you'll be to welcome André home."

"I better pack."

When Coco started for the bedroom, Spatz placed his hand on her arm, stopping her.

"Have you heard recently from Brian Wallace?" He was a British diplomat Coco had befriended years earlier during her affair with Bendor.

"Not in a long time. I'll send him a cable."

"Maybe you can see him at his office at the British embassy. Keep your eyes and ears open. I'd like to know what your friends are saying."

"My friends are my business."

"Your friends are my business, too. Another thing—Vaufreland will be accompanying you on the trip."

"I won't travel with that horrid man!"

Spatz insisted she needed a chaperone. The Nazi guards at the Spanish border in Hendaye had been alerted to give her safe passage, but he argued that the journey would be dangerous—what if the train was attacked or bombed?

"I agree he's unpleasant," Spatz said. "But you'll be safer if you're not alone."

"Why him?"

"I'm afraid there's no one else."

Several mornings later, Spatz drove Coco to the Gare Austerlitz himself. The August sky was black and heavy with humidity. Coco walked into the station past the ticket booths and the wooden benches with brass fittings. A red-jacketed porter trailed behind carrying her suitcases, two under each arm. Vaufreland met her on the platform beneath the dirty glass dome.

"Mademoiselle Chanel," he said, bowing slightly and leading Coco to a first-class compartment. Coco leaned into the plush seats and stared out the window as the train lumbered loudly out of the station, passing utility poles and apartment buildings, then villages, farms, and the open country.

"Are you comfortable?" asked Vaufreland. He sat across from Coco in the red-and-gold jewel box compartment and held out an open cigarette case.

"It's hot," said Coco in an icy tone. She took a cigarette, and as she leaned forward to accept a light from Vaufreland's silver lighter, she got a whiff of Bal à Versailles, a heavy perfume. He smelled like an expensive whore.

"Not as hot as second-class." Vaufreland smiled tightly.

As the train rolled on, Vaufreland tried to cover the awkwardness between them with small talk. "I missed you and Spatz last night at the Berthelots' dinner. The champagne flowed, and it was the usual collection of Second Empire old crones." He leaned conspiratorially toward Coco. "You know, I've always thought Pauline Raynard had a touch of something. Last night, I was seated next to her, and I had this overwhelming sense of being in the presence of a Jew. She picked up that I was uncomfortable and looked down that large nose of hers. 'Why are you staring at me?' she demanded. And I said, 'Because in that awful wig, you look like Louis XIV.'"

Vaufreland laughed, shaking his whole body. He looked expectantly at Coco, who stared back at him with an arched eyebrow. She said nothing.

"Of course, I didn't really say that to her. I did tell her, though, that I couldn't take my eyes off her necklace. It was a stunner of emeralds set in platinum. I was tempted to ask her to sell it to me."

Coco opened her mouth as if she was about to say something to challenge Vaufreland—Spatz had told her the man was broke—but decided against making a comment.

"I've a little money now," Vaufreland said, as if reading Coco's mind. "I sold my grandmother's house on rue de Courcelles. She put it in my name for tax reasons. She's in Vichy napping and playing pinochle, so why not?"

"And if she finds out?"

"She won't. And with luck, she won't last through the war."

Coco turned and stared out the window.

Vaufreland cleared his throat. "I hear your nephew has tuberculosis."

Coco whipped her head around to face Vaufreland. "André won't survive if he's not released soon."

Vaufreland examined the nails of his right hand for a moment, then turned his gaze back to Coco. "I'll see what I can do, if things do go well in Madrid—for us."

"Us?" Coco said.

"My friends—and von Dincklage's friends."

"I know. You want me to keep my eyes and ears open."

"That would be a start."

After parting with Vaufreland at the Atocha rail station in Madrid, Coco made her way by taxi to the Ritz. Brown dust hung in the air; the heat was insufferable. Heavily armed police slouched against the hotel's towering iron gate. In the lobby—as luxurious as the Paris Ritz—men with swastika armbands, Spanish military officers, and couples speaking a variety of languages milled about. The atmosphere felt tense.

A stack of invitations waited for Coco at the front desk. The next weeks passed in a whirl of dinners, luncheons, receptions, and meetings with the men responsible for distributing her perfume. She continually ran into Vaufreland, and she wondered if this was by chance or if the unsavory man had somehow discovered her schedule so he could follow her around. One afternoon, he asked her to have tea with him in the Ritz restaurant. He wanted to know if she'd "heard anything interesting?"

Coco gave him a heavy dollop of gossip she'd picked up (and embellished): The French ambassador to Spain and his wife were rabidly anti-British, while the English ambassador was intensely anti-French. Both were sympathetic to Germany. In the French ambassador's home, where she attended a cocktail reception, he displayed a picture of himself skiing with high-ranking Nazis. (Actually, they were German businessmen, and the picture had been taken before the war.) Coco had no clue how such trivialities could be useful to the Abwehr. Several times in her conversations with Vaufreland, she brought up the subject of André's imprisonment, and he assured her that everything would be done to secure the young man's release.

Coco relied on morphine every night to fall asleep. After injecting herself, she lay on the pillow and looked at the framed photo of André and his family that she always carried with her and that she'd propped up on the hotel nightstand. When she thought of André, though, she saw him as a child, digging in the sand with his little shovel on the beach at Deauville next to the blanket where she lay reading a book. Or André absorbed in putting together a puzzle on the floor at her feet while she draped fabric on a mannequin. When the picture of him coughing and shivering with fever in a dank German cell filled her head, she shoved the image aside.

As the weeks wore on, however, Coco grew increasingly anxious. Her strenuous socializing wasn't picking up anything she thought would be useful to the Germans. She was running out of gossip and anecdotes, and she feared Vaufreland would punish her inability to provide valuable intelligence by reneging on his promise to help André.

It was in this agitated state on her second-to-last night in Madrid that she attended a dinner at the home of British expatriate Christopher Whittlespoon and his wife, Hermione. He was an art dealer whom Coco knew from his sojourns in Paris over the years. When Coco entered the Whittlespoons' vine-covered villa on the outskirts of Madrid, she was not surprised to see Louis de Vaufreland. Most of the other guests were British, including the diplomat Brian Wallace.

Vaufreland bowed to Coco, then looked directly at her with a grim expression. He was angry she hadn't come up with better intelligence. Coco knew he would be watching her, expecting her to draw her friends into making indiscreet confessions. And if she failed? He hadn't said it in so many words, but she understood that otherwise he wouldn't help her.

She tried to avoid his gaze for the rest of the evening, which included cocktails on the stone terrace with polite chitchat and no talk of the war. Her anxiety led her to drink too much, and, as usual after several glasses of wine, Coco grew loquacious. During dinner—a traditional British meal that started with a bland pea soup—Hermione Whittlespoon asked

Coco what had brought her to Madrid. "I had to get a break from Paris. The situation is very bad," Coco said.

"We've been looking forward to hearing your views, Mademoiselle. You always have the most astute observations," said Christopher Whittlespoon.

The compliment relaxed her. She reasoned: *You have to give something to get something.* "The Germans hate the French, even more than the French hate the Germans," Coco said.

"I wouldn't expect it to be any different," said Christopher.

"The French provoke the Occupiers constantly. Humming the Marseillaise in the Métro, scribbling 'Death to the Occupiers' on the walls. The Germans are threatening to shut the Métro down completely. Parisians should just leave well enough alone and accept that France has got what she deserves for going soft."

Coco didn't notice the amazed expressions on the faces of the other guests and continued talking. "Very few Frenchmen realize they've lost the war. 'You wait until we've got rid of the German swine,' they say. If you point out to them that France has been defeated, they accuse you of being anti-French!"

Coco's friend Brian Wallace, a bespectacled, smoothly shaven man of fifty, spoke up from the opposite end of the table. "What do the Germans say about us?" he asked.

"They hate and fear Churchill, but aside from him, they are pro-English," Coco said. "In general, they admire English culture, and they believe the British citizens want peace, unlike the bloodthirsty French."

Coco was so brain-fogged by wine and anxiety that she was completely unaware of how far she'd gotten carried away. Most of the other guests were stunned into silence by her candor and regarded her with stupefied expressions as she nattered on, ignoring the steamed asparagus, roast beef, and biscuits on her plate. "To cover their anxiety, the French fake extreme gaiety," Coco said. "The Germans want to know, 'Why are you so happy, since you lost the war?' And the French want to know, 'Why are you so sad, since you won?' Well, the Germans are miserable because they can't stop fighting among themselves. The civil and military authorities hate each other as much, maybe more, than they hate the French, and they take a perverse pleasure in undoing each other's work. They are frightened; they are watched, and the watchers themselves are being watched."

When the plates had been cleared and chocolate cake served with the coffee, Coco stopped talking long enough to light a cigarette. Blowing smoke into the center of the table, she glanced across the flower arrangement to Vaufreland, sitting opposite her. He stared back at her with a hard, unblinking gaze.

She knew she had talked too much at the Whittlespoons' dinner. To make up for her careless babbling, she determined to be nice to Spatz's friend Herman Schmidt, a German candy manufacturer who was living in Madrid. Spatz had asked her to see him, so Coco met Schmidt for lunch at the Embassy, a fashionable tearoom, on her last day in town. They discussed nothing of consequence, though at the end of the meal, Schmidt handed Coco a letter for Spatz, which she promised to deliver. On her way out of the restaurant she noticed Vaufreland at a corner table, drinking coffee and trying to hide behind a newspaper, like a detective in a bad novel.

The next day, Vaufreland accompanied Coco on the train back to Paris. The pudgy chaperone who'd been so garrulous on the arriving trip now stayed largely silent. Coco wondered what he would report back, and she worried that she'd lost a chance to rescue André. The two travelers arrived after midnight. A man in a dark suit driving a black Mercedes met them and took Coco to the Ritz. Spatz was waiting up for her. "I'm exhausted," said Coco, dropping into a chair.

"Do you want a drink?" Spatz asked.

"That would be nice."

Spatz poured Coco a glass of red wine from a bottle on the bar cart. "A good trip?" he asked, handing her the glass. His tone was cold and his blue eyes hard and expressionless.

Had Vaufreland already told Spatz that she'd made a fool of herself at the Whittlespoons? That she'd failed to come up with information useful to the Germans? She saw her relationship with Spatz crumbling and along with it her life in Paris. She saw herself exiled from the Ritz, her building on rue Cambon confiscated, and André growing weaker in prison. She took a large sip of wine. Her instinct was to lash out, to put Spatz on the defensive.

"Tell me who you slept with while I was gone," she said.

He smiled slightly.

"It couldn't have been here. I'd smell it."

"There's no one but you," said Spatz, his voice coated in irony.

"You don't seem happy to see me." Coco took another large sip of wine. "I couldn't care less if you're unfaithful. It's unhygienic. But it means nothing. Are you seeing Hélène Dessoffy again? That nitwit is still mad for you." Coco paused, as Spatz sat in silence. "Tell me," she continued. "It would amuse me. I'm not jealous."

"Your lack of jealousy is the least of your charms."

"No need to flatter me."

"What makes you think I'm unfaithful?"

"You're a man."

Coco pulled an empty packet of cigarettes from her jacket pocket, crushed it, and tossed it in the trash can under the desk with an angry flick of her wrist. She opened one of the suitcases the porter had left at the door and retrieved a new pack. Fumbling with it, she finally ripped it open. She lit a cigarette. "Tell me, I want to know," she said.

"Stop it," said Spatz impatiently. He took a deep breath and spoke again in a calm tone. "Tell me about your trip."

"I didn't get any sleep," said Coco.

"No wonder. People stay up all night in Madrid."

"I tried to do too much."

"I heard you also talked too much."

"You heard that from my *chaperone*, I suppose."

"At the Whittlespoons' dinner, you talked nonstop, apparently, about the bitter divisions among the Germans, how the civil and military authorities are at each other's throats."

"It's true, isn't it?"

"You were supposed to listen, not talk."

"You had the wrong woman for *that* job. I was trying to get the British to relax so they'd express their opinions."

"You went on for three hours, I'm told. Wallace and the other diplomats heard all about how scared and wretched and disorganized we are."

"You're spying on me?"

"I wouldn't put it that way."

"It's confusing. I don't like confusion."

Spatz refilled his wineglass, then held the bottle up. "More?"

Coco shook her head and put her hand on Spatz's groin. He pulled away and walked across the room. "Did you see Schmidt?" he asked.

Coco sighed. "He took me to lunch. He was a bore, talked about nothing but his real estate interests in Baden-Württemberg."

"Did he give you something for me? A letter?"

"It's in one of my bags—somewhere."

"Would you get it?"

"Tomorrow."

"Now—please."

Coco shot Spatz a murderous look. She rummaged through her largest suitcase, pulled out a white envelope, and tossed it toward Spatz. He picked it up from where it landed at his feet, then disappeared into the bedroom to read the contents alone.

Coco never found out what was in the Schmidt letter, or whether the information she provided Vaufreland was useful. But one afternoon soon after she returned from Madrid, Spatz showed up at the Ritz with the best possible news: André was on his way home. Her nephew had been released from a German prison after two years in captivity.

Coco was on the platform standing at the Gare du Nord when André's train pulled in from Germany. The young man stumbled from the car coughing, his emaciated body hidden under ragged clothes. He was ravaged but alive. André stepped onto French soil at exactly nine in the morning, as church bells marking the hour rang out across Paris. Coco would always remember this moment. It felt as if the bells were chiming deep within her own heart.

"Aunt Gabby," André said in a quavering voice.

"My darling, you're home!" Coco cried, drawing the young man to her. His arms were as thin as a child's. A sob rose in Coco's throat with a sharp memory of André as a little boy. She managed to choke it back.

Coco drove with André in a car supplied by Spatz to a clinic in Versailles where she'd arranged a private room for him. It was a cool Friday in late fall. Maple trees waved them up the winding drive to the clinic, a large stone building with cheerful blue shutters. Redstarts and sparrows perched on the wrought iron gate, while a party of blackbirds slanted and tipped above the slate roof. Coco couldn't recall the last time she'd seen a bird in Paris. A new population had not replaced those asphyxiated at the start of the war. Perhaps the birds were as afraid to return to the city as the thousands of Parisians who remained in exile. She thought of lines from a poem by Emily Dickinson, an American whose work Pierre Reverdy had introduced her to: *Hope is a thing with feathers.* André was home, and now here were the birds.

Coco escorted André past the Nazi guard at the door. A doctor met them in the front office. He was a kindly, elderly man in a spanking white coat with a stethoscope around his neck. "Monsieur Palasse is in good hands," he said, taking André by the elbow and leading him toward a double door with a sign reading NO VISITORS BEYOND THIS POINT.

André hugged Coco tightly. "*Merci pour tous,*" he said.

"Catharina and the girls are on their way. I've rented a house for them nearby," said Coco, kissing her nephew on each cheek.

She stepped out into the bright afternoon, her heart feeling lighter than it had in two years. As she walked toward the Mercedes, she heard a gunshot, then another. The Nazi guard had moved a few yards from the entrance and was shooting birds out of the sky. Lifeless black clumps fell to the asphalt, like coal dropped from the clouds. One landed on the Mercedes windshield. The driver removed it with a gloved hand and tossed it in the bushes. *Sore must be the storm that could abash the little bird,* Dickinson had written. *Horrific is more apt,* thought Coco. As the car pulled away, the call and response of popping sounds grew fainter and fainter, then stopped as they reached the main road out of town.

TEN

"Bonjour, Westminster." Baron Vaufreland smiled demonically at Coco. He was sitting in a chair near the entry to her boutique and had been waiting for an hour for her to come downstairs.

"What did you call me?" Coco scowled at the nasty man. With her purse crooked in her right arm, she tugged at the hem of her gloves, pulling them tighter over her fingers.

"Didn't Spatz tell you? It was his idea to give you the code name of your old lover."

"What do you mean, *code name?*"

"My dear, you're a registered agent of the Abwehr now. Number F-7124. I memorized it before our Madrid trip, and now it's seared on my brain."

"That's preposterous! I don't want to have anything to do with you or your so-called Abwehr military intelligence."

"How's your nephew?" Vaufreland grinned viciously.

Coco stiffened and looked past Vaufreland to the door. "I have to go."

"I don't think you'll feel that way when you see this." Standing, Vaufreland handed Coco a large brown envelope. "Let me know if I can help you in any other way." He placed his hat on his head and, still smiling, walked past Coco and out the door.

Coco tore open the envelope. It was a copy of a bill of sale, dated a year earlier. The Wertheimer brothers had sold their 70 percent stake in Chanel Parfums—their controlling share—to Félix Amiot, a Christian Parisian industrialist.

Coco hurried across the street and burst into her apartment, where Spatz lounged in the salon. "Look at this!" she cried, waving the document.

Spatz put down his newspaper and took the bill of sale from Coco's hand.

"It's a sham!" Coco's face had turned bright red. "Amiot is just a front man!"

Spatz studied the bill of sale with a furrowed brow. "It looks like an attempt by the Wertheimers to avoid the law," he said. According to the laws of the Third Reich and Vichy, Jewish businesses were subject to confiscation. When Spatz looked up, his face had brightened with a smile. "Darling, this could be the opportunity you've been waiting for."

"Now that I'm an Abwehr agent? Vaufreland says you've registered me as a spy with the code name Westminster."

"It doesn't mean anything. I had to do it to arrange the Madrid trip."

"Well, I'm not doing any more favors for the Germans."

"No. It's our turn to do more favors for you."

Coco had complained bitterly to Spatz about her attempts over the years to wrest full control of her company back from the Wertheimers. She had met the brothers in 1923, when they already owned the largest perfume company in France. Coco was impressed with their worldwide business network, and they were impressed with Chanel No. 5, which Coco had been selling out of her boutique. They offered her 10 percent of the profits if she sold them the rights to the scent. She agreed, never imagining the perfume would turn into an international hit, and she soon became convinced she'd been cheated. The truth was, the Wertheimers, through their brilliant marketing of Chanel No. 5, had made it the most popular perfume in the world, and Coco one of France's richest women.

Coco and the dashing Pierre had been having an affair at the time the perfume deal was struck, but that ended when Coco began to think she wasn't getting enough from Chanel Parfums. In 1933, she sued the brothers, arguing that she deserved more of the profits. It was the first of many lawsuits she filed against them. Nothing ever came of these legal proceedings.

The Wertheimers arrived in New York after escaping occupied France through Spain. From their new home, they produced 350,000 bottles of perfume from a production facility in Hoboken, New Jersey, and sold the fragrance throughout the United States. Coco assumed that the American version of the perfume was a poor fake. Moreover, the French division of Chanel Parfums had shrunk considerably during the war as the American division expanded, diminishing Coco's profits even further.

Spatz spoke to his superiors, and the Germans launched an investigation. The Gestapo dragged Amiot in for questioning and warned him that he was playing a naïve and dangerous game—that he could be imprisoned for his complicity in hiding a Jewish business from German authorities.

Spatz also arranged for Coco to meet with Kurt Blanke, the German lawyer in charge of enforcing the Nazi race laws and ridding the French economy of Jews.

As the date of the meeting approached, Coco had second thoughts. She abhorred the Nazi program to seize Jewish businesses and property. She knew those Jewish owners were sometimes seized themselves—and never seen again. Still, she knew the Wertheimers were now safely in New York. This was simply a chance to earn what she deserved from a perfume she created.

Early one Monday morning, Coco climbed into the back seat of an Abwehr Mercedes parked outside the Ritz. It took twenty minutes to reach the Hotel Majestic on avenue Kléber. Over the years, Coco had attended many lavish events here in the vast gilt ballroom, which now served as headquarters for the German military command. A young man in uniform met Coco at the door and led her through the echoing marble foyer into a small office crammed with file cabinets. A pretty blonde in a green silk dress sat behind a big black typewriter stabbing the keys with her index fingers. The familiar scent of Chanel No. 5 floated up from her rosy skin. It was the smell of elegance, slightly astringent, like jasmine and rose misted with alcohol. "Mademoiselle Chanel! This is such an honor," said the blonde, her face reddening with excitement. "He's expecting you." She stood and opened the heavy double doors behind her.

Coco entered a huge, high-ceilinged salon with walls the color of a frozen lake. The blue silk upholstery covering the chairs and settees and the cut crystal dripping from the immense chandelier and sconces added to the room's chill. Not even the flames struggling for life in the enormous stone fireplace could dispel the shivery feel.

The man in the gray suit who sat at the mahogany table in front of the windows was so dwarfed by the room that he looked like a figurine in a dollhouse. He'd been scribbling in a journal, which he now closed. Kurt Blanke regarded Coco with dead eyes behind black horn-rims. He was a slim man in his late forties, with a pocked face and cardboard-colored hair slicked back from a high, deeply lined forehead, and a small, thin mouth.

"Ah, the famous couturière," said Blanke, rising to shake Coco's hand.

The blond secretary hurried in with a document and placed it on Blanke's desk. "For your signature, sir," she said.

"Fraulein Silber, you should thank Mademoiselle Chanel for the perfume."

"Merci," said the girl, curtsying slightly.

Coco had sent a crate of Chanel No. 5 to Blanke's office the previous week—greatly diminishing the supply in her boutique—and Blanke had distributed the bottles to his staff.

"I'm not sure how your office operates, but I understand you're very successful," said Coco.

"We are acting in the best interest of France," said Blanke with a tight little smile. Shadows from the fire streaked the wall behind him, and the room took on motion.

Coco cleared her throat. "Am I correct that the purpose of your office is to return property to Aryan citizens?"

"You are correct." He wasn't making this easy.

"My company is worth more than four million francs, and it is still the property of the Wertheimers." Coco paused.

Blanke looked at her but said nothing.

"They're Jewish," Coco said. She stared at the floor a moment, then raised her eyes to meet Blanke's gaze. "I have an indisputable right of priority. My profits are disproportionately small, as Chanel No. 5 is *my* creation. Here are the documents from my lawyer."

Coco removed a sheaf of papers from her purse and handed them to Blanke. Included was a letter from Ernest Breaux, the chemist who'd worked with Coco to create a fresh, modern scent that reflected the pared down elegance of her fashion. As Breaux explained, the secret to Chanel No. 5 was the combination of florals with aldehydes, a rare and innovative ingredient that was made up of molecules harnessed from the florals. The aldehydes made Chanel No. 5 extraordinarily expensive to manufacture. The perfume was an exclusive luxury, and, during a time of rationing and deprivation, a time when all other luxuries fell away, it became a potent symbol of the good life that might never return.

A toilet flushed somewhere in the building. As if that were the signal for Coco to go, Blanke rose and straightened his tie. "We want to help," he said. "I will look into this immediately."

A week went by, then another, and still Coco heard nothing from Blanke's office. One day, she had Misia to lunch on rue Cambon. Afterward, the older woman said she wanted to buy a negligee for her niece who was getting married, so they took a stroll around the corner to Baruch's lingerie shop on rue des Capucines. Gustave Baruch had been forced to relinquish his business to the Nazis, and now the shop was run by a Christian Frenchman appointed by the Germans.

The shop door swung open, and out stepped a stout middle-aged woman in a brown wool dress capped by a fluff of gray curls. She was Victorine Balsan, the wife of Coco's first lover, Étienne Balsan. When they'd first met, Victorine was a glamorous young demimondaine. Coco was a scrappy twenty-three-year-old seamstress. Balsan had rescued her from the tailoring shop in Moulins where she'd been repairing seams for a pittance. He came in one day to have his trousers mended, a pleasant-looking young heir to a textile fortune, and struck up a flirtation with the dark, wiry shopgirl. The next thing Coco knew, she had quit her job and moved into Balsan's estate. He had several mistresses. Coco was his *irregulière,* hidden away in an attic bedroom.

She cringed now to think of her humiliation, how she'd never been allowed in Balsan's salons or invited to his dinner parties. One evening, however, after she thought all the guests had left, she slipped into the dining room. She'd been out all afternoon riding through the woods on one of Balsan's horses, and she had eaten supper in the kitchen with the servants, as she always did when Balsan entertained. On an impulse on her way to her attic bedroom, she opened the door to the dining room. She heard moaning from a far corner and saw Balsan and a shapely blonde leaning against the wall. The woman was covered in laces and ruffles and billowing skirts, her waist corseted within an inch of her life. Balsan had his hand down her bodice. Coco had no power over this luminous beauty except her contempt, which she expressed by going to Balsan's closet and cutting up his clothes. She didn't cut them to shreds. She cut them to fit herself. She stayed up all night sewing, while he was with *her.* The next day, Coco showed up at lunch in a simple white shirt, plain jacket, and a pair of jodhpurs. That got her lover's attention. "Don't you look smart," he said. "Let's take the horses out." Coco had Balsan to herself that afternoon. But by evening, he'd gone back to his silly blonde, with her privilege and wealth and stifling, ridiculous clothes.

Now Victorine Balsan was a frumpy dowager in a shapeless dress. "Coco, it's been ages. I haven't seen you since you closed your house," she chirped.

"Is Étienne with you?" Coco kissed the air beside Victorine's powdered cheeks.

"I left him in the country trimming our rosebushes. I'm here for only a few days. I was hoping to pick up some lingerie. But there's nothing to buy. Not even one nightgown." Victorine nodded toward the shop entrance, then lowered her chin and looked at Coco over the tops of her rimless spectacles. "Perhaps you could come over—we still have the townhouse on Place Dauphine—and go through my closets with my maid. Advise her on what to keep and what to give away."

Coco wasn't about to play assistant to Victorine's lady of the manor. "I'll send my vendeuse over after the boutique closes," Coco said in an imperious tone. "Say bonjour to Étienne for me."

"There's no point in going in," said Misia. "I'm tired. I should go home."

"We can share a taxi, if we can find one," said Victorine.

As the women waited on the curb, a beggar appeared at Coco's side, wafting a foul stench and holding out a greasy, stubby palm. Opening her purse, Coco realized she had no change, only large bills. "I'm sorry, not today," Coco said. As Misia and Victorine scrabbled through their own handbags for coins, the beggar grabbed Coco's arm. "The Kraut whore doesn't have any money!" he yelled.

Coco caught Victorine's eyes. Madame Balsan glared at her. Did she know about Spatz? "Ignore him," said Misia.

"I think I'll walk," said Coco, then to Victorine: "Please see that Misia gets home." Coco hurried away as the beggar continued to shout "Kraut whore! Kraut whore!" A little crowd had gathered on the sidewalk. People were staring at Coco and whispering behind gloved hands. She knew they agreed with the beggar. She was nothing but a Kraut whore.

That evening, Coco met Spatz at Bignon's. The maître d' showed the couple to their usual table in front of the fireplace. Their usual black-haired waiter handed them menus, and, as usual, he stepped slightly to the side and hovered.

Coco was still reeling from her encounter with the beggar, and distress etched her face. "You look terrible. I suppose you heard," said Spatz.

"Heard what?" Coco lit a cigarette and took a long, calming drag.

Spatz turned to the waiter. "A bottle of Côtes du Rhône." The waiter bowed and slunk away.

Spatz leaned across the tablecloth and took Coco's hands. "I'm afraid I have bad news about Chanel Parfums. Herr Blanke issued his decision this afternoon. He decided that it can't be considered a Jewish company."

"Why not?" Coco felt a surge of disappointment. Around her, glasses clinked against cutlery, the ringing sound mingling with the low hum of voices.

"According to Blanke, your company passed into Aryan hands in a manner that was legal and correct."

"The Wertheimers backdated the stock transfers to 1938 so it looked like it was done before the war. Any fool can see through that ruse." Coco sat back and crossed her arms over her chest. "Pierre's surrogate must have bribed Blanke."

"Possibly."

"There's nothing to be done?"

"I'm afraid not, darling."

The waiter returned with a bottle, pulled the cork, poured Spatz a taste, and served the couple.

Parisians were starving, but Bignon's larder never lacked: steak, roast beef, lamb, veal, caviar, the finest cheeses, the best wines, fresh vegetables and fruits flown in from Spain.

"May I describe the specials?" the waiter said.

"We'll share the bouillabaisse," Coco said quickly.

The waiter bowed with deference and disappeared into the kitchen

"I was thinking of a veal chop tonight. Why did you do that?" asked Spatz, annoyed.

"To get rid of him. He's a pest. He doesn't let us dine in peace."

"You might appreciate the service. He's right there to pull out your chair and light your cigarette. He's efficient."

"He probably thinks I'm a Kraut whore."

"What?" Spatz scowled.

"A beggar outside Baruch's lingerie shop today called me a Kraut whore. You should have seen the looks on the faces around me on the street. The hatred. I could tell they were thinking the same thing."

"Had you ever seen this vagrant before?"

"No."

"I'm sure he had no idea who you are. He was a crazy old man who probably insults every well-dressed woman who doesn't give him a handout."

"Perhaps."

Spatz studied Coco's face. "You seem more upset about the beggar than your company."

Coco shrugged and gave an exhausted sigh. Spatz smiled slightly. "None of this will matter when we win the war."

Several days later, Coco and her nephew were in her rue Cambon dining room picking at the heavy lunch of steak, potatoes, buttered green beans, and bread that Coco had ordered from the Ritz dining room in her ongoing effort to fatten André up. Coco never ate much, and the robust appetite André had enjoyed before the war hadn't yet returned. He'd been released from the hospital months earlier after a stay of six weeks, but he was still too weak to resume full-time work. Before the war, he'd been the director of a branch of her company that made silk, but that business was mostly defunct now. So when André was up and around again, Coco gave him an office below hers on rue Cambon. He spent a few hours there every day looking over the books and handling correspondence before returning to his family in the nearby apartment Coco had rented for them.

She watched him cut a piece of meat and push it to the side with his fork. "You don't like steak anymore?" she asked.

"No, it's just . . ." André put his hands in his lap and looked hard at Coco. "It looks bad, Aunt Gabby. You should break up with Spatz now."

"You owe your life to him," Coco said.

"I owe my near death to his countrymen," said André.

Coco flinched at the comment. Her nephew had met Spatz just once, soon after he'd left the hospital, at an awkward dinner in that very dining room, during which André had sulked like a churlish adolescent. Spatz had brought presents for André's daughters, matching rose velvet dresses from Galeries Lafayette that Spatz had chosen himself. André accepted the brightly wrapped packages and thanked Spatz (a little too grudgingly, Coco thought), but later he refused to take the gifts home. Coco ended up stashing the unopened parcels in the closet of an empty atelier.

André had always pushed back against Coco's right-wing political views, matching her arguments with arguments on the liberal side that were bolstered by his knowledge of history and close reading of contemporary newspapers. She never minded being bested by André in these discussions. For his part, André knew how glowingly proud Coco was of his intelligence and seriousness, and he basked in her unshakable love. They talked often about many things—not just politics and business, but also André's daughters, art, and literature. There had been fewer of those conversations since André had returned. Coco told herself it was because André's energies were focused on his recovery. But a sense that he was pulling away from her nagged at her heart. She couldn't help but feel Spatz was to blame.

These troubling thoughts occupied Coco as she passed André a large box of Ladurée macarons; he selected a chocolate one but laid it on his plate without taking a bite. "I don't want to see you go to jail," he said.

"I'm not going to jail!"

"No? What do you think will happen when this is all over?"

"What if the Germans win?"

"Open your eyes, Aunt Gabby. The Germans are never going to win."

ELEVEN

Coco prided herself on having a sixth sense about events, but she felt wracked by uncertainty about the war's outcome. She'd closely followed the Nazis' march from triumph to triumph at the start of the war, but recently, it looked less likely they'd take over the world. There were many signs of trouble for the Third Reich: the Americans had entered the war with all their power and determination; the Royal Air Force of Britain had begun relentlessly bombing German cities; the Allies were holding the Nazis back in Africa and the Soviet Union. She let herself imagine a future in which Paris would be Paris again and she could forget the Occupation. She refused to think about where this would leave Spatz.

At the same time, Coco saw the war draw closer in Paris. Resistance fighters shot German soldiers on the street and in the Métro. The Nazis retaliated by executing French prisoners. Tanks lumbered up the boulevards, their open gun turrets manned by middle-aged soldiers—most of the young Nazis had been sent to fight on the Russian front. Allied bombing in the Parisian suburbs had destroyed train lines and airports and made it nearly impossible to send food and other supplies to the city. Coco watched her vendeuse Angeline grow thinner and thinner, despite the chocolate, bread, steaks, and eggs Coco bought her on the black market. "I'm sharing it with my neighbors, and there's not a lot to go around," Angeline told her one day, as Coco handed the young woman a tin of cookies.

It was May 1942, the chestnut trees fluffed with pink, and families strolled the gravel paths in the Tuileries, where Coco had gone for some fresh air. She marveled at the good looks of one young couple she passed—the man, tall and lanky, his intelligent face framed by shiny dark curls; and his pretty companion, ginger-haired, mannequin-slender, and dressed in a chic navy wool crepe dress. The first thing Coco had noticed about her, though, was the yellow star sewn on her dress above her left breast. It was a vile mustard color as big as the palm of a hand with JEW written in black Gothic letters. Now, Coco couldn't help looking at the chests of everyone she passed. On the way back to the Ritz, she saw two more yellow stars—one on a man in his forties, the other on a teenage boy.

"It's barbaric!" Coco told Spatz when she saw him later that evening. "Why are you doing this, labeling people?" She had said vulgar things, yes. She had her feud with Paul and Pierre Wertheimer, yes. But this?

"*I'm* not doing anything," Spatz snapped, and went back to reading his newspaper.

As the spring and summer wore on, the German noose tightened. In retaliation for Resistance violence, the Nazis moved up the curfew earlier and earlier. Parisians who defied the order and walked around the city without an ausweis were as likely as not to be shot on the spot. Coco read several papers a day. All were controlled by the Germans, who specialized in lies and spreading phony stories. One day she read that the RAF had bombed the Vatican, another day that the Soviets were about to surrender to the Nazis. It was impossible to know the truth.

For Parisian Jews, life became darker and more perilous, as one after another of their civil liberties were stripped away. By the summer of 1942, Jews were forbidden even from waiting in food lines to redeem their ration tickets. One hot morning in July, Coco stood in front of the closed iron grille at Atelier Schwartz, the jeweler on rue des Capucines around the corner from her boutique, where she'd left a necklace for repair. She rang the buzzer again and again, finally holding it in with her thumb and causing a harsh, steady noise to fill the air. The shutters above the shop flung open, and an old woman in a faded floral housedress leaned out the window. "The Germans took Schwartz away with his wife yesterday," she said.

"Where?" asked Coco.

"I don't know. I was here cleaning the apartment and watching their son." She moved aside, and a pale little boy stepped out of the shadow, clutching a toy truck. He glanced at Coco and buried his face in the housekeeper's apron. "I heard the commotion outside and saw the soldiers with their guns drawn," she said. "Thank God, Alexi isn't yet six, so he doesn't have to wear the yellow star. When the soldiers came upstairs to search the apartment, I told them he was my grandson, and from the way the poor thing clung to me, they believed me." She crossed herself and held her hands together in prayer for a moment. "The Germans are monsters. They'd shoot a child in his bed as soon as they'd shoot a dog in the street."

The boy began to whimper, and the old woman banged the shutters shut.

Coco hurried back to the Ritz. "Was there a round-up of Jews yesterday?" she asked Spatz.

He looked at her over the top of his newspaper. "Of foreign Jews, yes." Spatz downed the last drops of his coffee and poured himself another cup from the silver pot on the coffee table.

"Henri Schwartz and his wife aren't foreigners. They're French," said Coco. "His family has owned that jewelry store since Napoleon's day. Still, the Germans picked them up."

"I don't know what to tell you, darling," said Spatz.

"Where are they?" demanded Coco.

Spatz sighed. "I heard that the foreign Jews are being relocated to an agricultural colony in the East. I'm sure it was a mistake that they took Schwartz." He shook out his paper, rattling the pages, and returned to reading.

"A mistake? Is that what he told you?" cried Misia over the phone that evening. "It was a mass arrest of thousands of Jews. Entire families are being held in the Vel d'Hiver stadium. Sert told me they're being transported in buses to the prison at Drancy, and from there, who knows!"

"Spatz says an agricultural community in the East."

"You ask him about murder, and he talks to you about farming?"

"No one's talking about murder."

"The Germans aren't talking. They're doing it!"

"You don't know that."

"Do you think we'll ever see those people again?"

Coco hung up the phone. She had let Misia rant, interjecting a few gentle "Nos" and "That can't be trues," assuring her friend that she was misinformed. But Coco wondered. When weeks passed and the Schwartzes never returned, she began to fear that something terrible had happened to them. The same thing, no doubt, that had happened to Max's relatives. Coco pressed Spatz to make inquiries, but he insisted he was powerless to help the couple. "My office has nothing to do with the persecution of the Jews. It doesn't concern us. We hold ourselves aloof from it!"

TWELVE

One night in November 1942, while Spatz was in the bathroom preparing for bed, Coco turned on the radio and heard a BBC reporter announce that British and American forces, after storming the beaches of North Africa, had taken control of Algiers and Morocco. "This is an important breakthrough for the Allies," came the clipped British voice through the speaker. "The prime minister will now address the nation."

"Turn it up," said Spatz. He appeared in the doorway with his toothbrush in his hand. Though the Nazis forbade the French from tuning in to the BBC, Coco often hunted for their broadcasts. Who would report her—Spatz?

Coco raised the volume and sat on the edge of the bed with an unlit cigarette. "This is not the end," boomed Winston Churchill through the scratchy airwaves. "It is not even the beginning of the end. But it is perhaps the end of the beginning."

Spatz clicked off the radio. "This is awful for Germany," he admitted.

Coco lit her cigarette and, as she puffed, considered her situation. The war seemed to be turning against the Nazis. They were stretched thin in Russia. The Americans were just starting to unleash the full potential of their power. The Allies might yet win. Misia had warned Coco constantly: any woman who lived with a German would be marked for vengeance. Reverdy had told her she was already on a blacklist of collaborators. Coco felt her chest tighten. The cost she might have to pay for loving Spatz took her breath away. In the past, she had overcome every obstacle that was placed in her path. She always thought she could outsmart the universe if she had to. Now, she wasn't so sure.

Spatz was too restless to sleep, so he grabbed a newspaper and went to the salon to read. Coco downed a couple of narcotic pills, and as she started to drift off, she thought about Churchill. Wasn't she still his good friend? She recalled the admiring way Churchill looked at her the last time they'd dined together right before the war. How he laughed at her witty remarks . . .

The next thing she knew, Spatz was shaking her shoulder in the dark bedroom. "Coco, wake up," he said.

She opened her eyes. Her head felt like it was stuffed with cotton. "What time is it?" she asked.

"Four thirty." Spatz turned on the bedside lamp. "Teddy Momm is here."

"Momm?" She was sitting up now and rubbing her eyes.

"He needs to talk to us."

"Now, in the middle of the night?"

"Yes, *now*." A note of panic had edged into Spatz's voice.

"Let me get dressed."

"No time for that." He stood by the bed holding open her white silk bathrobe. "Come on, get up."

In the salon, a balding, blue-eyed man in a gray suit sat in an armchair by the fireplace. He was Abwehr Captain Theodor Momm, a close friend of Spatz's since their days fighting together on the Russian front in 1917.

Coco had had dinner with him a couple of times at Bignon's and found him intelligent and easy to talk to. Momm sat with his feet planted firmly on the carpet and his fingertips frantically tapping his knees. When Coco and Spatz entered, he jumped up. "I'm sorry to disturb your sleep like this, but I'm on my way to Berlin, and it was crucial I talk to you before I left," he said. "It's no longer safe for either of you in Paris."

Momm's light blue eyes bored into Spatz. "You should leave as soon as you can for Turkey. You can work with my brother at the Abwehr headquarters in Istanbul. More agents with your charm and polish are needed, if we're ever going to seduce the Turks to our side."

"Istanbul is the last place I want to go." Spatz plunked down on the settee and ran his hands through his hair. His bathrobe had come undone, and he wore nothing underneath but a stained white T-shirt and striped cotton shorts. Coco had bought him several pairs of silk pajamas, but he insisted on sleeping in his underwear. Growing up in a mansion in Saxony, Spatz was used to luxury and order, so Coco expected nothing from him but discipline and elegance. Usually, it annoyed her when he behaved like an ordinary slob. Looking at him now, she felt a rush of tenderness.

"British intelligence has reports on you," Momm said. "They know about your activities on the Côte d'Azur and your meeting with Hitler."

Coco gasped. He'd never told her he'd met Hitler. "You talked to the Devil himself?" she asked.

"At a dinner in Berlin on that trip I made last year. I spoke to him for only a few minutes."

"Germany is doomed as long as he's in power," said Momm.

"Hitler is a madman," said Spatz.

Coco looked from one man to the other. She'd never heard Spatz speak so harshly about Hitler to a fellow German. The war must be getting even worse for them than she'd assumed.

"And we're not the only ones who think so," added Momm. "There's a growing number of officers in the high command who'd love to see the Führer gone."

Momm lowered his eyes. When he lifted them again, he looked hard at Coco. "As for you, Mademoiselle, I'd go to Switzerland while you still have the chance." He took from his briefcase a copy of *Life* and handed it to her. "Look at page eighty-six."

The American magazine had published a Resistance blacklist of thirty-nine Frenchmen "condemned . . . for collaborating with Germans: some to be assassinated, others to be tried when France is free." Coco scanned the list quickly. When she didn't see her name, a current of relief shot through her. First on the list was Mistinguett, a music-hall star who'd performed in Germany and was the mistress of Maurice Chevalier, also on the list. The third and fourth names were Corinne Luchaire and Nicole Bordeaux, both actresses and mistresses of the German ambassador Otto Abetz's. Others included Maréchal Pétain, Pierre Laval, a smattering of lower-level Vichy officials, and several right-wing journalists and politicians. Coco's heart sank when she saw the name of René de Chambrun, the son-in-law of Pierre Laval and for many years Coco's lawyer. "Chambrun is here," she said grimly.

"It won't be long 'til you're on the Resistance blacklist, too," said Momm with conviction.

Coco didn't tell him she already was. *Life* just hadn't discovered it.

"The axe is falling," said Momm, as he stood and headed toward the door.

"Maybe I *should* go to Istanbul," said Spatz, when Momm had left.

"And leave me here to the wolves?" Coco clutched the lapels of her robe as she paced the room.

"God, don't be so dramatic." Spatz moved toward Coco and put his arms around her. "Let's get some sleep. We can talk about it later."

Coco lay in bed next to Spatz, listening to him snore softly. She felt comforted with him by her side. A woman who wasn't loved was lost. She'd always believed that, built her career on the notion. After all, the true subject of fashion was romance—alluring women in alluring clothes. She was no different than any other woman. She needed to be cherished.

Especially in these perilous times, she didn't think she could face old age without a man to make her feel young. Spatz wasn't brilliant like Boy Capel or fabulously connected like the Duke of Westminster. He didn't speak to her creative soul like Pierre Reverdy. But he kept her profound loneliness at bay. She couldn't bear the thought of being separated from him.

A few days later, Coco decided to go to La Pausa to escape the pressures weighing on them. Spatz said he had business to attend to in the city, and he would join her on the weekend. Coco was in the middle of packing when Céline called. "The Germans are here!" the maid shouted over the phone.

"In the house?" asked Coco. She was about to fold a silk blouse she'd just removed from a hanger.

"No, in town," said Céline. "I was at the pharmacy when an entire regiment of them arrived with their tanks!"

Coco sat on the bed, the blouse crumpled in her lap. "*Merde*," she muttered.

In response to the Allied invasion of North Africa, Hitler had ordered that all of France be occupied. Coco put her suitcase away. Now there would be no point in rushing off to La Pausa to hide.

For Coco and Spatz, the winter passed in a fog of worry. Conditions in Paris worsened, even at the Ritz. The heat and electricity went in and out. The menu at the restaurant shrunk. There was no steak, no cream, no fresh vegetables or fruits. Beyond the hotel, people had trouble getting enough food to survive. The reports Coco heard from her vendeuse Angeline were grim. Children were dying of hunger; the elderly were freezing in their beds at night. The icy cold continued into spring, and snow blanketed the city well into March.

As Coco pondered the bleak situation, an idea began to bloom in her mind. A bizarre, crazy idea, but one she believed might actually work. She told Spatz about it one night in April as they sat in her salon at the Ritz sharing a bottle of red wine. "What if I could get to Winston Churchill and convince him to negotiate with the Germans to end the war and stop the killing?" she said.

Spatz's eyes widened. "You're not serious," he said.

"I am."

"How in the world would you do it?"

"Through Samuel Hoare, the British ambassador in Madrid. He's an old friend."

Coco took a gulp of wine and placed her glass on the coffee table. "The British might not know there are people like you and Teddy Momm, and those even higher up in Berlin, who want Hitler gone. Churchill has insisted he'll accept nothing but total surrender from Germany. But what if I could persuade him to soften his position and initiate peace talks?"

Spatz stared into his glass, swirling his wine, as Coco pressed her argument.

"You know if Germany collapses, the Soviets pose a severe threat to all of Europe. The British aristocracy fears a communist Europe even more than a fascist one," said Coco.

Spatz shook his head. "It's too dangerous."

Coco urged him to take her plan directly to the dissident officers in the Nazi high command who'd lost confidence in their Führer, if they ever had any. With their backing, she would approach Churchill. Negotiations would go on behind Hitler's back, culminating in a coup. If the plan worked, Churchill would save lives and enhance his legacy. It would also make Coco a global heroine—the woman who ended a world war!

Even discussing the idea risked death, and Spatz balked at suggesting the plan to his superiors. Coco saw this as more evidence of his weakness. Her previous lovers had been men with ideas and ambition—men she could learn from. She knew she was much smarter than Spatz. *But he's so handsome! And he's good to me*, she thought with a stab of tenderness whenever she looked at him. What did it matter that she couldn't respect him? He was by her side, and that was enough for now.

She kept bringing up her idea, and, eventually, Spatz warmed to the plan. Finally, he agreed to talk about it directly to Teddy Momm.

The Abwehr captain was skeptical, too, but despite the risks, he agreed to pass Coco's plan along. He even gave the venture a name: *Modellhut*, or Fashion Hat. When Momm broached Coco's scheme to the German secretary of state in the foreign office in Paris, however, he was rebuffed. At Coco's and Spatz's urging, Momm next approached Major Walter Schellenberg, the head of the Nazi SD intelligence service, whom Momm knew was eager to see Hitler gone. At thirty-three, Schellenberg was one of the youngest high-ranking Nazis and a glamorous, dynamic man. Schellenberg thought Coco's idea intriguing. He asked Momm to send her to Berlin so he and Coco could discuss the proposed mission.

As Coco and Spatz prepared to travel to Germany, Coco felt confident they would win Schellenberg's approval. As it happened—and as the couple heard on BBC radio—Churchill was scheduled to stop in Madrid in early December on his way home from a conference in Tehran. Coco would use her connections to get a meeting with the prime minister. As cover, she would go to Spain with an aristocratic Englishwoman named Vera Bate, who'd once worked for Coco in Paris. They'd say they were in Madrid to scout locations for a new Chanel boutique. Vera had been a close friend of Churchill's since childhood. If Coco ran into trouble getting access to him, Vera could help.

Most of the hotels in Berlin had been bombed to rubble, so Spatz arranged for Coco to stay at a villa outside town, where the mistress of Momm's boss, a young woman named Karin Mertin, lived. Spatz would bunk with a friend in a house near the Tiergarten. "Karin is clothes-mad. It'll be a huge treat for her to be with a real Parisian couturière," Spatz said the night before they left Paris. "And you'll help our cause if you're nice to her."

The couple's "cause" was to keep Spatz in Paris. Momm was threatening to transfer Spatz to Istanbul if Spatz didn't volunteer himself for the assignment in Turkey.

The next evening, Coco sat opposite Karin Mertin at a corner table in the dining room of a villa outside Berlin. Karin was young, barely in her twenties, and exceptionally pretty with white skin and pale gold hair.

"Do you think this color washes me out?" Karin asked as she fluttered her hands over her yellow chiffon dress.

"It's lovely on you," Coco lied. The dress was the hard hue of a child's crayon and not at all becoming. Usually Coco had no qualms about speaking her mind. But since Karin was the mistress of a high-ranking German, flattery seemed wise.

Also, Coco was Karin's guest at the villa. A rambling white-stone affair with lavish gardens under a cover of fresh snow, the house sat on a lake surrounded by pine forests. The wealthy Jewish owners had abandoned the home, and it now served as a safe house for the mistresses of high-ranking Nazis, far from the Allied bombs and the prying eyes of wives.

Coco would be here only one day. Just long enough to convince Walter Schellenberg, head of Nazi intelligence, to approve Modellhut. But first she had to get through dinner with Karin.

In the rectangular dining room, a fresh pine scent hung in the air. Wagner wafted in from a gramophone in the foyer. A portrait of the Führer hung over the mantel, and one wall showcased two Monet landscapes that Coco recalled seeing in a drawing room in Paris. Ugly green brocade drapes lined the tall windows; a fresco of cupids holding flower garlands surrounded the high ceiling. "It came from a château in France and cost a fortune," bragged Karin. Her voice had the sweet, round tones of a child.

Her body, though, had a womanly grace. She was small and curvy, with an oval face dominated by large green eyes. Though the Nazis frowned on makeup, Karin wore heavy cosmetics: pancake foundation, rouge, goopy black mascara, eyebrow charcoal, stoplight-red lipstick. "I'd get stared at if I went out like this in Berlin," she said. Karin checked her face in her compact mirror and fluffed her silky hair. Then she clicked the compact shut and dropped it in her beaded purse. "No one cares out here."

Coco wore heavy makeup, too. Fending off a stab of envy, she thought if she had Karin's youth and flawless complexion, she'd only wear a little lipstick and, maybe, a touch of powder on her nose.

Beyond the windows, the sun had disappeared into the lake. The room was dark, warmed by candles at the center of each table. Through the blue haze of cigarette smoke, a few faces loomed—middle-aged men in Nazi uniforms and pretty young women. Some were very young, still in their teens. They'd landed here from farms and villages, plucked by some German officer in a Mercedes as they herded sheep or served meals in a roadside café.

Their clothes were too expensive, the diamonds in their rings too large, the cars that had brought them and were parked outside with chauffeurs napping at the wheels too shiny and new. None of the girls were used to having money, and as soon as they got some they spent it on jewelry and clothes, on furs and leather luggage with silk linings and built-in cosmetic trays. Coco had once been as penniless as the poorest of these young women, but she never let her fortune go to her head.

"You will never have money. You will be lucky if a farmer will have you," the nuns had told Coco when she was a child. She began to understand that without money, she'd always be nothing. She wasn't so stupid as to dream of being rescued by a rich man who came along and proposed to her. That was for other girls, lesser girls. She'd seen what marriage and motherhood had done to her mother, and she vowed to make her own way without a husband. But to be truly free, she had to have money. This became her mantra: *Money is the key to the kingdom*. It wasn't about buying objects. She had to buy her independence at any cost.

When the food arrived, Coco was dismayed to see it was typical heavy German fare: venison schnitzels, potatoes smothered in cream, and streusel and cherry tortes for dessert. Coco ate little, puffing on a cigarette, while Karin devoured her meal and nattered between bites. "I'm so bored here," she said. "There's just so many walks you can take, so many novels you can read—anyway, all the juicy ones have been banned. I can't go to Berlin because of the bombing, not even to see my poor mother. The last time I was there, she had my dead uncle laid out on the kitchen table. He'd died of a heart attack while visiting her, and she couldn't get anyone to remove the corpse. It happened during an air raid; part of her building was hit. The lights went out, and when they came on again, the windows had shattered, some walls had caved in and my uncle was dead. I wanted her to come here, but she wouldn't leave her brother."

Karin emptied her wineglass and called for the waiter to bring her a refill. She emptied that one, too, and ordered another. "Mother doesn't approve of my lover, though she took the cash he gave her," she continued. "He's so generous. He gave me an entire suitcase of banknotes for the couture shows last fall. But you know what? I only bought three dresses. God, the selection was horrid."

Karin lifted her big, mascaraed eyes to the heavens and sighed deeply. "There was nothing at Maggy Rouff or Schiaparelli. Finally, I found this dress and two others at Jacques Fath for eight thousand francs each." She grabbed a glass of champagne from a tray that floated by on the arm of a waiter. "What snobs those vendeuses are. When the woman at Fath told me the price, she had her nose in the air so high, I thought it would hit the ceiling. She didn't think I could afford it. But I didn't flinch. I took out the money and slapped it on the counter in front of her. A few banknotes floated to the ground, and, boy, did I enjoy watching her grovel around on her bony knees to pick them up."

Karin was slurring her words now. But she kept downing glasses of champagne. She drank because she was bored, because her lover was married, because she missed her friends in Berlin, because even with her silly, frivolous brain, she sensed the shift in the air, that the Nazis were in trouble, that the high life she'd been enjoying for the past few years was coming to an end.

"Snobs, all of them." Karin leaned forward, blowing her sour wine breath in Coco's face. "You know who else snubbed me at Fath's? Isabelle Mayer, that skinny witch who's married to the rich Jewish banker. I was assigned the little gilt chair next to her in the front row, but as soon as my bottom hit the velvet cushion she jumped up, looked at me like I was the Devil himself, and stormed off to the opposite side of the room."

A cold severity crept into Karin's girlish voice. "I told my lover about it, and the next day the Gestapo knocked on her door, arrested her, and sent her away." Karin straightened her shoulders and drew herself up proudly. "I showed her. No one's heard from Madame Mayer since."

Another person deported. Madame Mayer was a sometime client of Coco's. She was a tall, slender woman with a cool, aristocratic air. It was hard to picture her as a prisoner in a dank cell. Perhaps she'd disappeared to a house in an obscure corner of France, or even to America. Probably not, though, Coco thought with a dropping feeling in her stomach.

It was one a.m. before Coco got away from Karin. She took a couple of narcotic pills and fell into a long, deep sleep under the down comforter. The next morning the chauffeur who'd brought her to the villa the evening before drove her to Schellenberg's office. Weaving through the burned-out streets of Berlin, Coco shivered. The city looked apocalyptic. Entire blocks had collapsed. On one boulevard a large crowd had gathered to watch a group of men with ropes pulling down the only wall still standing. On other streets, exposed stairways stopped in midair. Huge craters marked the spots where Allied bombs had taken out entire buildings. Patches of blackened snow piled up, and dense yellow smoke hung in the cold sky. Pedestrians trudged through the rubble in overcoats, their faces hidden behind scarves to stifle the gaseous fumes. Sirens blared, and intermittently, planes roared overhead. Coco thought about the possibility of being burned alive in a bomb blast with no one able to find her.

Schellenberg's office stood unscathed on Berkaerstrasse in a sleek Art Deco building that had been a Jewish nursing home before the war. Spatz was waiting for her in the lobby. He looked gray and anxious, but he forced a smile on seeing her. "How did you sleep, *mein liebling*?" he said.

"I had a dreadful evening with Karin Mertin. How was yours?"

"Uneventful. Are you ready?"

"Yes."

Coco and Spatz took the elevator to the second floor. A brisk secretary ushered them into the intelligence chief's office. Schellenberg sat behind his immense black lacquered desk. Spatz had confided to Coco that the desk was tricked out with secret compartments holding automatic weapons that could be fired by the touch of a button. Next to Schellenberg's big, important desk, a humble military camp bed had been set up so he could catch a few hours of sleep. He didn't have time to go home for a proper night's rest.

The intelligence minister stood and greeted the couple with handshakes. No raised arm. No *Sieg Heil* or *Heil Hitler.* "Mademoiselle Chanel, Herr von Dincklage, so nice to see you," he said in beautifully accented French.

Schellenberg was tall, slim, and movie-star handsome with abundant straight brown hair and elegant, chiseled features. Next to Spatz, he was the best-looking German man Coco had ever seen. Schellenberg wore a crisply pressed uniform and shiny black boots. Spatz had also confided in her that the intelligence chief had one cyanide capsule hidden under the stone of his blue cabochon ring and a second implanted in a back tooth, so he could kill himself if captured.

Schellenberg smiled warmly at Coco. "My wife is a big fan of your perfume."

"The next time you're in Paris, stop by my boutique—I'll give you a few bottles for her," said Coco.

"Merci. You are very kind." Schellenberg nodded. When he raised his chin, his smile had disappeared. "Now, let's get to the matter at hand."

Schellenberg motioned to Coco and Spatz to take armchairs and settled himself in the swivel chair behind his desk. "Captain Momm has briefed me, but I'd like to hear more about exactly what you're proposing," Schellenberg said.

Spatz let Coco explain. Speaking in French, she told Schellenberg she would go to Madrid and request a meeting with Churchill through the British ambassador, Samuel Hoare, "an old friend of mine," she said. "I'll tell Winston about the opposition to Hitler in your high command. I'm sure he doesn't know how extensive it is. I'll tell him there are people willing to negotiate, to bring an end to this war. I can put the English in touch with them. I'm sure Winston will listen to me. He trusts me. And he knows how awful this war is for everyone."

Schellenberg tented his hands in front of his face and leaned back in his chair. "Herr von Dincklage, what do you think?"

Spatz hesitated. He shifted awkwardly, uncrossing his legs, before crossing them again. "I think it's worth your consideration," he said finally.

Both Spatz and the intelligence chief knew it was treason to even talk to the enemy. Men had been shot for much less than planning crazy schemes like Operation Modellhut.

Coco fixed Spatz with a severe look, silently urging him to say something stronger in defense of her plan. But just as Spatz opened his mouth to continue talking, an air-raid siren howled. The lights went out, then came on again, as an auxiliary generator whirred. A shapely nurse entered with a first aid kit and put it on Schellenberg's desk. She exchanged a glance with Schellenberg that made Coco wonder if the nurse wasn't also sleeping on the camp bed at night. A strange pang of jealousy buzzed through her. Why couldn't Spatz have more backbone, more authority, like this man? She sensed that Schellenberg was more on her level.

A plane rumbled overhead, drawing Coco back to the conversation. They discussed the details for fifteen minutes. Then Coco said, "There's one more thing. I'd like to take a friend to Madrid. Vera Bate. She's related to the British royal family, but she lives in Rome."

"Yes, Captain Momm told me," said Schellenberg, shaking his head. "I don't know. . . . Bringing in another person, an Englishwoman, complicates matters."

Coco cut him off. "I've never traveled alone in my life, and I'm not starting now!"

Schellenberg crinkled his brow. Coco feared she'd gone too far. Her heart hammered in her chest, and her hands felt clammy. She needed Vera because Vera was much closer to Churchill than she was. No matter what, Churchill would certainly agree to see his old childhood chum. But

Coco knew she should have tempered her request with more politesse. Her instinct was to bulldoze her way through obstacles. But Schellenberg wasn't someone who could be flattened easily.

Still, he offered no further objections. "We will arrange for your transportation and accommodation in Madrid," he said, rising and extending his hand to Coco, then to Spatz. "I don't need to remind you"—Schellenberg looked solemnly from one to the other—"total discretion."

They nodded. "Of course," said Spatz.

"And now, you should return to Paris immediately," said Schellenberg. "The Führer is coming."

"Today?" said Coco.

"I was just informed a few minutes before you arrived. He's at the chancellery and is expected here before lunch."

Coco thought she'd like to meet the monster who was ruining Germany and France, but Schellenberg wasn't about to let her and Spatz dawdle. How could he possibly explain why a French fashion designer and her lover were in his office? Grabbing Coco's elbow, Schellenberg pushed her toward the door as Spatz followed. "Good luck, Mademoiselle Chanel," he said.

"Why must you take Vera along?" asked Spatz in the car on the way to the train station. "She lives in Rome, and you haven't seen her in years. She could ruin everything."

"I want her," Coco said flatly. She wouldn't tell Spatz that she worried about her ability to get an audience with the prime minister.

"If you must take a companion, take Karin Mertin," Spatz persisted. "Momm says she's bored to tears at the villa and could use a change of scene."

"I won't spend another moment with that moron," Coco said.

"What if Vera won't come?"

"I'll figure it out."

"It makes me nervous."

"I go with Vera or the mission is off."

From there, the quarrel escalated. Coco flung insult after insult at Spatz. He was weak and inept. No wonder his superiors were threatening to transfer him to Istanbul. They probably just wanted to get rid of him. All he did in Paris was play cards and golf with his friends and go out to lunch. He was ineffectual. There was a darkness in Coco that made her say wicked things, untruthful things, but also sometimes terrible truths that no one wanted to hear and that were better left unsaid.

At the end of Coco's tirade, Spatz glowered at her but said nothing. They rode in silence on the train to Paris. When they finally returned to the Ritz, Coco left Spatz in the salon while she took a bath. Afterward, she turned down the satin comforter on the bed, which had been freshly made up with creamy linen sheets, and slipped in. As she drifted off, Spatz entered the room and sat on the edge of the comforter. "Darling, this is silly—not talking," he said in English.

"I'm sorry I said those things in the car. I didn't mean them," said Coco.

"I know, darling."

Spatz removed his shoes, then his jacket, shirt, and trousers, and got in bed beside her. He kissed her. Slowly, she relaxed and responded. She was glad the lights were out and he couldn't see her. With her clothes on, her body looked fifteen years younger than it was. Naked, her age was obvious. Skin hung loosely around her belly, upper arms, and knees. Her small breasts had flattened out and sagged. Coarse black hairs had begun sprouting where they'd never been before. Every day she inspected her face in the natural light in front of a window as she held a hand mirror. Just that morning she'd plucked a hair from her chin. *I'm turning into an old hag*, she'd thought. With the lights out, she could pretend she was once again a firm, supple beauty, younger even than Spatz.

The fantasy kindled her need, and she finished quickly. Afterward, Coco turned away to light a cigarette. Spatz sat up on one elbow and kissed the top of her head. "I still don't think it's a good idea to take Vera to Madrid," he said.

"Don't worry," said Coco, blowing smoke toward the windows. "I know what I'm doing."

THIRTEEN

As a honey-haired, blue-eyed, and peachy-skinned young woman, Vera Bate had epitomized English rose beauty. Her looks were enhanced by her aristocratic connections. Her godmother was the daughter of a duke, and through her mother's second marriage to a cousin of King George, she was distantly related to the Crown. Coco had become close to Vera in the 1920s. At the time, Vera was divorced from her first husband, an American military officer she'd met while working in an American hospital in Paris, and she needed money. Coco gave her clothes and paid Vera a small salary to wear them to society parties and openings, where she was photographed by the press. She also gave Vera the use of a little house at the back of the garden at La Pausa. Later, Vera had married an Italian cavalry officer and captain in the National Fascist Party, Alberto Lombardi, and moved to Rome.

Out of the blue one day soon after Coco's trip to Berlin, a German officer arrived at Vera's Rome apartment with a dozen red roses and a letter from Coco. The letter said Coco urgently needed Vera's help to find a location for a new boutique in Madrid. Would Vera meet her at the Ritz in Paris to discuss the plans further? *Don't forget, I'm waiting for you in joy and impatience. All my love,* Coco wrote. Vera hadn't heard from Coco in years and had no interest in helping her or in leaving Italy. Since the fall of Italian prime minister Benito Mussolini the previous July, her husband, who feared reprisals from Allied forces, had been in hiding in Salerno. Vera knew his location and was preoccupied with being reunited with him. She declined Coco's invitation emphatically.

A few days later, the Fascist secret police arrested Vera at her apartment on the trumped-up charge that she was an Allied spy. She spent a few nights in a black, rat-infested cell with prostitutes and pickpockets and was given a choice by the Fascists: join Coco in Paris or stay in jail.

Vera arrived at the Ritz on a cold, clear evening. Coco met her in the room she'd secured for Vera a few doors away from Coco's suite. Vera had changed since her years in Paris as Coco's house model. At sixty, she had gained weight. Owlish glasses perched on her nose. Her hair had gone gray, and she wore it in short curls.

The women embraced. "It's good to see you, Coco," said Vera with a tight smile.

Coco doubted her sincerity. She'd expected a torrent of abuse from Vera for being dragged to Paris, and she wondered if Vera had a secret agenda.

The former model had brought one small, battered suitcase and only two rather worn dresses. "Don't you have anything else?" Coco said with dismay.

"I just grabbed any old thing from my closet," said Vera. "I was too worried about my dog, Teague, to think straight. The Germans took him when they arrested me, and I don't know where he is." Vera handed Coco a picture of herself and her husband with Teague between them. He was a savage-looking, bristly-haired creature the size of a bull calf.

"I'll find out where Teague is," said Coco. As a dog lover, she sympathized with Vera's anguish.

"Won't you be glad to go to Spain, where the Nazis aren't in charge?" Coco asked.

"I suppose so," said Vera.

Coco counted on Vera's doubts disappearing and her old affection for Coco returning. Vera wouldn't completely forget her friend's kindness, would she? Surely she'd remember how, when Vera walked out on her first husband in the 1920s and struggled to make a living painting folding screens, Coco had bought many of the screens and given them as presents to friends. Of course, Vera had helped Coco, too. She was a stellar advertisement for the House of Chanel, a real beauty in those days who always drew the attention of photographers and reporters.

With Spatz's help, Coco managed to locate Teague and arranged for the beast to be cared for in Vera's absence by dog breeders who lived on a farm outside Rome. With Teague safe, Vera's mood brightened. She nodded while Coco talked fabric and trimming, shop layout and work-room organization, seemingly unsuspecting that Coco had no intention of opening a Madrid boutique. Coco wondered how she could be so gullible. There was no good reason for Coco to expand her business in the middle of a war. There was no tourism. No one was traveling around buying couture.

Vera should have discerned something fishy when Coco kept her trapped at the Ritz, not letting her leave the hotel. "I'd like to see Misia," Vera said one morning after breakfast in Coco's suite.

"She's not well," Coco lied.

"I'd like to talk to her, at least."

"Don't make any calls. The phone is risky; it could be tapped."

Coco continued to talk fashion on the train to Madrid, where the friends checked into separate rooms at the Ritz. "Why don't you have a bath and take a nap?" Coco said, as they parted in the hotel lobby. "I'll see you in a couple of hours."

Coco watched Vera step into the elevator, followed by a porter carrying her bags. As soon as the door slid shut and the elevator had begun its ascent, Coco handed a banknote to the porter holding her luggage.

"Please take everything to my room," she said, and dashed to the street to hail a cab.

At the British embassy, a receptionist ushered Coco into the ambassador's office overlooking a leafy square. Samuel Hoare, whom she'd met many years earlier through the Duke of Westminster, sat at a large mahogany desk piled with papers. "What a nice surprise," he said, rising from his chair to kiss Coco on each cheek. He looked genuinely happy to see her. They chatted amiably for a few minutes before the ambassador, concerned about getting back to his work, asked Coco what had brought her to Madrid.

"I'd like you to give this to Winston—to the prime minister," she said, and handed Hoare the letter she'd written to Churchill requesting a meeting to discuss the war. Hoare read it, crumpling his brow like corrugated cardboard. When he was done, he pushed his spectacles in place with a crooked finger. "I'm sorry to disappoint you, Mademoiselle Chanel, but Winston Churchill will not be coming to Madrid."

The color drained from Coco's face. "Why not?" Her voice came out in a breathy gulp.

"The prime minister is gravely ill with pneumonia in Tunisia. His doctors have forbidden him to travel."

"And when he's recovered?"

"He'll return immediately to London." Hoare handed the letter back to Coco.

She snatched it from Hoare's hand and stuffed it in her purse. For this she had risked being killed by a bomb in Berlin? Or murdered by rabid Nazis? Coco took the stairs to the ground floor, and as she crossed the lobby to the exit, she ran into Vera Bate. They stood, feet firm, looking fiercely at each other like two bulls in the moment before a violent charge.

Coco spoke first. "What the hell are you doing here?"

"You tell me why *you're* here," demanded Vera.

Coco sighed, defusing the tension. "Let's go back to the Ritz. I'll explain everything."

Over tea in the hotel restaurant, Coco told Vera the entire story—there was no point holding back now. She admitted that the plan to open a boutique was a ruse. She had a much more important mission. She told Vera about visiting Schellenberg in Berlin, about her plan to end the war, about her letter to Churchill and her discovery—just a few minutes before—that the prime minister was ill and would not be stopping in Madrid. Vera then confessed that she, too, had a secret plan. Once in Madrid, she hoped the British embassy would help reunite her with Alberto.

"You betrayed me," Vera snapped.

"You weren't exactly being open with me," said Coco. "But what's done is done. We're going back to Paris tomorrow."

"I'm staying in Madrid."

"With what money?"

"I have friends here—*real* friends."

"You also have a passport stamped with a German visa. How do you think that's going to look when you try to get back into Italy?"

"I'll figure something out."

"I'm only paying for one more night at the Ritz." Coco removed an envelope from her handbag and handed it to Vera. "Here's your train ticket. I'll see you tomorrow." She took a final sip of her tea, flung her napkin on the table, and marched off to her room for a nap.

Early the next morning, Coco called Vera's room. When there was no answer, she asked the concierge to knock on Vera's door. The concierge reported that the room was empty. At the Atocha rail station, Coco stood on the long gray platform, her eyes darting about in search of Vera. When the train rumbled in at eight, the Englishwoman had still not appeared. Coco boarded a middle car and settled into the plush seats. "That ungrateful cow," she muttered as the whistle blew and the train sputtered out of the station, headed toward Paris.

On the long trip home, Coco felt beaten, crushed, depressed, and alone. She dreaded facing Spatz and his inevitable "I told you so." She wanted to be comforted, but she knew she would not find solace with her friends. Cocteau would probably make a joke out of the debacle, and Misia would no doubt scream at her for being a megalomaniacal idiot. As the train sped north, Coco's thoughts turned darker still. If the Allies won, and Spatz, Momm, and Schellenberg were arrested and revealed the Modellhut scheme under questioning, Coco could face charges for treason.

She wanted to make these wretched thoughts disappear, but her morphine was in her suitcase in the luggage rack above her head. She couldn't get to it without attracting the attention of the Nazi guards who patrolled the train. Then, an idea struck her. What if there was hard evidence that she really had gone to Madrid to scout boutique locations and that instead of abandoning Vera, she'd tried to help her? It would be her word against the Germans' (and Vera's, for that matter). She removed the letter she'd composed to Churchill from her handbag, ripped it into tiny pieces, and stuffed them in her pocket. Then she took a fresh sheet of Ritz Madrid stationery from her purse and began a new letter to Churchill, partly in English and partly in French, which Churchill spoke fluently:

My dear Winston,

Excuse me for disturbing you at such a grave time as this. I had heard that Vera Lombardi was not very happily treated in Italy on account of her being English and married to an Italian officer. You know me well enough to understand that I did everything in my power to pull her out of that situation, which, indeed, had become tragic as the Fascists had simply locked her up in prison. I was obliged to address myself to someone rather important to get her freed, and to be allowed to bring her with me to Madrid, where I am planning to open a boutique. That I succeeded placed me in a very difficult situation, as her passport, which is Italian, has been stamped with a German visa, and I understand quite well that it looks a bit suspect. You can well imagine, my dear, after years of

occupation of France, it has been my lot to encounter all kinds of
people! It would please me to talk over all these things with you!

    In short, Vera wants to return to Italy with her husband. I think
a word from you would settle these difficulties and then I could
return untroubled to France.

    I hope your health has improved.

    I remain always affectionately,

    Coco Chanel

When the train stopped at the border in Hendaye, Coco gave the letter
and one hundred francs to a French porter sweeping the platform. The
porter stashed the envelope and the money in his pocket. He promised, as
soon as he had the chance, to post the letter, which Coco had addressed
to 10 Downing Street, London.

Settled once again in her seat as the train left the station, she wondered
if the porter would mail the letter after all. Perhaps he would discard it.
Perhaps the Nazis patrolling the platform had seen him talking to her
and searched his pockets. A fresh wave of worry washed over her and
stayed with her, keeping her awake on the long journey home.

When she saw Spatz again at the Ritz the morning after her return, his
eyes were as hard and cold as blue agate, and she knew he'd understood
the cable she sent: "Friend unavailable. Coming home."

"That was a disaster, as I knew it would be," Spatz said. He stood
several feet away from her to avoid kissing her. "You've placed me—and
Teddy Momm—in a terrible position."

"I thought it was worth a try."

"This isn't your world. This isn't fashion. In diplomacy, if you make a
grave mistake, you can't rip out a seam and start again to make everything
right. Schellenberg will be furious."

"You'll think of some explanation, since you, unlike me, are so expert
in diplomacy," said Coco with icy sarcasm.

"No," said Spatz, anger pulsing in a vein in his right temple. "*You* are
going to explain it to him."

A week later, Coco was back in Berlin, sitting in a chair opposite Schellenberg's desk at SS headquarters. "Who knows about this?" the intelligence chief asked.

"You, Herr von Dincklage, and Captain Momm," said Coco. She made a point of looking directly into Schellenberg's eyes and keeping her voice steady.

"And this Lombardi woman?"

"No," Coco lied.

"She doesn't suspect anything?"

"Nothing."

Lying came so naturally to Coco, as naturally as breathing, and usually she assumed her lies were accepted as truth. Now, though, she saw suspicion in Schellenberg's narrowed eyes. Her heart began to pound, and her face grew hot. She felt her cheeks turning red and the flames spreading to her neck and chest. She looked out the window to escape the intelligence chief's gaze. Black cars lined the curb. A few men in Nazi uniforms strolled by. Coco took a deep breath and told herself not to worry. She'd always been the nimblest of liars. All she had to do was pretend she was telling the truth. It was easy.

The trouble was, she was not herself this morning. She felt old, exhausted, disheveled. The long train journey from Paris had been a nightmare, her car jammed with snoring soldiers and old men. Many tracks along the way had been destroyed by bombs, causing a series of lengthy delays, as the train had to wait its turn to be rerouted. Finally, the train arrived in Berlin at midnight, six hours late. An SS agent had met her and driven her to a small house on the edge of town where she was to spend the night. A glowering old woman, the owner of the house and the widow of a German official, showed her to a room on the top floor. It was small and unheated, with only one dim lightbulb hanging from the ceiling. When Coco had asked for water to wash, communicating by pantomiming a pitcher and basin, the old woman shook her head furiously and flailed her arms. "*Kein wasser, kein wasser*," she cried, saying in German that there was no water, and waddled out of the room.

In the morning, Coco dressed in a fresh set of clothes, combed her hair, applied a thick layer of powder and lipstick, and sprayed herself with No. 5 perfume, hoping it would hide her animal stench. She might have overdone it with the perfume, as the driver who transported her to SS headquarters kept glancing at her in the rearview mirror and rubbing his nose.

Schellenberg looked handsome and rested. *Oh to be young again*, thought Coco with a fierce yearning. If she were still in her thirties, it wouldn't matter that she hadn't slept or washed, that the powder she'd applied over her stale layer of makeup had cracked. That she had smudged mascara under her eyes. Nor would the disaster of Modellhut matter. He would still want her. Maybe he would lock the door and make love to her right there on the camp bed next to his desk, the horror of the war and all they had been through giving urgency to their passion. Her imaginings helped distract from her fear.

"You've gotten in way over your head, Mademoiselle Chanel." Schellenberg's voice drew Coco out of her fantasy, back to harsh reality. "I was wrong to trust you, but what's done is done. The important thing is that no one knows, that you never speak of it." He stood and walked around his desk, signaling that he had nothing left to say. "The mission never happened. Do you understand?"

"Clearly," said Coco. She'd come all this way just to be scolded like a naughty child. She shivered with humiliation.

"Good day," said Schellenberg, extending his hand to Coco and nodding his head with an elaborate politeness that hid his glacial disdain. "Have a safe trip home."

A few nights after Coco returned from Berlin, Spatz took her to Bignon's for dinner. Their usual waiter was absent, and they enjoyed a pleasant evening free of his hovering presence. As they left the restaurant, a gaggle of Nazi officers entered, talking loudly as they stomped snow from their boots. Coco and Spatz stepped into a waiting Mercedes, but they'd traveled only a few blocks when a cavalcade of police cars with lights flashing and sirens wailing sped past them toward Bignon's.

The next morning, they read in the papers that a group of Resistance fighters had burst into the restaurant soon after Coco and Spatz left. When the Resisters began shooting, the Germans returned fire. In the end, the death toll was twelve: four Nazi officers, three Resisters, and five innocent French citizens shot in the cross fire, including a young couple and their three-year-old daughter.

A week later, Bignon's reopened, but Coco refused to dine there again. "It's cursed," she told Spatz. "Besides, I never liked the food."

The Germans retaliated by executing twenty of the hundreds of Resisters being held at Drancy—five Resisters for every Nazi killed at Bignon's—lining them up in the courtyard at dawn and shooting them down. The Resistance struck back with more violence still. One morning, Coco walked out of the Ritz to find the body of a German soldier lying in the street, his uniform soaked in his own blood. After that, she refused to leave the hotel.

"People shouldn't live like this," Coco complained to Spatz.

"Then don't," said Spatz.

"You don't hear the bombs going off? The guns? The city is a battlefield."

Coco remained cooped up for weeks, spending long hours on the phone with Misia, the two women griping to each other about the Germans, the French, the state of the world. Her boredom was broken one day in January 1944, when Cocteau stopped by the Ritz. "I need you," he said. "I'm reviving my *Antigone* at the Paris Opera, and I want you to design the costumes."

"*Antigone*? It's all about defying authority, about a young girl breaking a king's law. What will the Germans say?"

"They're too stupid to understand the symbolism. And they're hoping some of the glory will blow back at them." Cocteau's 1922 adaptation of

Sophocles's tragedy, with sets designed by Picasso and costumes by Coco, had been a huge hit, widely recognized by the critics and the public as a stunning work of art.

"I don't know. . . . I'll think about it," said Coco.

Cocteau had no time to waste while Coco dithered, so he played the card he knew would bring her to his side. "We're using the same sets from 1922," Cocteau said. "Picasso, the genius of the art world, will be at the rehearsals."

"I was a genius before he was," Coco snapped.

"I know, my dear."

Coco thought of the wiry little Spaniard—Max had introduced them decades earlier, and she'd used all her wiles on the painter. Nothing had worked. "Pablo doesn't like aggressive women," Max had explained.

During rehearsals for the 1922 production, Coco had thrown extravagant dinners at her apartment on rue du Faubourg Saint-Honoré, hoping to lure Picasso to spend the night. He would show up for the food—hams and turkeys, caviar and pastries laid out on the table in Coco's dining room—but he rarely stayed longer than an hour. "Why am I always the one throwing the party?" Coco grumbled to Max one night after the guests had all gone.

"You've got the money," Max said.

"Sometimes, I'd like someone else to pay. . . . Like Picasso. He's rich."

"In his head, he's still a starving artist," Max explained.

"*You're* the starving artist, Max."

"*You're* starved for love."

That was cruel. Max apologized, and Coco brushed off the comment.

It had been years since she'd seen Picasso. Coco knew from her friends he'd stayed in Paris, tolerated by the Nazis because of his fame, despite what they considered the degeneracy of his art and his half-Jewish mother. "Oh, all right, I'll design your damn costumes," Coco told Cocteau.

He came over and hugged her. "We'll all be geniuses together again," he said.

One afternoon, during the final dress rehearsal of *Antigone,* as Coco sat at the back of the gilded Opera, Picasso burst through the door and jogged to a seat in the front row.

At the sight of the famous artist, cheers and applause rang through the house—from the actors onstage and from the group of society swells in the balcony who'd been invited to create excitement about the soon-to-open revival.

Coco abhorred being overshadowed by Picasso, especially since his rejection of her still stung. She stood to yell at Cocteau across the seats, half of them empty. "I have a question about costumes."

Cocteau blinked into the lights. "I can't be bothered about that now," he said sharply. "We need to rehearse."

Coco rushed the stage, making straight for the actress playing Antigone. She grabbed the hat she'd designed—a smart navy cloche with a brown ribbon—off the young woman's head and threw it on the floor.

Coco removed her own hat—a more structured beige felt model—and plopped it on the actress's head. "That will make the play," Coco said, as she strode triumphantly back to her seat.

Coco's costumes were extravagantly praised in the press, and she felt something she hadn't in a long time—the pleasant buzz of accomplishment. She attended a couple of performances a week and enjoyed soaking up the audience's applause. At the same time, the hard right wing heaped scorn on Cocteau. One critic excoriated him for his "effeminate" rendering of a Greek classic, with actors—in skimpier costumes than those worn by the actresses—mincing and gyrating across the stage. On the evening when fifty seats had been reserved for the PPF, the Fascist party, catcalls flew, and two members of the Milice, the French Gestapo, showed up toting machine guns on their shoulders. When the doorman refused them entrance, they punched him in the stomach and walked over his moaning body. Coco happened to be in the audience, but when she saw the Fascist thugs, she grabbed her handbag and fled.

In the following weeks, Spatz didn't press her to go out with him, until one night in early February he insisted she join him at a French-themed party at the home of German ambassador Otto Abetz and his wife, Suzanne. A French meal would be served and only French would be spoken. The invitation specified white tie for men and gowns for women—an exception to the government ban on long dresses, which the Reich had ordered to conserve fabric for the war.

"A French party? How deluded are they? Don't they know they're losing the war?" Coco griped to Spatz.

"A little delusion goes a long way," said Spatz.

"I'm staying home."

"Trust me, Coco. You want them to think you're still their friend."

Coco and Spatz argued about it for a couple of days. Eventually, she agreed to go, but she told Spatz, "This is the last time."

On the night of the party, Coco retrieved from her rue Cambon store-room a dress she had designed in 1939 for her last collection—a flouncy, ivory organdy gown with patriotic red, white, and blue floral embroidery. From a trunk, she pulled out a pair of shoes and an evening bag. She was not looking forward to the evening. The very idea of Germans playacting at being French disgusted her. But Captain Momm would be there, escorting his boss's mistress, Karin Mertin, and Momm was expecting Coco and Spatz to attend, too. Their failure to appear would be seen as disrespect to German officials. Above all, neither Coco nor Spatz wanted to do anything that might provoke Spatz's bosses into transferring him to Istanbul, as they continued to threaten.

The Hôtel Beauharnais sat on rue de Lille, where a shiny necklace of black cars blocked the street. Doors opened, and out stepped women in glittering gowns and men in white tie and black tails. Coco and Spatz mounted the elegant stone steps to the entrance, which was flooded with light from torches held by sentries dressed like Napoleon's soldiers in tall visored hats and blue coats. Inside, a long line of party guests waited at the lift, so Coco and Spatz took the curving staircase to the third floor. When they entered the Abetzes' apartment, the redheaded ambassador was standing on a gilt chair in the salon giving a toast—in French, of course. "Tonight we celebrate Paris, which stands for beauty and romance. We salute the beauty and romance in our lives."

As Abetz raised his glass high to spirited applause, Spatz leaned down to speak in Coco's ear. "No one's allowed to mention the war tonight," he said.

"What a relief," said Coco in a sarcastic tone.

"Or the Occupation."

"Not a word. Nor will we talk about the German defeat at Stalingrad."

"Please, Coco, keep your voice down."

"Or the British dropping several tons of bombs on Berlin. Or all the German ships that have been sunk."

"Hush."

The salon was jammed to a standstill with Germans chattering in French, trying to show off their mastery of the language and correcting one another's grammar. It hurt Coco's ears to hear beautiful French words spoken in croaking German accents. A sonata played by musicians buried behind a screen of potted palms wafted over their chatter. "Coco!" a voice behind her called out. She turned to see a small, shapely blonde gliding toward her—Suzanne Abetz. "We have the best of Paris here tonight," said the ambassador's wife, her eyes glittering. She wore emerald green floor-length satin by Lucien Lelong, head of the Chambre Syndicale de la Couture. "Lucien made this just for me," she said, holding out the skirt of her dress and twirling. "He's here, over there." Madame Abetz pointed her chin to the opposite side of the room.

Coco spotted the couturier, immaculate in his bespoke white tie and tails, talking to a German woman with an ermine stole draped around her marble shoulders. Though Lelong had persuaded the Germans to let high fashion stay in France, the Nazis had chipped away at French couture until there were only a handful of houses left. Recently, they'd ordered the closure of the few that remained.

Now, here was Lelong, chatting up a gorgeously dressed fraulein, as if the war wasn't happening, as if most of his customers weren't the wives of Nazis and war profiteers, as if he wasn't about to be put out of business entirely. Coco thought him arrogant and untalented. "What do men know about dressing women?" she'd often said. In general, she found fault with all designers, men and women. Still, she did not want to see Maison Lelong or any other French fashion house shut down. Paris without couture wouldn't be Paris.

Suzanne Abetz smiled at Coco and leaned to whisper in her ear. "I still prefer the clothes you made for me to anything Lelong or anyone else does. I wish you'd reopen." She straightened and spoke normally. "Isn't this marvelous? You'll see many of your friends here tonight."

Coco broke away and found Spatz in the crowd talking to Jean Cocteau. "Did you bring Marais?" she asked.

"He's on the terrace, fending off a mob of women," Cocteau said.

She glanced across the salon through the French doors and glimpsed Jean Marais, resplendent in a black tailcoat, signing autographs on cocktail napkins and gloves shoved at him by bejeweled, manicured hands. The actor's most recent film, *L'Éternel Retour*, had caused a sensation when it opened in Paris in October. It was a modern retelling of the Tristan and Isolde myth written by Cocteau, and Marais had played the doomed lover, Tristan.

Fans mobbed Marais wherever he went. Recently, a group of students, recognizing him in the Bois de Boulogne, had torn the actor from his bicycle and carried him to the Porte Dauphine Métro station, where Marais caught a train home.

"There's one particularly avid fan who keeps showing up at our apartment leaving letters and presents for Jeannot," said Cocteau. "Not only is she madly in love with him, but she wants him to help her become an actress. She's a silly little German named Karin Mertin."

"Oh, no." Spatz emitted a deep, unhappy sigh.

"You know her?" asked Cocteau.

"She's the mistress of his best friend's boss," said Coco. "Jeannot better watch out—she's here somewhere."

"Does the best friend know what she's up to?"

"Captain Momm? I doubt it," said Spatz. "Karin's only been in Paris a couple of weeks."

"Maybe you can tell us what to do. She comes over at all hours of the day and night. Disturbs the entire building."

"Coco will speak to her."

"I will?" Coco looked at Spatz as if he'd asked her to climb to the top of the Eiffel Tower.

"We'll discuss it later, my dear."

Coco and Spatz got champagne at the bar and strolled out to the large, glass-walled winter garden overlooking the grounds. Outside, bright moonlight suffused the black satin sky. The room was warm and jumping and filled with the siren smell of perfume mixed with the scents of exotic plants. German couples wandered in and out. They all seemed to know one another, and they laughed lightly as they spoke (in German, ignoring the party's French theme) about their children, their weekend plans, their country *schlosses* in the motherland. They acted as if they owned the world.

The party made Coco uncomfortable. She should have stayed home and dined with Misia in her Ritz suite, as her friend had suggested. Misia made a point of not attending German parties, but Coco's other friends were happy to be included. At least Coco wasn't as cozy with the Germans as Cocteau or Serge Lifar. Earlier, Coco had spotted the ballet master on the dance floor pushing an old German dowager around the parquet.

Dinner was a five-course feast served in the wedding cake dining room painted frosting white. Gilt boiserie drifted up the walls and around the ceiling. Paintings by Rembrandt, Velázquez, Rubens, and Titian, stolen from a Rothschild château, decorated the panels. "At least the Nazis have good taste in some things," Coco grumbled.

"You promised to be nice tonight," Spatz reminded her.

The guests sat on silk cushioned chairs at oval tables. Much to her dismay, Coco was seated next to the blustery, paunchy German Consul

General Rudolf Schleier. He brushed the back of Coco's hand with his prickly ginger mustache, bowing low and rattling the collection of medals on his breast pocket.

When the food arrived—potages à legumes, followed by fillet de sole—the general ate heartily. "In times like these, to eat well and eat a lot gives one a feeling of power," he said in gravelly bad French.

Coco took a bite of her sole, discovering it to be overcooked, and pushed her plate toward the center of the table so aggressively that she scrunched the white linen tablecloth and almost toppled her wineglass.

"There are far too few evenings like this," said Schleier. "It's a pleasure to see so many women in beautiful dresses." General Schleier paused long enough to shovel a pile of potatoes rissolés into his mouth. "I suppose they'd all be in Chanel if you hadn't retired."

"I'm never in retirement in my heart," said Coco.

"You should reopen in Berlin. As you might have heard, we're shutting down couture completely in Paris," said General Schleier.

"Are you also paving over the vineyards in Bordeaux and setting fire to the perfume fields in Grasse?" asked Coco. She smiled insincerely.

The general took a gulp of wine. "Mademoiselle Chanel, have you heard the German word *Lebensraum*? It means the space Germany is entitled to by the laws of history. It includes France."

Ignoring the crème brûlée a server had placed in front of her, Coco lit a cigarette and puffed on it distractedly, as General Schleier turned to chat with the woman on his left—the white-haired, elderly wife of a German colonel. A few moments later, he spoke again to Coco. "It's wonderful to see so many figures from French culture here tonight, embracing the nation of Goethe and Wagner," Schleier said. "I include yourself of course, Mademoiselle Chanel."

The lyrical notes of a waltz floated into the dining room. Spatz touched Coco's elbow and stood. "Let's dance, darling."

In the salon, Spatz pulled Coco to his chest and spun her across the room. "You were about to start an argument with the general, weren't you?" he said.

Coco tilted her head up to look into Spatz's eyes. "How can he be so smug?"

"He's a powerful man."

"I'm not afraid of him."

"You should be. His niece is Fraulein Lichten."

Coco dropped her hands from Spatz's shoulders. "So?"

"Every time I run into her, she asks me if you've been back to Saint-Benoît to visit your friend, the *monk*."

The waltz ended, and the little orchestra slid into a tango. Spatz reached for Coco's waist, but she stood like a statue. "Why is that suspect?"

"She doesn't believe Max is really a monk."

"Who does she think he is?"

"A Resister. I told her she was mistaken."

"Good."

"It's not good," said Spatz angrily, as he led Coco off the dance floor. "She knows it was a lie."

FOURTEEN

S oon after the Abetzes' party, Coco decamped to La Pausa. She was eager to lose herself in the peace and beauty of the country-side. Since all of France was now occupied, however, signs of the Nazis were everywhere: in the checkpoints manned by uniformed guards, in the swagger of the tall, fair-haired German soldiers strolling the dirt lanes with pretty French girls, in the swastika banners hanging from the front entrances of humble village halls, in the haunting emptiness of the homes and shops of those who had disappeared.

A few miles outside Roquebrun, Coco's car came upon a truck lying on its side in the middle of the road with the engine still smoking and the driver dead behind the wheel. A group of Nazi soldiers surrounded the truck. Their own jeep was parked a few yards away. Was the dead man a Resister delivering weapons or transporting Jews across the border? Had the Nazis run him off the road and shot him? She thought of Reverdy, of

GIOIA DILIBERTO

the British parachute buried in her garden, and his transmitters, which she'd flung into the river. She told herself she'd done that as much to protect him as herself and Céline. Where was he? Was he safe?

A wail of sirens filled the air, and a cavalcade of French police cars appeared at the crest of the road. The vehicles screeched to a halt by the truck. Coco's driver slowed down to get a closer look. "Move on!" she ordered.

As the Rolls speeded up, Coco looked over her shoulder and saw the Germans remove the body from the truck and lay it on the ground. That the dead man could have been Reverdy hit her with a jolt. Then she recalled she'd never seen him drive a car. She didn't think he even had a license. It wasn't Reverdy. It couldn't be. She wouldn't let herself imagine more disasters.

At La Pausa, the phone was ringing when Coco walked through the door. Cocteau was on the other end, asking if he and Marais could visit. The actor's crazed fans continued to stalk him day and night, and the couple wanted to escape the city. "Stay as long as you like," Coco told Cocteau. "It's quiet, and you'll be able to write."

On a cool Tuesday afternoon, Coco's driver fetched Cocteau and Marais from the Roquebrun train station. Winter still enveloped the Riviera, and the bare brown branches of the olive trees stretched against a gray sky. Cocteau and Marais found Coco in the large, white-walled salon, reclining on a sofa, reading a book. "My two Jeans!" she cried, jumping up to greet them. She was dressed in beige, wide-legged trousers, a black sweater, and flat shoes. "I've set up a writing studio for you next to your room," Coco told Cocteau. "There's everything you need—typewriter, paper, pens, ink. I ask only that you write something that requires costumes by Chanel." Designing for the *Antigone* revival had left her hungry for more work.

"I'm planning a new film project," said Cocteau. "A retelling of the classic fairy tale *Beauty and the Beast*.

Coco closed her eyes. "Already I see how Beauty should look."

Cocteau told Coco that the talented young actress Josette Day had been cast as Belle. "Perfect," said Coco. "Who's the Beast?"

"Me," said Marais.

"Jean wants to hide under a fur suit, as if that'll fool his fans," said Cocteau.

"I got mobbed in Saint-Benoît yesterday. It's as bad as Paris."

"You were in Saint-Benoît?"

"Visiting Max."

Coco sat up and lit a cigarette. "How is he?"

"Mourning his family," said Cocteau.

"They're all gone now," said Marais. "The ones who aren't dead have been arrested or deported. Max is sure he'll never see any of them again."

The handsome actor looked sternly at Coco. Though he would never criticize her to her face, Coco knew he deplored her relationship with Spatz. Cocteau had confided that Marais thought it unconscionable for her to be sleeping with a German when so many Frenchmen were suffering. "Well, you shouldn't be sleeping with *him*. You're way too old for him," Coco had shot back.

Marais had seen the suffering firsthand. He had volunteered for the army in September 1939 and fought the Germans on the Maginot Line before being demobilized after the armistice ten months later. As soon as Marais returned to Paris, he tried to join the Resistance. But the leader of the Parisian cells turned him down. "You live with Jean Cocteau, and Cocteau talks too much," the leader had said.

"There was a German captain billeted in Saint-Benoît who admired Max's poetry," Marais continued. "This gave Max a protector for a while. But the man has been transferred out of town. Max still has the priests on his side, and they're probably the reason he hasn't yet been picked up in one of the round-ups."

"We took him out to dinner," added Cocteau. "I don't think he'd had a decent meal in weeks."

"He has enough money?" Coco asked.

"He had to sell your bracelet," said Cocteau. "We gave him some cash."

"I can send him more."

"What he'd most like from you, Coco, is a visit."

"Perhaps on my way back to Paris."

Coco knew, though, that she would not be visiting Max again. Since Fraulein Lichten had told Spatz about seeing Coco with Max, Coco knew it was too risky. Lichten would probably suspect Coco, too, of working for the Resistance.

Céline set out a buffet of black-market food—lettuces, roast beef, shrimp in aspic, and fruit tarts—on the long table in the dining room. Only Marais ate heartily. Afterward, the friends played cards for a couple of hours in front of the fire. At ten, they went to bed.

Cocteau and Marais slept in the guest wing far from Coco's room. In the middle of the night, she was astounded to find herself standing in the hall with them outside their room. The men wore blue terrycloth robes and slippers. Coco was in white silk pajamas with black stripes and bare feet. In her right hand she held a large pair of scissors like a dagger. "What happened? How'd I get here?" she asked.

"You were sleepwalking," said Cocteau.

"What did I say?" Coco looked at the scissors she held, as if she'd never seen a pair. "Did I say anything embarrassing?"

"Nothing more than usual," said Cocteau.

"Tell me what I said," Coco pressed.

"You woke us up with a fugue-like monologue," said Marais. "You were standing by our bed waving your scissors and repeating, 'I closed my house! I never did business with the Germans! The others did—Fath, Lelong. They are the true collaborators!'"

"Oh God," Coco moaned.

"What did you take before bed?" asked Cocteau, his tone turning solicitous.

Coco stared at the carpet.

"The morphine is making you sleepwalk," said Marais.

The actor hated drugs. He'd been urging Cocteau for years to give up opium, and he hoped that finally Cocteau had kicked the habit for good. He had not smoked a pipe in two months. "If Jean can quit, anyone can."

"Come on, Coco Macbeth, time to go back to bed," said Cocteau, gently taking Coco by the elbow.

Coco let the men escort her to her bedroom. They watched from the doorway as she slipped under the beige satin quilt and pulled the sheet up to her chin. "With luck, I'll stay asleep now," she said.

At eleven the next morning, Coco burst into the dining room where Cocteau and Marais were drinking coffee. She opened a drawer in the sideboard, peered in, then slammed the drawer shut. "Where are all the scissors?"

"We gathered them up this morning and hid them," said Cocteau.

"I need a pair to cut flowers in the greenhouse."

"You'll have to ask Céline, or whatever you're calling your maid these days."

"You'll get rid of your drugs, too, I hope," said Marais.

Coco frowned at the actor. "I don't sleep without drugs."

"It's making you sleepwalk, which is dangerous. You could hurt yourself," said Marais.

"Or worse, one of us," said Cocteau.

"I only do it when I'm without Spatz."

He had promised to join her at La Pausa on Sunday, now four days away. Until then, she couldn't risk another sleepwalking episode with gossipy Cocteau in the house. Then she got an idea.

That night, after Cocteau and Marais had retired to their room, Coco went to her bedroom. She padded across the plush brown carpet and drew the satin drapes closed. She undressed, slipped on her pajamas, got into bed, and as Céline looked on, she injected herself with morphine. "I'm ready," Coco said.

Céline pulled two long pieces of rope from her pocket. First, she tied Coco's right ankle to a wrought iron spike in the footboard, then her left ankle. "Are you sure this is a good idea?" asked the maid.

"Yes," said Coco, not adding that it was what the nuns did when she sleepwalked as a child. She laid her head against the pillow and closed her eyes. "Stay with me, please."

Céline sat on a wood chair by Coco's bed, holding her employer's hand. Beyond the windows, a gentle rain had begun to fall, glistening the olive trees and the bricked courtyard. Coco thought she heard a nightingale, but it couldn't be—the nightingales had flown south for the winter and not yet returned. Maybe she already was asleep and dreaming of a long-ago time at La Pausa, a warm summer night, when she had a houseful of friends, laughing and drinking on the terrace. There were no Nazis in France then, and none now in her dreams.

FIFTEEN

The letter from Max was waiting for Coco when she returned to Paris. She sat on the settee by the window in her suite at the Ritz and tore open the envelope. The Gestapo had arrested him on February 24, and he was in prison at Drancy, awaiting deportation to a German concentration camp. A sympathetic guard had mailed the letter, which Max had written on a piece of notebook paper:

How ironic that I was at my desk writing my daily thoughts on Christ when the Germans came for me at eleven in the morning. I stuffed my rosary in my pocket, but when I turned to gather some of my books and other possessions, a German in a trench coat stopped me with a meaty hand on my arm. Outside, a little crowd, alerted by my landlady, had gathered on the sidewalk. An elderly doctor, who'd once treated me for shingles, handed me a bottle of scotch and a pair of wool long johns. I knew this day was inevitable. Though my neighbors might have closed their eyes to the horror unfolding around them, I could not. I had already lost my family to the evil unleashed in the world. I thought the priests could save me, but I'd been wrong. No collective expression of strength and courage could have stopped my arrest, no protestation from my landlady, from the doctor or the students I noticed lingering at the back of the crowd.

At the intake office at Drancy, the clerk asked me to empty my pockets. I had 5,520 francs, which I placed on the counter. He took them, then pointed to my wrist. I removed my grandfather's gold watch and gave that to him, too. They put me in a dank cell with two coughing, wheezing old men, and soon I was also coughing and wheezing. The doctor's scotch, which I shared with my cellmates, offered some relief, but the long johns little defense against the wet, bone-chilling cold.

This is my darkest hour, and I need your help. Isn't there something you can do?

Coco sat with a cigarette burning in her fingers and Max's letter in her lap. She stared out the window at the rooftops and windows that suddenly looked unfamiliar, like rooftops and windows in a foreign land. She imagined Max in a cell crammed with old men, a yellow star hastily sewn to his monk's cassock. Coco herself had taught him how to sew one rainy Sunday afternoon, when she was still living on rue du Faubourg Saint-Honoré. Max said he wanted to be able to mend his own shirts, so Coco showed him how to make small, even stitches in a square of linen. Only Max's stitches weren't very small or even. "You'll never be a tailor," she'd told him. "And you'll never be a teacher!" he'd shot back.

She wished he'd stopped wearing the cassock and cross, wished she'd pushed him harder to give them up. Everyone knew Max was a Jew. His pose as a monk only drew more attention to himself, made him stand out. He should have left France long ago, escaped to Switzerland when he had the chance. Now it was too late.

In the next hour Coco's phone rang twice—first it was Misia, then Cocteau on the other end. They'd received letters from Max, too, and Cocteau had started a petition that he hoped would persuade the Nazis to release their friend. Spatz urged Coco not to sign it. "Don't do it!" he'd told her. "The Germans are desperate, lashing out at anyone they think isn't with them 100 percent. Who knows what they'll do to you."

"Or *you*," said Coco. "This is Max. We have to act! Cocteau is coming by tomorrow."

The following afternoon, as a storm pounded Paris, Cocteau showed up at the Ritz with the petition for Coco to sign. He stood in the salon, rain dripping from his coat and puddling on the carpet. Coco had not asked him to remove the wet garment because she didn't want him to stay. Spatz was in the next room, and he'd be listening to every word of their conversation. She had to get Cocteau out of there fast so she could hide the petition and sign it when Spatz was out.

"You're not looking well," Cocteau said in a snide tone. His hair was freshly dyed an artificial auburn color, and white powder covered his face like a Kabuki mask.

"Neither are you." Coco stepped closer to Cocteau and peered at his chalky face. "What are you covering up with that powder?"

"This dreadful rash. I've got it on my back and legs, too."

"A guilty conscience reveals itself on the skin."

"Like your lines. And the circles under your eyes. And what became of your flesh? You've become an old bag of bones, Coco."

"I don't have a guilty conscience."

Cocteau removed a document from a pocket inside his jacket, unfolded it, and handed it to Coco. "You know why I'm here," he said somberly.

Coco read quickly:

Max Jacob invented a language of poetic images that expresses the depths of our French language. He is revered by all admirers of

literature and most especially by the youth of France, who respect
him as a great teacher.

He has been a Catholic for twenty years and long ago
renounced the world to live for God. The priests of the abbey
of Saint-Benoît will attest to his regular attendance at church.
They are among the many who salute his nobility, his wisdom,
his inimitable grace.

Our love for this dignified old man commands us with all our
hearts and our minds to do all we can to free him. We urge the
authorities to release him immediately.

"Poor dear Max," said Coco, as she laid the petition on the coffee table.

"Someone must have given him up to the Gestapo," said Cocteau. "He's been sick for a week now, and he grows weaker by the hour. I had extra blankets sent, but I doubt the guards delivered them. Before I came here, I stopped at the embassy and offered to take Max's place, but Abetz refused me."

Coco shook her head. "You knew he would. They only want *Jewish* inverts."

"I'm grateful I'll never be as cynical as you," said Cocteau.

"Did you really see Abetz?" asked Coco.

"I saw Von Rose, the Nazi in charge of pardons at the embassy. He's a reader of poetry, and he's assured me he can put pressure on Abetz."

Coco turned away and stared out the window. A raging rain splashed against the glass, clamoring to get in and drown her, wash her away with her carpets and antiques.

Coco's eyes scanned the twenty-five signatures at the bottom. They included Misia and José Maria Sert, Michel and Amélie Pelissier, and several French celebrities, including the popular actor Sacha Guitry, whose name had appeared on *Life*'s blacklist of collaborators.

"I don't see Picasso here," she said.

"He's not. I went to his studio earlier, but he was working and wouldn't see me." Cocteau stared hard at Coco, trying to catch her eye. "I haven't given up on Picasso, but your signature is more important. It would carry more weight with the Nazis. The Germans think Picasso is a degenerate. They'd love to get rid of him. But you have highly placed German friends. Won't Spatz help?"

"He isn't here," Coco lied.

"Did you even ask him?"

"No."

"My God, Chanel! One word from Spatz, one phone call to the embassy, and Max is free."

"You think it's that easy? You know what's going on. The Germans might shoot Spatz just for asking. Leave him out of this." They might also shoot *her*. Schellenberg had certainly looked like he wanted to kill her over the Modellhut disaster.

"What are you afraid of? That he'll leave you if you help a Jewish friend?" Cocteau pulled a pen from his pocket and held it out to Coco. "Spatz never has to know."

"What am I—a love-sick adolescent? I make my own decisions."

"Then sign!"

"It's dangerous." Oh, why hadn't Cocteau come when Spatz was out?

"This is Max!" Cocteau began pacing nervously around the small salon. "Are you still thinking that the Germans will win? So, you want a clean record, no pesky petition signatures to suggest you weren't on board with the Nazis?" His tone was brutal.

While Coco rummaged in a desk drawer for a new pack of cigarettes, Cocteau took a moment to compose himself. When he spoke again, his voice was low and humble. "I'm begging you. Do not turn your back on Max. This is your chance to stand against evil."

Coco blew out a cloud of smoke. "In case you hadn't noticed, evil is here to stay."

"It's redeemed by love and courage."

"You sound like Max."

"He used to say he was good at cheating God. Well, he no longer is. He needs you." Cocteau stared at Coco with a harsh, unflinching gaze.

"Think about it. You *have* to sign. I'll come back in a few hours. For once, Chanel, don't be selfish."

A moment after the door closed behind Cocteau, Coco slipped the petition under a sofa seat cushion. Spatz entered wearing a silk dressing gown and slippers. "Where is it?" he asked. His eyes darted to the coffee table, to Coco's tortoiseshell spectacles lying on top of a magazine, and a vase of faux camellias.

"Cocteau took it." A cigarette dangled from Coco's mouth as she fingered the strands of pearls looped around her neck.

"Usually, you're a good liar," said Spatz, upending the cushions on the chairs, then the sofa. When he found the petition, he ripped it up and tossed the pieces in the trash bin under the desk.

Turning her back on Spatz, Coco walked the length of the carpet to the hall and disappeared into the room beyond.

When Cocteau returned later that afternoon, the maid told him Coco was out. He asked for the petition, but the maid knew nothing about it. The next day, Spatz left for Berlin. He didn't tell Coco the reason for his trip, only that he had "business" to attend to. He was gone a week.

Coco passed the time smoking and reading. She barely left her suite at the Ritz, ordering her meals in and seeing no one but Serge Lifar, whom she knew wouldn't ask her about Max's petition. One night she awoke at three a.m., certain she'd heard faint screams coming from somewhere deep in the Ritz. In the morning she questioned the night maid. The old woman had also heard the screams. "Oh yes, Mademoiselle," the maid said. "The Nazis took away Madame de Kerdreor on the floor below. I saw them with my own eyes! She was in the Resistance and a communist, it turns out. Imagine, a communist at the Ritz!"

So, the Germans had been watching Madame de Kerdreor, the wealthy heiress of a family in Burgundy. They were watching Coco, too, she was sure. A chill shot through her as she recalled how Goering had showed up at her boutique the day after she failed to appear at one of Otto Abetz's parties.

Misia sent Coco an icily formal note to tell her that Cocteau had circulated a new petition, which he didn't even bother asking Coco to sign. He'd collected thirty signatures, five more than on the original document, and he'd submitted it to Ambassador Abetz that day, March 4.

Coco heard nothing more for a week. Then, on March 13, Misia called. She was sobbing so hard she could barely get the words out: Max was dead. He'd succumbed to pneumonia while the petition was still on Abetz's desk. "I want to organize a memorial mass," Misia said.

"I'll help you," said Coco.

"You'll help, but you wouldn't sign the petition."

"I hid it under the sofa cushion to sign after Spatz left. But he found it and ripped it up."

"And still you stay with him."

Coco had no answer.

"Don't ever bring him near me again!" Misia shouted, and hung up the phone.

Coco felt a heavy shame spreading through her body. *Max would have died in any case. He was sick*, she told herself.

Misia arranged a service for Max at Église Saint-Roch, the beautiful baroque church on rue Saint-Honoré. The earliest date available was March 21, a week hence. Without consulting Misia, Coco ordered flowers and hired a hearse. *I'll make the funeral beautiful. At least I can do that*, she thought.

The morning of Max's memorial Mass, Spatz urged Coco to stay home. "It's a bad idea to draw attention to your friendship with him," he said, standing in the doorway to their bedroom.

Coco pawed through the hangers in her closet. "I'm going." She slipped a black silk dress over her head. "If you won't call a car for me, I'll take my Rolls out of the garage."

"I'll call a damn car."

A half hour later, as Coco entered the church, dripping melted snow from her fur coat onto the stone floor, the Latin prayer for the dead rang out.

Requiem aeternam dona ei.

Grant unto him eternal rest.

The priest's low baritone bounced off the towering pillars and climbed to the domed ceiling. He waved a silver chalice, releasing a sharp tang of incense that hovered in a blue haze above him. Coco took a deep breath and fought the urge for a cigarette.

Strolling the long center aisle through bars of gray light slanting in from the vaulted windows, she scanned the pews, spotting Misia and Cocteau in the second row. Coco removed her fur and draped it over her arm. Melted snow seeped through the sleeve of her dress, and she shivered. The past week had been among the coldest of the war, with below-freezing temperatures and mounds of snow, coal in short supply even at the Ritz. She nodded to her friends and slipped into the pew beside them. They stared at the coffin in front of the altar surrounded by flowers and flickering candles.

Coco had designed the service as she'd designed her fashion collections, as a symphony of style with everything working in harmony. She erased all that was black in Max's death in a service that was all white: white flowers on the pews, white cloths on the altar, and white horses to pull the white coffin to the white eternal light.

It was all for show. There was no body to bury. The coffin was empty. Max's jailers had placed him in a pine box and lowered him into the ground in the municipal cemetery in a grave marked with a simple wood cross.

After Max's death, Cocteau never spoke to Coco about his petition. These were wretched times, when selfishness and opportunism collided with history. Who was Cocteau to judge Coco? For the past four years, they'd both been swimming through filthy waters. They'd both howled with the wolves.

Coco knew Misia would never forgive her. She also knew, though, that Misia would never stop loving and needing her. They were locked to the death in a battle of wills.

Ex lux perpetua luceat ei.

Let eternal light shine upon him.

After the service, Coco followed Misia and Cocteau outside into the cold afternoon. They strolled past the Nazi soldier standing guard on the church steps to keep an eye on the proceedings. All was quiet. Only a trickle of mourners had showed up. Pallbearers loaded the empty coffin into the waiting hearse. Pulled by the white horses, it would clatter around the block several times, then head back to the rental stable.

At the curb across the street idled a big black Mercedes with a chauffeur behind the wheel in a brimmed cap and white gloves. In the back seat, Spatz sat in a camel cashmere coat watching Coco through the frosted window. As she parted from her friends and strode toward the Mercedes, a wave of disturbance surrounded her. Women who recognized her stopped to stare. Men hurried away, made uneasy by the familiar Mercedes, the car of the Gestapo and almost the only car still on the streets. Couples folded into each other tightly. Bicycles wobbled by on the icy pavement.

Spatz reached across the seat to open the car door, and Coco stepped inside. He glanced at her for a moment with a blank expression, then looked away, as if she were someone he recognized but no longer wished to know. As the Mercedes glided from the curb, Coco sunk deeply into the dark leather seats. It was like floating on a black cloud, soft and languid, but also ominous.

A storm was coming, a storm against her, and it would be here soon.

SIXTEEN

Coco awoke to loud shouting from the street. It was still early. The pink light of dawn leeched through her bedroom shutters. Looking out, she saw barricades of broken furniture and cobblestones manned by shirt-sleeved young men and girls in summer dresses, a few wearing old World War I helmets, probably swiped from their grandfathers' closets. In the distance, gunfire. The low buzz of aircraft. Eleven weeks earlier, Allied troops had stormed the beach at Normandy. Soon, they'd be in Paris.

In the salon, Spatz sat with his suitcase in front of him, puffing frantically on a cigarette. He hadn't dressed down for the long journey ahead in the August heat. He wore a crisply pressed navy linen suit, a white shirt with gold cuff links, and a silver striped Hermès tie. "Get ready. We have to leave now," he said.

Coco pulled her robe tight across her body and shook her head.

"I'm tired of arguing with you," Spatz said. "You can't stay. You'll be arrested!" He crushed his cigarette in an ashtray. For two months, he'd been pressing Coco to leave with him when they still had a chance to get out of Paris safely. Though not impossible, it would now be much more difficult. Since the failed plot to assassinate Hitler on July 20 by a group of mutinous Nazis, it had become complicated for Germans to travel across borders, especially with Frenchwomen in tow.

"You know the Resistance has been keeping files on collaborators," said Spatz gravely.

Coco winced at the word.

Seeing her stricken look, Spatz softened his tone. "Please, darling, come with me."

For the past four years, he'd been Coco's constant protector, when she might have been thrown out on the street. Without his help, her nephew would have died in a German POW camp. Spatz had pursued her, and she'd fallen in love with him. But the disaster of Modellhut and Max's death had chilled her feelings. There was no way she was going with Spatz to Germany. She couldn't exist outside France. She'd rather be dead. *I'd blow my brains out, if I had to live one day in disgraced Deutschland.* She'd promised herself not to commit suicide while André was still alive. The young man was recovering steadily from tuberculosis and his ordeal as a prisoner. Coco often lunched with him and never let him know the horrible weight of worry and fear she now carried with her, like a pile of stones in the pit of her stomach. Even so, she'd take her chances in Paris.

Spatz grabbed Coco's arms and pulled her to him. She smelled the starch in his shirt and felt his heart beating. "We belong together," he said. He smiled at her, showing his boyish dimples, and for a moment she almost gave in. "I'll meet you in Switzerland, when everything blows over," she said.

She wasn't at all sure, however, that they would ever see each other again, and she saw in Spatz's narrowed eyes that he sensed the doubt behind her words.

Coco disappeared into her bedroom and returned a minute later with a wad of French money tied with a string. She handed it to Spatz. "This should get you across the border."

Spatz put a few franc notes in his wallet and slipped the rest in his suitcase, under a pile of neatly folded shirts. "Are you still going to your mother's home in Kiel?" Coco asked.

"It's as good as any place to hide out until the war is really over. I'll get word to you when I reach Lausanne," he said.

A boom shook the air, followed by whistles. A bomb dropping somewhere in the distance. "I better leave," Spatz said. He kissed Coco quickly and slipped out the door.

When he was gone, Coco felt a deep breath of freedom. In an instant, her status had changed. She was no longer living with a German. Her sense of solace, though, soon vanished, replaced by a profound emptiness more complete than anything she'd ever known or imagined.

She thought of Spatz lying on his side with his back to her in bed, one smooth, sculpted shoulder moving slightly under the white silk sheet with the rise and fall of his breath. There was nothing as intimate as sleeping with someone. She was old now. Her allure was gone. No one would ever want to sleep with her again. Tears welled behind her shut eyes. Holding her fists to her forehead, she fought the tears back.

She wouldn't indulge in misery. Her instinct was to act, to do something to cancel her pain. Pierre Reverdy had told her to call if she ever needed him, and now she dialed the number he'd given her. An unfamiliar male voice answered. "Please get a message to Reverdy as soon as you can. Tell him I need to see him," Coco said.

The man didn't ask Coco anything else and seemed eager to end the call quickly. "All right," he said, and hung up.

Two days later, on August 24, the French army marched into Paris, liberating the city. German General Dietrich von Choltitz surrendered, mercifully deciding not to destroy the City of Light, as his troops departed. Looking out the window, Coco saw young men tearing down the swastika from the entrance of a bank and hoisting a tricolor flag in its place. She watched a boy clamber up the pole at the corner of rue Cambon and rip the German street sign from its post.

Coco decided to view de Gaulle's victory parade from the balcony of José Maria Sert's apartment, which had a perfect view of the Arc de Triomphe. Leaving her suite on the morning of the parade, she found the lift out of service and took the front stairs. The hotel had been steadily emptying for several weeks. In their haste to flee, the Germans had left behind a mountain of clothes and documents, and hotel employees were burning them in the bathtubs. Snowfalls of gray ash swirled through the long carpeted halls. The lobby resembled a train station—porters hauling luggage, trunks stacked near the entrance. At the checkout desk, lines had formed twenty deep.

Outside, the streets were unpassable. Not even a bicycle could get through the raucous crowds. People talked about the twenties as *les années folles,* yet Coco had never seen anything as crazy as what she witnessed now. In the doorway of an elegant hat shop, a couple was having energetic sex. When Coco looked away, she saw a dozen women stripped to their underwear and shackled together being led up the street by two laughing FFI soldiers.

Coco crossed the Place de la Concorde just ahead of the victory parade. In Sert's apartment she found Misia and the artist on the balcony, with a small group of friends waving little French flags. Coco leaned against the iron railing and saw de Gaulle, exceptionally tall and regal, standing in an open car. The crowd below roared, and the little party on the balcony cheered. "Everything about him is larger than life—his ears, his nose, his hands," said Misia.

"How do you know? You can't see in front of your face, let alone to the street," said Coco.

"I *feel* his presence," said Misia.

"De Gaulle's speech yesterday was so stirring." A man's voice came from behind. Coco turned and saw the lawyer Michel Pelissier. He looked elegant in a crisply pressed linen suit and a tricolor cockade pinned to his lapel. "I caught the speech on the BBC, and it almost made me cry. '*Paris ravaged! Paris broken! Paris martyred! But Paris free!*' I was glad the general gave credit to the Resistance, and all the sons and daughters of France, except, as de Gaulle put it, a few unhappy traitors who gave themselves over to the enemy." He looked directly at Coco, and she felt her face burn.

"Everyone's in the Resistance now!" she blurted. She knew she should have kept her mouth shut, but she couldn't help bludgeoning her way through arguments. "Every outlaw in town has taken up arms in the name of the FFI. It's just an excuse to raise hell."

Misia frowned at her. "I wonder if Cocteau and Marais are getting a better view than us. They're watching the parade at the Crillon."

Shots rang out from a nearby rooftop, and the tanks surrounding de Gaulle fired back, violently shaking the air. The cigarette dangling from Coco's lips fell to the floor.

At the Ritz, the concierge handed Coco a message from Pierre Reverdy. She was to meet him at the statue of Hannibal in the Tuileries at two. It was now one forty-five.

Coco hurried through the streets under a lurid blue sky. The blazing heat took on a sinister feel. Her blouse was soaked, and her skirt clung to her legs. She found Reverdy sitting on a bench in the shade of a chestnut tree. Great shafts of white sun slanting through the branches cast his face in a saintly glow. He stood as Coco approached. "You wanted to see me?" He looked sharply at her.

"You've heard of Baron Louis de Vaufreland?" Coco said.

"We've been looking for him for four years. He was responsible for the arrest of ten of our men in Morocco. The Gestapo shot them all," Reverdy said.

"I know where he is."

Reverdy's eyes widened, and Coco continued. "He's staying with Count Jean-René de Gaigneron."

Coco handed Reverdy a slip of paper with an address. He studied it a moment, then ripped the paper in tiny pieces and dropped them in his pocket. "I have to go," he said. No "merci." No kiss. He stood, and, turning quickly on his heel, walked away.

Coco sat on the stone bench and lit a cigarette. Her eyes followed Reverdy as he hurried down the long, tree-lined allée, until he was nothing but a black dot in the distance. When she finished her cigarette, she smashed it on the ground and started home.

It felt good to turn over Vaufreland to the Resistance. *If he rats me out, it'll be his word against mine,* Coco thought, *and who will believe a nasty parasite like him?* With Vaufreland out of the way, she could breathe easier. She had helped the Resistance nab a reviled enemy! They wouldn't dare arrest her now.

Coco skipped dinner, swallowed two Seconals—she was running out of morphine—and went to bed early. As she drifted off, she thought of Spatz. She wouldn't worry about him. His perfect French, his sunny charm, his extraordinary good looks would carry him safely across the border. In a few months, they'd rendezvous in Switzerland, where they'd enjoy a lovely, romantic holiday. She let herself feel comforted, safe.

Six days later, the doorbell rang.

AUGUST 30, 1944

ehind the table in the dingy room at the Prefecture of Police, the Interrogator pressed his mustache with his lower lip. Nazis had occupied the building until a few weeks before, and the pungent smell of the black goop they used to shine their boots still hung in the air. Coco puffed on a cigarette and with her free hand worried the gold buttons on her jacket. Finally, the Interrogator asked, "Did you and von Dincklage first become intimate that night in July 1940 when you returned to Paris?"

Coco couldn't believe his rudeness. The Germans had been chased out of Paris, only to see French brutes like this man take control. With no real authority and no higher power to answer to except his God, he could do anything to her he wanted: shave her head, strip her, beat her, shoot her. A cold current of panic coursed through her. She felt dizzy, as if she might pass out. Fighting to steady herself, she took a deep breath and willed herself to be strong. "Do you know Pierre Reverdy?" she asked. "He's a close friend of mine, and a member of the Resistance. I gave him some very important information recently, and he'll vouch for me."

"Never heard of him," the Interrogator said.

The Resistance was a jumble of separate organizations with no central control. Reverdy wasn't part of the FFI. "You have heard of Winston Churchill, though." Coco rummaged through her handbag and pulled out a small, framed photograph of herself with the prime minister. "That's Winston and me boar hunting in the Aquitaine," she said, setting the silver frame on the table.

On her way out that morning, she'd grabbed the photograph off her bedroom bookshelf. She'd also jotted down the prime minister's private phone number from her personal address book and taken a cache of his letters from her lingerie drawer. "Winston will tell you. I'm as much of a patriot as de Gaulle."

Coco dropped the packet of letters on the table and pushed it toward the Interrogator. "Please, look at the letters."

The Interrogator frowned but took the packet.

"We were good friends, as you'll see from our correspondence," Coco said confidently.

The Interrogator opened the top letter, read it quickly, and tossed it aside. "This is nothing—a thank-you note for gifts you sent Churchill's wife—typed by a secretary, probably."

"There are many notes handwritten by Winston himself." Coco's voice came out more shrilly than she intended.

The Interrogator glanced through several other letters.

"Churchill loves me," Coco continued. "He admires smart women. I was a change from all those British snobs he was meeting at country house parties, those silly women who did nothing but get drunk and sleep with other people's husbands. English *men* are different. They're gentleman, civilized. Spatz got his polish from his English mother. To me, he was an Englishman."

"I suppose you thought those other Nazis who stayed at the Ritz—they were Englishmen, too? Goering, Goebbels, Himmler. You passed them every day, in the lobby, in the dining room, on the stairs."

"I didn't see them. For me, they weren't there."

"You could have gone to another hotel."

"All the best hotels in Paris were taken over by the Germans."

"But not every hotel had a giant swastika hung over the entrance."

"The Eiffel Tower had a giant swastika hanging off it! It was impossible to avoid the damn swastika!"

"But you didn't even try to avoid Nazis. You and Spatz dined out every week at Bignon's, the Gestapo's favorite restaurant."

Coco hesitated. How much did these *salauds* know about her? "Spatz liked the food. But we stopped going after that awful shooting incident—four French citizens killed and a baby girl!"

Coco detected the Interrogator's lips quiver slightly under his mustache.

"Four Nazi officers eliminated," he said.

Coco shook her head. "I hate violence."

The Interrogator glared at her a moment, then moved on. "You have a house in the country. You could have stayed there."

"Where did you spend the war? Here in Paris, like me?"

"Please answer the question," the Interrogator persisted.

"I had a very good reason for staying in Paris. I was working hard to have my nephew released from a German prison. Spatz helped me. He notified German officials on my behalf, and we managed to secure André's freedom. Otherwise, he would have died."

"Your nephew was released two years ago, and still you stayed with your Nazi at the Ritz."

Coco didn't respond, but glanced at the boy scribbling notes, his head bent over his notebook, one beefy forearm lying at an angle on the table, his thick wrist and fingers as white and smooth as a baby's. He looked nothing like her nephew, who, like all the Chanels, was dark, short, and slender-limbed. Yet there was something in the boy's expression, an innocence and gentleness, that recalled André.

"Young man," said Coco, nodding toward the boy.

He looked up.

"You remind me of my nephew. He's left-handed, too. A good boy, as I'm sure you are."

The boy glanced nervously at Coco, while the Interrogator leaned back in his chair and regarded her carefully. "A very touching observation," he said. He continued to stare, studying Coco's face. She had the feeling he kept waiting for her to do something or say something—some kind of acknowledgment or confession. But she was a hard stone no one could crack. She'd made sure of that.

Coco removed a slip of paper from her purse and laid it on the table in front of the Interrogator. "That's Churchill's private line," she said, nodding toward the paper.

The Interrogator sat motionless with his arms crossed over his chest.

"This is ridiculous," said Coco. She lunged for the phone, grabbed the receiver, and held it out defiantly. "Call Churchill. Ask him about me."

The Interrogator took the receiver from Coco and replaced it. "Sit," he commanded.

Coco hesitated, then dropped into her chair. "Please call Churchill. He'll put an end to this wicked farce."

The Interrogator regarded Coco with smug authority. "I don't think Churchill can help you now."

"You think I was pampered by the Germans?" Coco said sharply. "Because of Spatz? Because they let me live at the Ritz? Well, you're wrong. They took my suite away and stuck me in a pair of maid's rooms. And that's where I stayed."

The Interrogator scowled. "Still, the Nazis were going to help you reopen your fashion house. You were dying to go back in business with the Germans."

"You're crazy!"

"Really?" The Interrogator reached in a file and pulled out a yellowing copy of *Ce Soir* with the article about Coco's relaunch. "What do you make of this?" He handed the clipping to Coco.

She glanced at it for a moment and handed it back. "I remember that story. I *did* think about reopening. The Germans were pressuring me, and I didn't feel I could out and out turn them down."

"You were willing to do business with the Nazis when you knew they were butchering Frenchmen?"

"I never met a dress that committed murder."

"You're rich. You didn't need the money."

"I'm not as rich as everyone thinks. Anyway, I never did reopen my house."

The Interrogator returned the clipping to his file, carefully arranging it in place, as if he had all the time in the world. After a while, he said, "But you did work with the Germans. You designed costumes last January for the Paris Opera's revival of *Antigone*—a production approved by the Nazis."

"*Antigone* was about an act of resistance! Which you'd know, if you'd paid attention in school."

"I'm well aware of the symbolism of *Antigone*."

"Then I don't have to tell you Antigone is a heroine, a brave girl who defies authority. She's willing to die for her beliefs." Coco drew herself up dramatically and recited from memory a line of the play. "*I can say no to anything I think vile, and I don't have to count the cost.*" She continued. "It's a play I know well. I designed costumes for the 1922 production at the Théâtre de l'Atelier. And my costumes got more attention than Picasso's set or Cocteau's direction, I'll tell you that!"

"You could have said no to the Nazis," the Interrogator argued. "You didn't need to work with them."

"It's very easy now, when the war is ending, to act brave and tough," Coco said. "But even just a few months ago, no one would refuse the Nazis unless they wanted to die."

The Interrogator stood abruptly. "Come with me. I want to show you something." He took Coco firmly by the arm and led her to the window. She looked out to the square below. Men wearing FFI armbands and rifles slung over their shoulders stood in small groups smoking and chatting. One had his foot on the empty chair where a half hour before a young woman had sat while her hair was shorn. Fluffy brown and blond clumps cluttered the ground. Coco thought of the little piles of fabric scraps that collected every day under the worktables in her atelier. The youngest of her workers, the adolescent apprentices, would sweep the scraps from the floor. The next morning, the snipping would start again, a cutting away that created beauty from disorder, unlike this barbaric shearing, which only added to the chaos of Paris.

"Within an hour, four women like you will be brought here for punishment," the Interrogator said. "A shopgirl from the rue du Bac, the concierge at the Hôtel des Marronniers, the cashier in the glove department at Galeries Lafayette, and the wife of a pharmacist who had a child by her German lover."

"You give haircuts more than once a day?" Coco said, jerking her arm free.

"France has a lot to avenge," said the Interrogator.

"On poor, helpless girls. Yes, avenge yourself on them."

"You're hardly a girl."

Coco glared at him. He was trying to goad her into an outburst. She fought to control herself and said carefully, "I'm Coco Chanel. France knows me. You can't put me up as a spectacle."

"Let the citizens of Paris see you for what you are. It's important for the nation to know that it's been betrayed by some of its most famous celebrities. You won't feel so arrogant after I parade you up and down rue Cambon with a shorn head. Your perfume customers will know what you've done, and Chanel No. 5 will start to stink to high heaven. It will be so worthless you might as well dump it all in the Seine."

Coco turned and strode back to her chair. She lit a cigarette with shaking hands. "I bet you spent the past four years hiding in the woods, while the Germans tromped all over France!"

The Interrogator resettled himself behind the table without responding. Growing more frantic, Coco continued. "What do you want from me?"

"To start, tell us where von Dincklage is."

"I've already told you, I don't know." Coco sighed deeply. "What else do you want?"

The Interrogator paused before responding. "Admit what you've done. You've collaborated with the enemy of France. You have aided the Nazis and supported their vicious cause to your advantage. You have used your fame and money to live in comfort while millions of your fellow citizens suffered. You have committed outrageous treason against your country and its people." He leaned forward while Coco recoiled. "Admit your guilt."

Coco couldn't breathe. The air had been sucked out of the room and now the walls were closing in. She looked at the floor for a moment and closed her eyes, summoning the strength of will that she knew was within her, the hard determination that had gotten her through every crisis of her life so far. She opened her eyes, and when she raised her head and saw the Interrogator's stony face with its ludicrous mustache, she knew how to respond. "Who are you to judge me?" she said in a firm voice. "Your pals in the Resistance did much more damage than I ever did. Look at the innocent people who died whenever they derailed a train or shot up a restaurant."

The Interrogator drew himself up proudly. "I'd rather sacrifice a few innocents and die myself to end Nazi rule."

Coco eyed him coldly. "Most people want to live no matter who rules."

"If you're not fighting the Nazis with every breath, you're one of them."

"You'd imprison the doctors who treated German children?"

"Yes."

"The bakers who sold the Germans bread?"

"Yes."

"And beggars who accepted coins from Nazi officers?"

"Yes."

"Even beggars need to eat."

The Interrogator picked up the scissors lying next to his files, and as he distractedly fingered the handles, the sharp tips pointed toward Coco. "Collaboration or resistance. That's what it comes down to in the end for all of us."

"You'd condemn an entire nation?"

"Not the ones who were deported."

Coco crushed her cigarette on the floor and made her voice steady. "Would you use those scissors on the *Mona Lisa*? You wouldn't, would you? Because she's a national treasure. Well, I'm as valuable to France as da Vinci's masterpiece."

"Because you've helped some rich women get dressed?" The Interrogator took a deep breath and, loosening his grip, let the scissors fall to the table.

"Everyone has to wear clothes."

"Not six-thousand-franc dresses."

Coco turned to the boy. He'd been writing furiously in his notebook, but he hadn't yet said a word. "Young man," Coco asked, "if you could afford it, what would you drink—champagne or table wine?"

The boy lifted his head and looked at her with wide eyes. "Champagne!"

"So, you can talk."

The boy's face brightened. "We always had champagne around the house. My uncle is a wine broker. He saved the cellars at Clos de Varlet from the Germans. Also Château René Chasse."

The Interrogator rapped his hand on the table. "That's enough, Raoul."

Sensing an opportunity, Coco pressed. "How exactly did he save the wine—by drinking it?"

The boy's expression fell, his round white face turning red. He was like a child, with a child's inability to mask his emotions.

At that moment the big black phone rang, and the Interrogator picked up the receiver. "I'm in the middle of—Give me a minute." He hung up and shot a pointed look at the boy. "I'll be right back. Keep an eye on her—and don't talk!"

The Interrogator left the room, shutting the door behind him with a hostile click.

Coco lit another cigarette. Her mouth was getting dry from all the smoking. She cleared her throat. "So your uncle was a wine broker," she said.

"He dealt with all the best Paris hotels and restaurants."

Coco let her eyes wander from his frayed shirt cuffs to his cheap cotton pants. "You must be from the poor side of the family."

"The Lebel family isn't rich, but we're proud."

Coco cocked her head. "Is your uncle Lebel, too? Antoine Lebel?"

"Yes." The boy looked at the floor, his voice a whisper.

Coco smiled slyly, pleased with herself. "I know Uncle Antoine. He sold wine at the Ritz."

"He's a hero." The boy scowled at Coco.

"He kept the wine flowing throughout the war in the Ritz dining room, all *les grands crus*. Your uncle Antoine also kept a very nice car, a gleaming, custom-built Hispano Suiza. I noticed it parked outside. Hard to miss that car."

"He bought two Jewish wine châteaux so he could save them for their owners and return them after the war."

"He didn't buy them so he could do business with the enemy?"

"Never! He saved the best wines for the French. He gave the Germans duds."

"You call the Château Ausone's Bordeaux a dud? Or the Château Lafleur Pomerol? I saw a lot of those bottles on the tables of German officers. Uncle Antoine dined every week with the *weinführer*. They'd walk arm-in-arm through the lobby."

The boy hesitated, then blurted, "He was putting on an act, pretending to be the Germans' friend."

"It's all right. You're not your uncle," said Coco in a gentle tone. "A nice man, by the way. Very cultivated. Speaks English *and* German beautifully."

"I would never speak German," said the boy. "I'm a Resistant of the first hour! I joined before Serge!"

Coco looked toward the door. "Serge—is that the name of your colleague?"

The boy nodded.

"Is he your boss?"

"I'm his assistant."

Coco made a small show out of considering this information. "So, as you were saying, Raoul, even though you are Serge's assistant, you joined the Resistance before he did."

"A couple of years ago, my best friend was arrested for refusing to sell tobacco to a German soldier at his parents' shop. When they took him to the Field Kommandant for questioning, I was waiting by the side of the road, so I could give him a basket of food my mother had prepared. His face had been beaten to a pulp. His eyes looked like blue-and-black balls. Ever since—"

The door swung open, and the Interrogator returned. "They've got two of the women, and they're waiting for two more," he said.

The boy shifted nervously in his seat. "Did you see the major?"

"No."

The Interrogator looked back and forth at Coco and the boy. "What's this?"

Coco smiled at the boy, and his face flushed. "Nothing. Your little deputy is a good soldier."

The Interrogator started rummaging through some file boxes on the floor. When he couldn't find what he wanted, he stepped into the hall, where more boxes were stacked.

"My uncle despised the Nazis," the boy whispered. "He loaned his car to the Resistance to transport weapons. He saved the Roths-child's wine cellar. We have a letter from Baron Philippe of Château Mouton-Rothschild."

Coco cocked her head toward the door. "Is your boss investigating Uncle Antoine, too? No special dispensation for friends and family?"

"He *will* be cleared."

"If they can find him. He's disappeared, no? I haven't seen him around since the Liberation. Where is he? Hiding in one of those Jewish wine cellars he bought?"

"My uncle is not a traitor." The boy's lower lip puckered out.

"Maybe I can help," said Coco.

The boy gaped at her. He seemed so young, still an adolescent barely out of short pants. "How?" he asked.

"Charlie Ritz, who owns the hotel, is a good friend of mine. He can keep Uncle Antoine safe until this madness blows over. I'll talk to him."

"Talk to who?" asked the Interrogator, reentering the room with a sheaf of papers.

"You. I'm afraid this boy has confessed that he's not very good at taking notes."

The Interrogator glared at the boy. "I told you, Raoul, no talking. Do you want me to throw you out?"

"Why are you employing children?" Coco asked.

"He's old enough."

"For what? To play at policeman, jury, and judge?"

"To judge you, yes, on your anti-Semitism."

"What?"

"You deny that you're an anti-Semite?"

"Where are you getting this information?"

The Interrogator stroked his mustache with his left index finger and thumb as he read through the papers he'd just brought in. When he found what he was looking for, he said to Coco, "At a dinner party at the home of Misia Sert you went into a long diatribe against the Jews, though a member of the Jewish Rothschild family was present."

"Who told you that?" Coco recalled how she'd gotten carried away that night. Even Spatz thought she was out of line. She wondered which of the guests had spoken against her to the FFI.

The Interrogator looked amused at what he was finding in the file. "Apparently, you made quite a scene, ranting about the Jewish furrier you claimed had been cheating you since you started your business."

"He *was* a crook."

"Given your anti-Semitism, I'm not surprised you lived with a German."

"I have many Jewish friends, many . . ." Coco stumbled briefly. "The playwright Henri Bernstein. Max Jacob . . ."

"Jacob, the poet?"

"We were very close." Coco stared into the Interrogator's dark eyes. "I'm not anti-Semitic. I'm anti–whomever is annoying me at the moment."

The Interrogator abruptly turned away to sift through his box of files. He pulled out folders, perusing the documents inside, and then returned the folders to the box. It seemed he was forever searching through his documents. Coco watched his expressionless face. He was just like any other dour, self-important Frenchman, she thought. He looked almost familiar.

Did he know about Modellhut? Were there any records of her trips to Berlin? Did he have copies? After several minutes of silence, Coco reached for her packet of correspondence from Churchill. It still sat tied with a pink grosgrain ribbon on the table in front of her. If the Interrogator was going to delve into his evidence, she would delve into hers.

As Coco began reading through her letters, the Interrogator glanced up. He regarded her for a moment, then, seemingly uninterested in what Coco was doing, returned to digging through his files. Coco scanned several letters, mostly short, all typewritten and probably dictated to Churchill's secretary. Then she came across one that was handwritten on thick ivory paper. Churchill's elegant, slanted handwriting suddenly struck her as odd, a contrast to his bloated, blustery self. From the embossed heading, Coco saw that this letter came from Château Woolsack, one of the Duke of Westminster's hunting estates in the Aquitaine. Coco slid the letter across the table toward the Interrogator. "Here's one you should see," she said.

The Interrogator looked up from the document he was reading but ignored Coco's letter. He had another matter he was eager to pursue. "You bought a lot of petrol," he said.

Coco frowned. "So?"

"It was severely rationed, yet you went way beyond the limits. How did that happen?"

"I have no idea. My driver bought it. I gave him the money, and he found it."

"You didn't think that was strange?"

"I didn't ask. He's very enterprising."

The Interrogator studied her for a moment, then returned to his files. A few moments later, he asked, "Did you use the gas to take trips in your Rolls-Royce?"

"The Rolls stayed in the garage." As soon as Coco said this, she realized she was caught. How else could she explain the gas? So she quickly added, "We took it out a couple of times, when I went to the country."

"Did you have a permit?" The Interrogator narrowed his eyes. "The Germans issued only a few thousand auto permits, and only to doctors, midwives, and firefighters."

"I don't know," Coco said. "Ask my driver." Then, after a pause, "No, I didn't have a permit."

"But you never got stopped when he drove you around?"

"That's correct."

"Wasn't it strange that you were able to drive around in a car, unlike almost every other French citizen?"

"Young man, everything about the last four years was strange."

The Interrogator dove back into his files for a moment, then lifted his head abruptly. "Did you ever consider paying a bribe to get the Germans to release your nephew André Palasse?" he asked, as if the idea had suddenly struck him.

"No!" Coco grimaced. "Why would I?"

The Interrogator shrugged. "People did."

"I wouldn't know where to begin. Besides, Spatz was working on André's release."

"But it moved slowly, didn't it?"

Coco sighed and ran her hands along her thighs, smoothing the wrinkles in her skirt. "You know the way the Germans operated," she said. "Everything very precise and official. Their bureaucracy worked slowly, like all bureaucracies."

The Interrogator lifted a file out of the box and fanned some documents on the table in front of him. "Why did you write a five-thousand-franc check to Countess Virginie de Fontenay?"

Coco's pulse jumped. He had her bank records! She couldn't believe the effort these barbarians had put into excavating her past. "I give away a lot of money. It may be hard for you to understand, but I believe in charity."

"She's a countess. She doesn't sound like a charity case."

"If you didn't notice, a lot of formerly wealthy people have fallen on hard times. Virginie worked as a newspaperwoman, but she couldn't do that during the Occupation."

"You only wrote the check on July 18 of this year, as the Allies were closing in on Paris. You didn't by any chance give her the money so she wouldn't write about you and von Dincklage?"

"No!" cried Coco, stamping out her half-smoked cigarette on the floor. "The countess visited my apartment, crying—she didn't even have enough money to buy bread. She was desperate." As she spoke, Coco recalled that rainy morning, several weeks earlier, when Virginie de Fontenay had shown up at the Ritz in tears. Coco went immediately to her desk and took out her checkbook. Of course, it had passed through her mind that the countess would never dare write a cruel word about her now. But nothing was ever said to cinch such an arrangement. It was just a passing thought. Coco told the Interrogator, "Your fury at the Nazis has warped your views of all mankind. You find the worst possible motive for every action. Sometimes people are simply kind. Can't you accept that?"

The Interrogator's demeanor remained impenetrable. "Mademoiselle, it's hard to accept kindness as a motivating principle from someone who spent the last four years living with a Nazi."

Coco's panic rose again. Everything she had done, everything she now said, would be twisted to cast her in an evil light. She nodded to the documents on the table. "If you have my bank records, you'll see that I wrote many checks to people in need. For many years I've been the chief benefactress of the Asylum of Saint-Agnes Orphanage. I'm always willing to share what I have."

The Interrogator pulled a stack of checks from a box on the floor and flipped through them. "A lot of these checks went to your friends who were higher than you on the social ladder. Jean Cocteau, Misia Sert."

Coco bristled at the idea that Misia and Cocteau were higher than she, but she held her tongue. "I gave help where it was needed," she said, pointing to her bank records. "You'll find lots of checks to Max Jacob there. He was hardly of high social standing. And he was a Jew."

The Interrogator continued to ask questions about Coco's finances—detailed, tedious queries on specific checks and deposits. Her payments to the Ritz, outlays for wine, royalties from her company, checks she wrote to people she now couldn't even identify. Was Felix LeClair the upholsterer? Or the man she hired to clean the drapes in the rue Cambon apartment? Coco's patience quickly wore down. "How am I supposed to remember now?" she demanded. "That was years ago, and we've all had a lot on our minds."

Ignoring her complaint, the Interrogator ran through several more payments. When he finally stopped, he meticulously gathered the checks and other documents into a neat pile on the table but didn't return them to the box. The boy took advantage of the pause to shake his arm, relaxing it after an hour of steady note-taking.

For a moment, Coco let herself hope they were finished with her. Then the Interrogator asked evenly, "Why do you think von Dincklage was interested in you?"

Coco frowned. "That's an idiotic question."

"He's a strapping, handsome fellow with a history of pursuing women. Even when he was married, he had many affairs. You've heard of Hélène Dessoffy?"

"What are you getting at?" Coco said icily.

"Why would such a dashing rake take up with a much older woman?"

Coco's rage roiled her stomach. She felt red blotches heating her cheeks. She knew what the Interrogator was trying to do—provoke her into an incriminating outburst. She took a deep breath and responded calmly, "I've had men after me my entire life."

The Interrogator nodded, as if accepting Coco's boast. "What exactly did von Dincklage tell you about his work?"

Coco snorted. "Work? Spatz didn't work."

·"Didn't he go out every day? What did he do?"

"He saw his friends. They played cards. Lunched. Smoked cigars. Sometimes they went golfing."

"Weren't there times when you dined with von Dincklage's friends?"

"Not often."

"When you did, you must have listened to some interesting conversations—perhaps you heard talk about Nazi business?"

"Yes, they discussed military maneuvers with me because couturiers are expert in such matters."

"Did you ever tell them things that would be useful to the Nazis?"

"I have no idea what would be useful to a Nazi. No, I never told them a thing."

"You don't think von Dincklage was using you?"

Coco swallowed and shifted in her seat. "I am my own person," she said. "No one uses me."

The Interrogator pressed. "It looks to me like a quid pro quo. Von Dincklage smoothed life for you in Occupied Paris. You helped him spy on your countrymen."

"That's absurd!" shouted Coco. "I hated having the Germans here. I gave them nothing. They didn't turn me into a collaborator!"

Cries and banging rang up from the courtyard below. The Interrogator and the boy looked at each other, and the boy scurried to the window. "They're bringing the women in now," he reported.

The Interrogator strode over and looked out. "The crowd is back—bigger than before. The citizens are demanding justice." He returned to the table and, opening one of his files, examined a note inside. "Why did you have a German visa issued for Madrid?" he asked.

He doesn't know about Berlin and Modellhut, Coco thought with relief. She could explain away Madrid. Coco pursed her lips, then spoke in a measured tone. "I had to go to Spain to discuss business with the people who distributed my perfume."

"You weren't spying for von Dincklage?"

"No!"

"You didn't report back to him about what you'd heard?"

"I told him I'd been to a lot of long, loathsome dinners."

"I understand you livened up a few of those dinners. At the home of Christopher Whittlespoon you said some pretty nasty things about France."

"You can't believe gossip," she said.

"This was reported by a member of de Gaulle's Free French Intelligence Service."

"He needs a hearing aid, or was it a woman who made that up? You can't trust women. I know, I've been dealing with them my entire life."

"You're a woman—are you lying?"

"I never lie."

"While you were in Madrid, did you meet any members of von Dincklage's spy network?"

"Almost everyone I met was British."

The Interrogator pulled another folder from his pile of evidence, opened it, and stabbed his finger on a document inside. "After you got back, on November 4, 1941 didn't you go to the avenue Kléber offices of the German military command?"

"How can I possibly remember what I did that day?"

The Interrogator's eyes roamed quickly over the document. "You spoke to Kurt Blanke, the German official in charge of ridding the French economy of Jews. You argued that since your partner Pierre Wertheimer was a Jew, the company you jointly owned, Chanel Parfums, should revert wholly to you, a Christian French woman."

"Wertheimer was taking 90 percent of the profits!" Coco said in a loud, shrill voice.

"You went to the Gestapo for blood!"

"Oh, please. Wertheimer and his family were safe in New York. They fled as soon as the Germans arrived. I never would have reported Pierre if I thought he was in physical danger."

"Your denunciation could have sent Wertheimer to his death."

"Pierre didn't die, and I didn't get my company back."

"Why not?"

"The Germans couldn't see through Pierre's ruse. Or else they were corrupt, like everyone else."

"You thought sleeping with von Dincklage would get you everything you wanted," the Interrogator said.

"Spatz only wanted to protect me and keep me safe. We weren't hurting anyone."

"Just a typical couple," the Interrogator said snidely.

"Have you ever been in love?" Coco asked.

The Interrogator's expression darkened, and Coco sensed the sorrow beneath his hard façade. "What happened? You were in love with a girl in the Resistance, and it turned out badly?"

The Interrogator stared at Coco with his mouth clenched, his lower lip peeking out from his mustache. His steeliness rattled her, and she reacted in a burst of words, filling up the silence with chatter. "Maybe your girl wasn't in the Resistance. Maybe she left you because you wouldn't quit. You young men are all alike. You want to be heroes. You'd rather throw petrol bombs in the Métro than make love."

When Coco stopped talking, the Interrogator kept his gaze on her for a moment. Then he opened a file and ran his fingers along a thick sheaf of papers, causing them to flutter.

Coco was growing fatigued from fending off the Interrogator's questions. Did he really not care that she had friends in high places? "Churchill understood my work. Whenever he came to Paris he visited me in my atelier. He sat on a little footstool and watched me drape and pin. He was fascinated by my creations—and it didn't hurt that he got to see the mannequins in their underwear." Coco paused a moment and nodded toward the packet of letters. "You don't believe Winston and I are good friends, do you? Read that one on top." Coco pointed to the letter she'd pulled out before. She hoped the Interrogator didn't notice her trembling finger.

The Interrogator unfolded the letter and looked it over.

"Winston always said I was the smartest woman he knew," said Coco. "You need to release me. I've shown you that I have important friends. What kind of future will you have, once I tell them how you've treated me?"

The Interrogator tossed the creamy sheet of stationery back onto the table. "I'm not going to waste my time reading this," he said.

"Then I'll read it to you." Coco snatched up the paper. "'My Dearest Coco,'" she began in heavily accented English.

The Interrogator lurched across the table and grabbed her wrist. "Drop the letter," he ordered.

Coco tried to pull her hand away, but the Interrogator stood, shoving the table and scattering his files on the floor.

"Serge!" cried the boy, springing up.

The Interrogator's grip was strong and painful. His eyes flashed. Coco dropped the letter. The Interrogator fell back into his seat as the boy hurried to pick up the spilled files and place them again on the table. Before sitting down, he said quietly, "Serge, can I talk to you a minute?"

The Interrogator scowled. "Not now."

"Just for a minute."

The Interrogator nodded toward a corner of the room, and he and the boy walked there. Though taller and bulkier than the Interrogator, the boy slouched and whispered nervously in his boss's ear. The Interrogator responded angrily. The conversation went back and forth like that for a minute or so.

Coco tried to overhear but could make out nothing. She sensed that the boy was taking her side, maybe urging her release or at least arguing that they hold off on further action until the mysterious major appeared. She thought she might find an opportunity and called out in a light voice, "What are you two whispering about? You know, I'm used to men whispering about me. There was a time I couldn't go anywhere without them following me down the street."

The Interrogator and the boy stopped talking and stared at Coco. Her tone turned solicitous. "I have a lot of admirers. Who would you like to meet? Churchill? It would be difficult, but I could arrange it."

The boy looked to the Interrogator, but he just glared at Coco. She added quickly, "Someday this madness will end. Then what will you do? There are a lot of people I could introduce you to. I know everyone."

"Yes, all the high-ranking Nazis who occupied Paris."

Coco shook her head in exasperation.

The Interrogator returned to the table with fury sparking in his eyes. For a moment, Coco thought he might hit her.

"You didn't meet Goering and Goebbels? Himmler? Did you meet Hitler when he came to town?"

"Don't be ridiculous!"

The Interrogator stretched back in his chair, watching Coco. She was pale and wide-eyed, sitting rigidly with her hands tightly clenched. When she spoke again, she forced herself to sound calm. "I'm a patriot just like you."

"You are nothing like me," snarled the Interrogator.

Coco unclenched her hands and leaned slightly forward in her chair. "No, I would never presume to play God."

"This is about collaboration, not religion."

"Ask his uncle about collaboration," said Coco, pointing her chin toward the boy, who was slumped in his seat taking notes. He looked up and stared at Coco with a panicked expression. "Ask Monsieur Lebel why the Germans allowed him a special permit to drive on Sundays."

"He had to work! He needed the income to live!" the boy shouted, canting up suddenly from his seat.

"On Sunday?" Coco snorted. Even she didn't work on Sundays during the years her fashion house was open.

A plane rumbled overhead. An Allied fighter jet flying low, throwing a shadow across the window. How long had Coco been inside this room? An hour? Two? She felt the day slipping away, and with it her freedom, her life. She thought about what she would be doing now at home, probably reading a book and smoking. A surge of nicotine need hit her, and she reached into her pocket for her cigarette case. The small gold rectangle encrusted with diamonds felt solid in her hands. Boy Capel had given it to her. After he was killed, she wanted to forget him, so she'd given the case to Misia, who'd admired it one night while they were dining in her apartment. "It's yours," Coco had said, placing the case in Misia's hands. It pleased her to be generous with her money and possessions—one of her few truly good qualities.

But soon after making a gift of the cigarette case, Coco realized she didn't want to forget Capel after all. So, one day, when Misia pulled out the lovely object during a fitting in Coco's studio, the couturière had demanded it back. Misia had thrown the case at Coco's feet and stormed out. The two friends hadn't spoken for several weeks after that.

What she should have done, Coco thought now, was to have simply asked for the gold case, instead of making a scene in front of the manne-quins and giving them something to gossip about behind her back. Why did she sabotage herself? The Interrogator was right. She should have sat out the war at La Pausa, or better yet, gone to Switzerland. She could have avoided arrest entirely. She would never have encountered Spatz.

Coco inhaled a long, calming drag, then pointed her cigarette at the Interrogator. "At least I was trying to do something positive."

The Interrogator snorted loudly. "You call consorting with Nazis *positive*?"

"I resisted in my own way. I certainly didn't contribute to the killing, which is more than either army or you and your colleagues can say. All those lives lost, innocent lives. You know, I almost got killed myself. I'd just left Bignon's on the night of the massacre."

At the mention of Bignon's, the Interrogator flinched, then lashed out at Coco. "Why is it everyone who knows you says you're a bitch?" he demanded.

"Am I on trial for being unpleasant?" Coco looked hard at the Inter-rogator. What had happened in his life, what sorrows had he endured, to make him so angry?

"This morning, when you looked in your shaving mirror, what did you see?" she asked. "In the middle of last night, when you couldn't sleep, what did you think about?" Coco had a genius for detecting weakness, and she was not surprised to see pain ripple across the Interrogator's face. In a moment, though, it shifted into an angry glare.

"I thought about you," he said, nodding toward the window and the square beyond. "Down there with the other German whores."

The Interrogator licked his thumb and ran it through a sheaf of papers from one of his files. When he found what he was looking for, he stopped and read a note pinned to the top of the page. "Did you enjoy yourself at the Abetzes' French party?" he asked.

Coco winced at the thought of having to defend her attendance at that dismal event. "Contrary to what you think, I did not like associating with Germans. Besides, it was a stupid party."

"Why did you go?"

"I felt an obligation to Spatz, to others. Remember, my nephew owed his freedom, his life, to Spatz."

Unmoved, the Interrogator continued examining his notes, flipping from one page to another. It struck Coco suddenly that he wasn't actually reading the materials, but just nervously shuffling papers around. "You ate dinner every week at Bignon's, the Nazis' favorite bistro," he said.

"It's a public place, for God's sake."

The Interrogator leaned across the table toward her. "Here's what you don't understand," he said. "In your world of luxury, of parties and restaurants, there was no war. You laughed and drank champagne that Nazis sent to your table. You raised your glass to them across the room and invited them to come to your boutique for perfume. You were one of them."

"Nonsense!"

"Really?" The Interrogator sat back, an amused expression on his face. "I myself have seen you saluting the Germans with a raised champagne glass."

"Were you at the Abetzes' dinner, too?" Coco's voice was hard with sarcasm.

"You should be careful what you say when dining out."

Coco stared hard at him.

The Interrogator bowed his head deferentially. "Would Mademoiselle care for dessert?" he asked.

Coco's eyes opened wide in a flash of recognition. "My God! The waiter! I knew I'd seen you before." The Interrogator's now-huge mustache hid half his face. If he'd been clean-shaven, she would have recognized him easily.

Coco shivered, as her evenings with Spatz at Bignon's came flooding back. The dark paneling and burgundy flocked wallpaper, the waiter hovering, standing too close to their table, listening to their conversations. Then she remembered who she was and drew herself up. "Is this all because I sent a fork back?"

The Interrogator smirked.

"You were a terrible waiter," Coco said.

"I'm no longer in that line of work."

Coco recalled the many times she'd been rude to this man at Bignon's. He was punishing her for her arrogance as much as anything, she was sure. That and her relationship with Spatz.

"Do you think arresting me is going to win you the Legion of Honor?"

"I am simply a patriot."

"You think I'm not?"

"I love my country."

"You think I don't? I've spent my life here. In my work, I've drawn on all I know, all I love about France, her traditions, her beauty, her elegance, and I revolutionized one of her great arts. I tapped what was in me, what I was born with, what my country had made of me. I *am* France!"

Shouts rose from the courtyard. The boy jumped to the window and looked out.

"What's going on?" asked the Interrogator.

"I don't know. I can hear people arguing, but I can't see them." The boy started for the door.

"No," said the Interrogator. He hunched his shoulders and tugged on the cuffs of his shirt as he stood. "I'll go."

When he'd gone, Coco turned to the boy. "Who is this mysterious major?"

"I don't know. He's in the Central Office. I've never met him."

"He sounds like a reasonable man," said Coco softly. "I heard you talking about him when your friends brought me in. He wanted you to wait for him, didn't he?"

The boy shuffled his feet nervously.

"When he finds out you didn't wait, you'll be in trouble."

"I've been taking my orders from Serge."

"The major is *his* superior, true?"

The boy looked at Coco but said nothing.

"I don't trust your boss, do you?"

"I don't know. . . ."

"They're looking for your uncle. What do you think the FFI will do to Antoine Lebel when they find him?" Coco leaned back in her chair and regarded the boy through lowered eyelids. His face contorted with worry. "I think you should call the major and stop this travesty before it gets out of hand. Do you have his number?"

Coco reached for the phone, picked up the receiver, and held it out to the boy. "Make the call," she said. "I think the major will appreciate your loyalty, and it could help your uncle. And once I'm out of this place, I'll do my best to help as well."

The boy remained fixed in his seat.

"Tell me," Coco said in the soft tone she'd used with her nephew when he was young. "How did you end up working in this place? I imagine you growing up in a quiet town with nice parents."

Like a guilty child, he leaned forward in his chair and poured out the story of how he ended up with the FFI in Paris. "At home, the most dangerous thing I did for the Resistance was join a raid on the town hall. I was given a rifle and told to stand lookout while the leader of the cell and a group of other Resisters broke the lock on the front door. They stole a few identity cards and ration tickets.

"Then one day after the Liberation, a group of fighters who'd been hiding out in the woods showed up at our farm. My mother fed them and put them up for the night. The next day I drove with them to Paris.

We ended up at the Prefecture, where I ran into Serge on the stairs. He asked me if I could take notes, and here I am."

Coco crushed the tip of her cigarette with her shoe and pushed it into the pile of butts on the floor. The smoky mess of ash and white stumps ringed in red lipstick revolted her, and she felt her stomach turn. "Can you get me a glass of water?"

During her working days, that simple request made during the *pose* in her studio had always struck terror in her seamstresses and mannequins. She'd never been known to ask for a glass of water when she was pleased with their work. The request for water was always a precursor to a litany of complaints about crooked pleats and ill-fitting sleeves, about too-wide hems and too-narrow seams.

The door opened, and the Interrogator strode in. He'd heard her request.

"No water," he said without looking at Coco as he took his seat behind the table.

"What? This enormous building, and there's no water?"

"You can have some when we bring you down."

The longer the Interrogator refused to look at her, the more Coco babbled on. "Doesn't anyone ever clean this place up? How difficult is it to mop the floors? On my way in I saw a heap of garbage in the entrance mixed with human hair." She lit another cigarette and talked around it. "Why punish women for behaving foolishly in love—something we've all been guilty of at least once in our lives? It's men who commit the atrocities of war. Look at what the Resistance did at Bignon's. Maybe you'd understand, if you'd been there and seen it."

The Interrogator looked up with an expression of smug satisfaction. "I planned it."

Coco pulled the cigarette from her mouth and stared at him. This stiff former waiter constantly shuffling through his files didn't seem capable of planning a road trip vacation, let alone a terrorist attack. But he had access to the reservation log. He knew when the German officers were coming in. She wasn't surprised he'd botched the job, with so many innocents killed.

"You're a murderer!" she cried.

The Interrogator sneered. "I killed Nazis. I didn't fuck them."

Coco turned away sharply. The Interrogator continued. "Someone informed, and the Nazis arrested me. Your friend von Dincklage was there in the townhouse where they'd brought me. He didn't see me, but I recognized him when they led me past the salon where he was talking and laughing with his friends. On the top floor, there were cells where they questioned and tortured prisoners."

"Spatz would never torture anyone," said Coco. She drew on her cigarette and expelled a lungful of smoke.

"No, he was too refined. He left that to others. They beat me so I could hardly stand. They wanted me to tell them where my colleagues were."

"Did you?"

"I didn't tell them a thing."

"I see you survived."

"I escaped."

"You escaped from a Nazi torture chamber?"

"They were so pleased with their savagery that they forgot to lock the door. I got out down the fire escape."

Coco regarded the Interrogator with an expression of stunned disbelief. She drew a deep breath, then laughed. "You fool! They let you escape. They followed you, and you led them to your colleagues."

The Interrogator's hands tightened into fists, and his jaw clenched.

Coco sensed her advantage now and pressed. "The Nazis probably killed them all. It's a wonder they didn't kill you."

Trembling, the boy asked, "Serge, there was a farmhouse of Resisters in Sarlat who all got shot. And your fiancée, Valentine—wasn't she there, too?"

"Shut up!" the Interrogator screamed.

"So, you're responsible for the death of your own fiancée? And how many others?" Coco said sharply.

"We were at war!"

"*I* didn't kill anyone."

His face red with rage, the Interrogator reached across the table, grabbed Coco by the hair, and jerked her head toward the files on his desk. "These are the innocent deaths," he cried. "Tens of thousands. Murdered by people like you who lived high while the Nazis crushed our country."

Coco struggled to pull free. She gripped the edge of the table and twisted her shoulders. After a protracted struggle, the Interrogator released her with one sharp yank of his arm. Coco fell back into her chair.

The Interrogator was still standing, leaning over her with a murderous look. "It's all here—your betrayal, your treachery, your corruption. Your guilt. You fucked the enemy and you liked it."

"How dare you speak to me like that."

Coco rose to her feet again. She wanted to slap the Interrogator hard across the face, but he lunged for her throat.

"Stop it, Serge!" The boy shoved the Interrogator, who stumbled backward, then righted himself, teetering from side to side.

Suddenly, the door creaked open, and the lawyer Michel Pelissier stepped into the room. "What's this?" he demanded.

Coco was astonished to see him. "Michel! My God, what are you doing here?"

"Are you the major?" cried the boy.

"That's right," said Pelissier.

He nodded to Coco and turned to the Interrogator, who was rubbing his chin. "What's going on? I was to question her, not you. And those women downstairs? You heard the orders. The head shaving is to stop! This comes straight from Colonel Rol-Tanguy. Haven't you seen the posters all over town? There are reprisals for soldiers who disobey his orders."

"I didn't know," the Interrogator told Pelissier. He covered his mouth with his hand, as if to hide his lie.

Pelissier spoke sharply. "We're not barbarians. We have more civilized ways to deal with collaborators. Once the government has been reestablished, we'll have courts for official trials."

Sweat beaded the Interrogator's face. Coco noticed that under the table, his knees were shaking.

As Pelissier took Coco's hands in his and kissed her on each cheek, her expression relaxed into a smile. She felt tears coming and tried to hold them back, but they overflowed in a single burst. "What are you doing with these *salauds*?" she cried.

"My dear Coco, these are good men," said Pelissier. He removed a handkerchief from his pocket and gave it to Coco. She wiped her eyes. Pelissier moved away to perch on the wood table with his hands folded in front of him. "We're on the same side, though they've been on the front lines, while I've worked behind the scenes. I've had plenty of time on my hands these past four years; my law practice hasn't exactly been thriving."

"I never dreamed you were part of the Resistance. Does Amélie know?"

"No. Wives don't know. I wanted to tell her, but it's necessary to follow the rules."

"What about Misia and Cocteau?"

"None of our friends know." He smiled without warmth. "Amélie, by the way, thanks you for the dress you gave her from your stockroom."

"Oh, that old thing."

"She still wears the clothes you made for her before the war. I especially love that navy silk gown splattered with silver paillettes. It reminds me of the night sky in Provence."

"I wore that dress myself. It was the hit of the 1939 spring collection, my last."

What a glorious career Coco had created for herself, defining the new with simplicity, purity, and cleanliness. And now look at her. She was sixty-one and exhausted. She knew she must look a fright. And what was to become of her? She closed her eyes. A fantasy défilé of gorgeous dresses floated around her, designed by her much younger self. But when she looked again at the filthy interrogation room with the stained walls and trash-strewn floor, she could no longer count on those memories of beauty that had always been her shield from despair.

Pelissier was not the only aristocrat in her social circle who spouted leftist views while enjoying a luxurious life of grand houses, servants, cars, bespoke suits, and couture. At dinner parties over the years, she'd heard these men and women voice their support for unions and labor laws, and, more recently, de Gaulle and the Resistance. But Coco hadn't thought Pelissier or the others would actually act on their beliefs. Still, at that moment, she was glad to see him. "It was nice to see you at Sert's the other day," said Coco. "I haven't seen you much—just at Misia's Bastille Day party and that time I ran into you at Bignon's." Was it a coincidence that he had been there? Or was he helping to collect information on her and Spatz?

"Amélie and I have stayed mostly at her mother's old place in Bordeaux, as far from the Occupiers as we could get," said Pelissier.

He removed a lighter and two cigarettes from a case in his jacket pocket. He clamped one cigarette between his thin lips and offered the second to Coco. She took it, glancing furtively at the Interrogator as Pelissier lit both sticks. "This man understands nothing," she said, taking a long, sibilant drag. "Collaboration or resistance. That's it."

"You and I know things aren't that simple." Pelissier blew a jet of smoke out the side of his mouth. He stood and moved away from the table, toward the window. "Has Spatz gone back to Germany?"

Coco shifted uncomfortably in her seat. "Yes."

"She knows where he is, but she won't tell us!" blurted the Interrogator.

"I don't," Coco said evenly.

Pelissier shot a fierce look at the Interrogator, then turned to Coco. "I remember when I first met Spatz. It was at one of Hélène Dessoffy's parties on the Riviera."

"She never paid her bills on time."

"Did you know that she and Spatz were lovers? Even recently? You must have heard."

Coco felt a coldness spread through her limbs with a sharp sense of betrayal. She fought against it. So what if Spatz slept with Hélène Dessoffy? Virile men always had women on the side. Boy Capel did.

The Duke of Westminster did. Reverdy was married, for God's sake! Fidelity was for lovers in cheap novels. Anyway, Dessoffy had nothing to hold Spatz, except her soft docility. *That* he could get from many others. But from her—only from her could he get elegance and sophistication matched by intelligence and achievement.

"I'm sorry, Coco."

"Dessoffy is a moron. She has fat arms, like white sausages," said Coco.

"I agree, she's not too bright. She thought Spatz was a harmless diplomat. He fooled me, too, all those years ago on the Côte d'Azur." Pelissier paused for a moment and moved away from the window, toward Coco's chair. He faced her directly. "Back then, Spatz chose Hélène because she had a house near the naval base in Toulon, where a lot of classified materials were kept. Her late father had been a high-ranking naval officer, a hero of the first war. Spatz was trying to learn secrets about French navy operations, a job made easier by the officers he met at Dessoffy's parties. Spatz told me he was working as a journalist. He said he'd been thrown out of the German diplomatic corps because he was married to a Jew, a Jew he no longer was in love with, so he'd taken up reporting for a newspaper on the Riviera. I felt sorry for him."

"Spatz can take care of himself," said Coco.

"But he needs women to cover for him. He needed Dessoffy. She helped him flee to Switzerland in 1939 when war broke out between France and Germany. Dessoffy wrote letters to Spatz in Switzerland, which French intelligence agents intercepted, and . . ."

"I know all about that."

"What I'm sure you don't know is that while Hélène was in prison, Spatz slipped over the border to visit her mother at her home in Toulon. When the maid showed Spatz into Madame's sitting room, he got right to the point. If Madame Dessoffy would agree to receive Spatz's German colleagues from time to time and share interesting information with them and arrange meetings for them with the French naval personnel who revered her husband, Hélène would be released immediately. Madame

Dessoffy refused, even at the cost of her daughter's freedom. A few weeks later, having no evidence against her, French authorities released Hélène. By then, though, Spatz had no use for her. He had you!"

Pelissier turned to gaze out the window. He sighed deeply. When he looked again at Coco, his face blazed with disgust. "You spent the war with a German spy!"

Coco looked at her hands folded in her lap and let her mind drift out of the interrogation room. She wondered where Spatz was, what he was doing. Had he reached the border yet? Would he be in touch soon? She imagined them together at the Beau Rivage Hotel in Lausanne, in a room on the top floor overlooking the lake. She fought to hold on to that vision, as an image of Spatz huddled in the corner of a prison cell with captured German soldiers filled her head.

Pelissier's voice brought her back to the present. "Spatz was perfect spy material with his charm and fluency in four languages," said Pelissier. "In Berlin he'd been trained in the finer points of spy craft. He'd learned to be empathetic, observant, enterprising, and secretive, and he soon warmed to his role. Espionage had its dangers, but it was better than being shot at on the battlefield."

Coco lifted her gaze and forced her voice to sound firm, confident. "Do you have your car? Can you take me home?"

She knew Pelissier wasn't there to help her, but if she *willed* him to have pity on her, if she applied the force of her ferocious strength of mind, he would save her. Perhaps.

Pelissier ignored her request. "Ordinarily, I don't fault a woman for falling in love, for being in the grip of a passion that leads her to act foolishly. I might even forgive her vile politics, especially if she's been manipulated by a lover. And I might—under certain circumstances—even excuse a woman's opportunism."

Coco scowled at the Interrogator. "*He* wouldn't. You saw how he attacked me. He's bullied and threatened me all morning."

Pelissier stood in front of the table, making his body a barrier between Coco and her accuser. "You think I should arrest him and forgive you?"

"We've all suffered these past four years. We've all been forced to do things we didn't want to do."

The Interrogator snorted loudly. "Like spy for the Nazis in Madrid."

Pelissier wheeled to face him with a stern frown. "Serge!"

"Like murder innocent people!" Coco cried.

"A sacrifice for France!"

"Enough!" Pelissier straightened his tie. He walked to the window, wiped the sill with his hand, and leaned against it as he addressed Coco. "You were fond of Max Jacob?"

"Max?" Coco said breathlessly. "We were close friends."

"Did you think that because Max was a Jew he deserved to die?"

"Of course not!"

"Max Jacob liked to play the clown. So many people mocked him to his face. But he was a talented writer. Your friend Jean Cocteau thinks Max's best poems surpass those of Apollinaire."

"Max was nuts. So are a lot of writers."

Pelissier held his hand out to the Interrogator. "Do you have the Jacob letter?"

The Interrogator pulled a wrinkled piece of notebook paper from one of his files and gave it to Pelissier.

"After he was arrested by the Gestapo last February, Jacob wrote to you," Pelissier said. "One of our men got it from your maid." He smiled at the Interrogator.

"You could have asked me, and I would have given it to you myself. I have many letters from Max," Coco said.

Pelissier held the letter out to Coco at arm's length, as if she had vicious germs he didn't want to catch. "Read it," he said.

Coco took the piece of paper and skimmed it quickly. "I remember this," she said, handing it back to Pelissier.

"What did you do for him?" he asked.

"After Max had been arrested, there was nothing I could do. There were lines you couldn't cross."

"Your Nazi lover wouldn't have approved?"

"I did what I could."

"Then why didn't you sign the petition Cocteau gave you for Max's release?"

"What petition?"

Pelissier strode to Coco's chair and peered into her face. "Your lies stop here, Coco. You know exactly what petition."

Coco shifted nervously. "Ask Picasso why he didn't sign it."

"I'm asking you. Jean Cocteau told me he urged you, he pleaded. Did you think he wouldn't talk? He's the biggest gossip in Paris."

"I could tell you a few things about Jean Cocteau. He wanted to marry me. There were rumors that he had! He thought I could cure him of his homosexuality as well as his drug addiction. He had more German friends than anyone. Every week he had lunch at the German Institute and got a hard-on for all the handsome Nazis in their black leather boots."

Pelissier narrowed his eyes and pointed at Coco with a long, pale finger. "I'll tell you why you didn't sign—you didn't want the Nazis to think you had even one shred of sympathy for a Jewish friend."

"Nonsense. I would have, but Spatz was watching me. . . ."

"While Cocteau circulated a new petition, Max grew weaker and weaker."

Coco felt Pelissier's words like a blow to her stomach, and she lashed out. "And what did you do?" Nodding toward the Interrogator and the boy, she said, "You let them do the dirty work while you sat out the war at your wife's estate."

Pelissier ignored her, as he would an outburst from a witness he was cross-examining in a real courtroom, during a real trial. "Max begged, and you turned your back. It would have cost you nothing, but you wouldn't even sign a petition."

"I wanted to sign it. After Cocteau gave it to me, I hid it, so I could sign it after Spatz left." Coco's voice rose. "But he found it and ripped it up!"

"You expect me to believe that?" said Pelissier.

"It's the truth." Coco felt a hot wave of shame turning her face red. *I could have done more*, she thought. *I could have sent for Cocteau, or gone to his rooms to sign the new petition. What is wrong with me? Why did I do nothing?*

The major nodded toward the Interrogator and the boy. "These men brought you in for your traitorous collaboration with the enemy—for spying for your German lover and for denouncing your business partner to the Gestapo. That's bad, but maybe you have excuses, maybe you can cobble together an explanation of sorts." Pelissier paused and let his contempt settle over Coco. "But you wouldn't even pick up a pen; you wouldn't take the slightest risk to help your friend, a man who had stood by you all those years, who adored you. You wouldn't even sign your name." As Pelissier spoke, he picked up the Interrogator's scissors and gripped them angrily. "We are done talking."

Turning to the Interrogator, he said, "Have the women in the square released. Their neighbors will take care of them." He loosened his grip, and the scissors dropped to the table. He strode across the room and opened the door. "As for her"—he jabbed his thumb at Coco—"do what you want."

The door slammed behind him. The Interrogator and Coco stared hard at each other, their eyes burrowing, as though whoever could stare the longest without blinking would be redeemed from sin, washed clean of all unspeakable acts, all unimaginable tragedy. The Interrogator's gaze broke first. He turned to the boy and cocked his head in Coco's direction. The boy pulled Coco to her feet, gripping her arm. She staggered forward toward the table and struggled to sound brave. "What will you do with me?"

"First a haircut," said the Interrogator. "After, we'll parade you around the Place Vendôme and maybe the Ritz lobby. Then you can stand in front of your boutique until dark. You'll spend the night here, in the Conciergerie, with murderers and thieves. Tomorrow you'll go to the prison at Fresnes."

As the Interrogator reached across the table for the scissors, Coco lunged forward and grabbed them. She held them up to the naked lightbulb suspended from the ceiling and regarded them as if they were a magical talisman. "Every day from morning until night for twenty-five years I wore scissors like these dangling from a ribbon around my neck," she said quietly. "Only when I removed the ribbon with the scissors did my staff know we were finished for the day. As long as I had my scissors, my power was safe. My scissors were my weapon against my enemies, all those who wanted me to fail."

The Interrogator held out his arm and made a cup of his fingers. "Give me the scissors," he said.

Coco stood erect, defiantly clutching the scissors. "I'm keeping them. I can always use another pair. When I reopen my house, I'll use them to cut away some annoying threads and think of you. Because I *will* reopen someday."

"Give me the scissors."

"In 1918, I was the first woman in Paris to cut my hair off. People were shocked. But I didn't need it. A woman's brain is her most alluring asset."

Coco's eyes were fixed on the Interrogator, her jaw was set, and every fiber in her body tensed. "I'll save you the trouble."

She lifted a lock of her dark hair, pulled it straight, and snipped it off at the gray root. She grabbed another chunk of hair and snipped again, then another and another, grabbing and snipping, grabbing and snipping. As the hair fell around her, she kept hacking away at her scalp. Coco hadn't been to confession since she was a charity ward in convent school, but now she felt compelled, not to confess exactly, but to explain away her sin. "I saw my mother die when I was twelve in the flophouse where she cooked and cleaned. I was raised by nuns who didn't give a damn about me. I fed on deprivation and anguish, and it made me strong!"

Her face was a smear of guilt and sorrow. Tears welled up in her eyes as she chopped her hair. The room was silent except for the sharp click of scissors.

Then the phone rang, a shrieking alarm. Coco, the Interrogator, and the boy all stared at it. Finally, the Interrogator lifted the receiver. "Yes?" As he listened, his face darkened. "No," he said. "No . . . I don't know." He slammed the phone down and fell back into his chair. Barely containing his fury, he turned to Coco. "You can go."

"What?" She couldn't believe she'd heard correctly.

The Interrogator looked at the ground and sighed heavily.

"Was that Churchill?" Coco demanded.

"I said you can go."

"Winston was on the phone, and you didn't let me speak to him? What did he say? Who was it? His secretary? Someone else?" Coco flung the scissors on the table. Her body felt cold and her legs were on the verge of collapsing, but her faith in herself was returning. She wasn't surprised. She had always believed she would survive. If she wanted something enough, she would get it.

"I told you, and you didn't believe me!" Coco shouted at the Interrogator. "Well, now you know whom you're dealing with, who you had the colossal nerve to arrest. You put me through this ordeal for what? You think you're so smart. Well, I'm smarter. When the doorbell rang this morning, I knew it was you. I have a sixth sense about these things. I wasn't going to hide in the closet or jump out a window. I told the manager of my boutique to call Churchill."

The Interrogator silently gathered his files and documents and scooped the pile—with the scissors on top—into his arms. The boy opened the door for him. Before stepping into the hall, the Interrogator turned to Coco. "If I were you, I wouldn't stay in Paris. Down there in the streets, it's open season on collaborators."

"Do you think I want to stay with the city in *those* hands," she said to the boy, after the Interrogator had left. Her tone turned mocking. "French Forces of the Interior. FFI. Fifis, that's what they are, little terrorist poodles. The Germans emasculated them, and what do they do? Attack the easiest targets—poor, powerless women. Wait 'til their precious de Gaulle finds out what they've been up to. He'd cut off their balls, if they had any."

Coco grabbed the picture of herself and Churchill, her letters and the bottle of Chanel No. 5 off the table, and dropped them in her purse. "I'm not a nice woman. Too bad. But I've done more good in my life than bad. It's true. Don't look so shocked." She smoothed her skirt and arranged her face into a neutral expression as she spoke to the boy. "Do you have anything besides that jeep your friends brought me in?"

He stared at her, a look of disbelief on his face.

Coco sighed. "All right, you can take me back to the Ritz in that."

When the boy failed to move, Coco snapped at him. "You've got something better to do this afternoon? Someone else to torture? I thought you wanted my help to save your uncle?"

"I don't want anything from you," said the boy.

"If you won't drive me yourself, at least call a taxi. You're capable of that, aren't you?"

The boy glowered at Coco, and she realized he wasn't going to help her. She reached for the phone. With one violent jerk, the boy snatched it away and ripped it out of the wall. He stared at Coco a moment, then, carrying the phone, walked past her and out the door, slamming it behind him.

Coco stood for a moment, staring at the blank door. Then she began to pull herself together. She took a mirror from her purse and checked herself, scowling at her hacked hair. She donned her hat, careful to cover the bald spots on her scalp. She applied her lipstick. When she was done, she replaced the lipstick and mirror in her purse and carefully pulled on her gloves. From the handbag draped in the crook of her arm, she removed the bottle of Chanel No. 5. Slowly and ritualistically, she dabbed perfume behind her ears and inside her wrists. Then she sprayed a silver ring of mist around herself and walked through it, as she made her way to the door.

Outside the Prefecture of Police, tricolors hung from the surrounding balconies. Tinny strains of the Marseillaise wafted from an invisible band shell in a park across the Seine. Bicycles clogged the street, slowing to a crawl a single car headed north on rue de Lutèce. Coco clutched her purse with one gloved hand, while she waved furiously to hail a taxi. She waited more than an hour for a cab to drive by and pick her up.

As soon as she entered her suite at the Ritz, she yelled at her maid to start packing. Then she phoned her boutique. "Did you call Churchill?" she asked the manager.

"Oh, Mademoiselle, I called the number you gave me and left a message for the prime minister. I don't know if he got it, but thank God, you're free! I was so worried," the woman said.

Coco hung up the phone. She paused with her hand on the receiver and wondered.

A moment later, she called her driver. "Get my car out of the garage. Make sure you've got gas. We leave for Switzerland tonight."

In the next room, Coco heard her maid banging drawers and pulling suitcases from the closet. She would not give up these rooms, humble as they were. She called Charlie Ritz and told him she'd be away for a while, but to keep her suite ready for her at all times with fresh linen and wood for a fire. She would pay the bill for a year's rent before she left.

When she hung up the phone, she started to cry. She lit a cigarette, but it failed to calm her. Puffing furiously, smoke enveloped her in a foul cloud of gloom that drew her back to her childhood. She was alone in the dark again on her cot at the convent. Her mother was dead, and she would never see her father again. No one loved her. She was a horrid little girl, and she grew up to be a horrid woman.

Unlocking the bottom drawer of her desk, she pulled out a syringe and a vial of morphine. Carefully, so as not to spill any and waste her supply, she filled the vial halfway. Leaning back against the chair cushion, she placed the syringe in a fat blue vein of her left forearm, injecting just enough poison to obliterate her shame.

Across the street, in Coco's boutique at 31 rue Cambon, the vendeuse Angeline was giving away Chanel No. 5.

An American soldier, one of thousands, would return home with a bottle in his rucksack. He would give it to his mother, and whenever she wore the perfume, as she would every day for the rest of her life, replacing this bottle many times over the years, she would think of the miracle of her son's return.

And this is how we forget. With each drop of golden scent. The golden scent of treasured life. The golden scent that masks the dishonor of the world.

AUTHOR'S NOTE

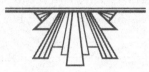

oco at the Ritz is a novel, though it is based on true events. In writing my story, I've tried not to contradict the known facts, though I've invented many details and the characters of the Interrogator, his assistant, and the major. The other main characters are based on real people.

Myriad books have been written about Coco Chanel, but almost nothing is known about her arrest and interrogation by the French Forces of the Interior (FFI) in late August or early September 1944—the various accounts of her life differ on the date. What is certain is that one morning two soldiers from the FFI, the loose band of Resistance fighters, soldiers, and private citizens who took up arms in the wake of the liberation of Paris, led Chanel from her suite at the Ritz Hotel in Paris to an undisclosed location for questioning and released her unharmed a short time later. What transpired during her interrogation, who was present, and why she was set free when so many other women who'd been involved with German men had their heads shaved or were imprisoned, remains a mystery. Chanel never discussed it, and there is no documentation of her interrogation, as there would have been in an official court proceeding.

I first became intrigued by this story while researching Chanel's life for my 2006 novel *The Collection*, set in Chanel's atelier in 1919 in the aftermath of the First World War. Her biographies rarely give a clear picture of her life during the Occupation, and her arrest is barely mentioned, owing no doubt to the scant record. I wanted to know more, and two details I discovered on a trip to Paris in 2007 set me on a course toward writing this book. The first I found at a museum near Montparnasse honoring the Resistance hero Jean Moulin. On a wall display of front pages from the Nazi-controlled press, an article about Chanel's plans to reopen her fashion house under German rule jumped out at me. (Of course, she never did.) The other was a footnote in a book I was looking through of Max Jacob's poetry. Even with my poor command of French, I clearly understood the simple note, translated roughly as "People say Chanel refused to sign Jacob's petition." Along with several other celebrated friends of the poet's, including Pablo Picasso, Chanel did not sign the document Jean Cocteau circulated calling for Jacob's release from Gestapo custody.

These revelations of Chanel's seeming willingness to do business with the enemy and her apparent refusal to go on record to save a Jewish friend raised serious questions about her loyalties and character. Was she a collaborator, and, if so, what was the nature of her collaboration? Since she left behind no memoir, letters, or diaries that might offer clues to her interior life, her motivations were accessible only imaginatively.

The Occupation offered a stark contrast between good and evil, yet few people were either heroes of resistance or villains of collaboration. Most citizens, as the writer André Gide noted, were like old shoes floating in murky waters: battered and torn, riding the turbulent flow, just trying to survive. It's impossible to discern to what extent, if any, Chanel supported Nazi ideology. She is on record making anti-Semitic remarks, but like most of the world, she almost certainly didn't know (or didn't want to know) about the death camps until the end of the war.

For many years in France after the end of World War II, the Occupation remained a raw, agonizing wound. Women who'd had relations with German soldiers were reviled pariahs shunned by their neighbors and even their own families. Chanel remained in exile for ten years, living on and off with her Nazi boyfriend, Spatz von Dincklage, who, having escaped arrest and prosecution, joined her in Switzerland at the war's end. The couple parted amicably in the early 1950s. Spatz moved to an island off the coast of Spain, where, supported by a trust set up by Chanel, he passed the time painting nudes. Chanel returned to Paris in 1954 to reopen her fashion house. Her countrymen weren't quick to forgive her recent past, and French journalists panned her first postwar collection. Americans, though, who were largely ignorant of Chanel's personal life and still revered her as the personification of French style, hailed her return as the second coming of the fashion messiah.

Fifty-seven years later, in his 2011 book, *Sleeping with the Enemy*, journalist Hal Vaughan published the contents of declassified intelligence documents that revealed Chanel's wartime activities. Executives at corporate Chanel were quick to deny Vaughan's charge that their founder had been a German spy recruited by her lover. The documents were real, yet the exact details of the schemes they revealed, including Chanel's efforts to safeguard her assets, and Modellhut, the harebrained plot she cooked up with Spatz to negotiate a separate peace, were hazy. To this day, Chanel's official bio on the company's website makes no mention of Spatz; the years 1940 to 1944 are mostly ignored on the timeline of her life. In Chanel Inc.'s many extravagant promotional films, including those starring Geraldine Chaplin as the mature Chanel and Keira Knightley and Kristen Stewart as young Coco, there is only one reference to Spatz. In *Once and Forever*, an eleven-minute fictional film directed by Karl Lagerfeld in 2015 about the supposed making of a Chanel biopic, Stewart's character asks, "What about Spatz? Is he going to be in the movie? . . . It's probably one of the most important aspects of her life." The actor playing the imaginary film's producer answers, "We will only cover the years of happiness and success."

After all, the several-billion-dollar Chanel brand thrives on the sense of chic its handbags, perfume, sunglasses, clothes, lipstick, and other products confer on women. No one understood better than Chanel herself that fashion is a form of escapism, "the most intoxicating release from the banality of the world," as the legendary magazine editor Diana Vreeland put it. Chanel strove vigorously to hide the ugly aspects of her life, even going so far as to bribe people who knew her darkest secrets. Nazi intelligence chief Walter Schellenberg was one. Chanel paid his medical expenses when he was suffering from cancer and then paid for his funeral. Schellenberg's posthumously published memoir, *The Labyrinth*, makes no mention of Chanel or Modellhut, which he authorized.

In a way, Chanel's story epitomizes the treachery of France during World War II. She's a kind of anti-Marianne, the symbol of French liberty, equality, and fraternity. In writing my book, however, I was mostly interested in exploring Chanel's particular sensibility. At its heart, *Coco at the Ritz* is a story about the choices one woman made when the stakes were at their highest, why she made them, and the consequences to those around her. In today's world, at a time when anti-Semitism, right-wing extremism, anti-immigrant violence, and hatred in general have exploded anew, I hope my novel can be read as a cautionary tale about the necessity of standing against evil when it stares you—seductively—in the face.

ACKNOWLEDGMENTS

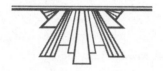

My obsession with the story told in these pages stretches back so many years that it would be impossible to thank everyone who helped me understand it, flesh out its details and unlock its mysteries.

That I found a way to tell it at all seems a miracle, and I'm grateful to Jessica Case at Pegasus for guiding the book into print. Thank you to Molly von Borstel for designing a stunning cover, to Andrea Monagle for her thoughtful, careful copyediting, to Maria Fernandez for the book's interior design, and to April Roberts for her work on publicity.

I'm fortunate to have Flip Brophy as my agent, and I'm deeply thankful for her support, patience, friendship, and wise counsel.

Though most of the dialogue in the novel is invented, the character Coco Chanel sometimes says things her real-life counterpart reportedly said, according to articles, web sites, and books. The quoted snippets of Max Jacob's poetry are authentic. Letters, newspaper stories, and other documents that figure in the novel are largely based on real records.

Following is a partial list of the books I found invaluable: *Jean Cocteau: A Life* by Claude Arnaud; *Coco Chanel: An Intimate Life* by Lisa Chaney; *Mademoiselle: Coco Chanel and the Pulse of History* by Rhonda K. Garelick; *Misia: The Life of Misia Sert* by Arthur Gold and Robert Fizdale; *Coco Chanel* by Marcel Haedrich; *Selected Poems of Max Jacob* by Max Jacob; *The Cost of Courage* by Charles Kaiser; *The Secret of Chanel No, 5: The Intimate History of the World's Most Famous Perfume* by Tilar Mazzeo; *The Allure of Chanel* by Paul Morand; *Chronicles of Wasted Time* by Malcolm Muggeridge; *Picasso: A Biography* by Patrick O'Brian; *Vichy France: Old Guard and New Order 1940–1944* by Robert O. Paxton; *Coco Chanel: The Legend and the Life* by Justine Picardie; *A Life of Picasso: The Triumphant Years 1917-1932* by John Richardson; *And the Show Went On: Cultural Life in Nazi-Occupied Paris* by Alan Riding; *When Paris Went Dark: The City of Light Under German Occupation* by Ronald C. Rosbottom; *Chanel* by Edmonde Charles-Roux; *Sleeping with the Enemy* by Hal Vaughan; *Fashion Under the Occupation* by Dominique Veillon; *Shorn Women: Gender and Punishment in Liberation France* by Fabrice Virgili; *Max Jacob: A Life in Arts and Letters* by Rosanna Warren.

Thank you also to Judith Sternlight, who read early drafts of *Coco at the Ritz* and provided crucial insights; James Bohnen, who taught me how to write a play, parts of which found their way into this narrative; and my dear friends Jonathan Rabb, Dinitia Smith, and Christine Sneed, brilliant novelists themselves. Jonathan gave me expert advice on structure and point of view. Dinitia and Christine read the book with incisive rigor and made many important suggestions.

I couldn't get through writing a book without my posse of forever friends: Jonathan Black, Maureen Dowd, Ted Fishman, Brenda Fowler, Victoria Lautman, Trish Lear (another talented writer who read an early draft), Ann and Phil Ponce, Kaarina Salovaara, Julie Shelton, Rachel Shteir, Sara Stern, and Monica Vachher.

Finally, and most profoundly, thank you to my husband, Richard Babcock, and our son, Joe, for everything. You are my life.